CW00840071

The ruins of Detroit were in the b[...]
mind as he touched down in Lond[...],
and drizzling November day. The psychogeography of what
he had left behind ghosted his consciousness: a vague mist,
the fog of decay, loss and emptiness. Cajmere had a
fondness for perambulating the city of his birth, of observing
and documenting the buildings in a state of entropy.

This city. This city that was once great. 1993. Thirty years
ago there was optimism, car factories, the music of Motown.
All was dream. The bright hopes of coruscating metal, the
tinny trebly musical uplift patented by Berry Gordy. Daniel
Cajmere's parents, his pretty white mother and his
handsome black father had arrived here with their hopes in
their pockets.

Since then, continual decline, slide, slide into nothingness.
The derelict buildings were totemic. There were deserted
streets, desolate neighbourhoods; abandonment,
desperation. The suburbs where Cajmere had grown up had
once been characterised by well-tended gardens and tidy
detached bungalows. Now there were burnt out cars outside
his mother's house, feral kids on the street and no one dared
venture out after dark.

And yet…. And yet… he found a strange melancholy beauty
in brick edifices with black spaces where windows once
were, like dental cavities in a rotted mouth. He spent
afternoons photographing the ruined interiors of 1930s
movie theatres, running his fingers over pitted plasterboard
Ionic columns, gilt paint and threadbare, claret hued velvet
seating where the stuffing was sprouting out impudently like
weeds between paving stones. All was grandeur desiccated,
pilasters crumbling; plaster peeling, detritus, rubble, spores
of dust.

It was from these remnants of a once imperious metropolis that the gleaming sound architecture of Detroit techno had emerged, a futuristic vector, Marinetti redux. It had been originated by the so-called 'Belleville three' – Derrick May, Juan Atkins and Kevin Saunderson - a trio of DJs and producers who met at high school and started making tracks in the late eighties. May once famously said that the sound, a smooth sheeny electronic cruise, sounded 'like Kraftwerk and George Clinton trapped in an elevator together.' And Cajmere, all hubris, brilliant smile and prodigious innovation was currently its greatest export of all.

He pitch shifted, sensorially, into the oppressive gloom of London in wintertime as he trudged through the airport immigration hall. The jet lag was enervating; an eight hour flight from Detroit could leave him wasted for days. The sigh of a serotonin rush he'd felt on the plane after swallowing an SSRI with a glass of red wine, was dissipating fast. The record label that was courting him, had arranged for him to stay at Kensington Garden Hotel. It was surprisingly corporate for a rock star haunt. He stared at the carpet as the receptionist checked him in, observing for a split second the ersatz rendition of 80s Memphis, pale pink and lemon hued lozenges, that someone had mindlessly designed to floor numberless anonymous corporate hotels, all over the world. And that would elicit the same feelings of vague recognition and anaesthetized gloom at the dated ubiquity of the anodyne environment.

Cajmere took the lift to his room on the 12th floor, suddenly aware of the dead weight of his reinforced record box as it swung about, leaden, corners occasionally denting his calves. He was used to hotel rooms by now. Two years of peripatetic DJing in Europe and the US had exposed him to varying outposts of corporate hospitality. His heart sank as he entered the room, it was a grey box, plastic fixtures and fittings, harsh fluorescent lighting. The kind of identikit bland multinational aesthetic designed to signify business class luxury of a supremely inoffensive and innocuous strain.

He crashed onto the bed and slept. The one consolation of these institutions was fresh white sheets and the narcoleptic pleasures they offered. And so he lay unconscious, fully clothed in his black Levis and fleece, without even having removed his brown caterpillar boots. Outside, the sky mutated from granite-hued cumulus to the black of night to the muted concrete of morning.

Around 1pm the next day Cajmere found himself ushered through more anaesthetised grey corridors in the large West London EMI building. Here were endless desks with paperwork, peopled by hot pant and lycra clad PAs, with the glossy centre-parted bobs that epitomised the era, hard plastic phones clamped to their ears or feeding fax machines with documents. As he strode through, waves of EMI's female employees found themselves momentarily distracted from their work by this tall confident strikingly good looking man – all sepia-toned fawn skin and annular mahogany eyes with long luxuriant eyelashes. He wondered what it might be like to work in such an office, a world away from the solipsism he found so difficult in his studio in a dilapidated warehouse in Detroit, with the small cluster of geeks and enthusiasts who came to hang out and experiment with sound.

He entered a small meeting room, again, grey, plasticised, velux blinds and harsh strip lighting. On a low sofa sat the two record company men who'd been courting him. They stood up.

'Hi Dan, I'm Simon Wanstall, A and R for the new label Fresh beats' offered one, 'we've been speaking on the phone for the last few months.' He was tall with dark hair in a bob and sunken eyes. Cajmere found himself cringing inwardly at his earnest over familiarity. The other man, who was older, silver haired and wore an expensive looking suit stepped forward 'I'm Miles Higginbottom, the MD of the label's new fledgling imprints.'

They talked at him for seemingly an infinity, Wanstall was astonishingly well informed, possibly more so than himself pondered Cajmere, articulating succinctly the sonic geography of the Detroit producers vogueish at that moment, which records had impacted in terms of aural progression and innovation and their sales demographics. Wanstall reminded him particularly of a studied Melody Maker journalist who'd been one of the first to interview him in Britain: shy, introvert, supremely intelligent. Too 'nice' to be a threat. He eyed them dispassionately, he knew innately, his name was on fire right now in dance music. They would be lucky to have him.

Whilst someone with integrity might have argued that this record label was a vulture upon a burgeoning youth culture, Cajmere could not have cared less, he had come here for money. He wanted it: the burgeoning cheque, the fame, the women, the cars, a futuristic mixing desk oh and endless records in his box. All of it. Yes he had striven hard for little monetary gain for a few years, so, he figured he deserved what was to come. If he was complicit in the commercialisation of his genre that was about to commence, he felt no guilt, no questioning, bring it on.

It was a simple deal. They needed the credibility of the brightest new star in the Detroit firmament to launch their new dance imprint. He wanted stardom and, in all honesty Dionysian abandon, parties in hotel rooms, endless blondes, fawning promoters, to be told once, twice thrice and again that he was the saviour, the genius of Detroit techno they had all been waiting for.

The deal was closing, he could feel it. Cajmere stared at the duo. Wanstall was too soft, he could relate to his college learning, Cajmere himself was an autodidact who loved to read, but he found Wanstall's gentle expounding on the seditious subtext of black techno rather grating. Higginbottom was money, statistics, power, corporate reach.

Impressive. He listened to Higginbottom, surefooted, expounding the omnipotence of the record label, it's chart successes, sophisticated distribution network, peerless A and Rs, PR and marketing team.

And suddenly the money was on the table. Cajmere found himself blinking in disbelief. It was a life-changing sum. He quickly calculated how it would change things: he could buy a house, a new car (oh how muscle cars coursed through his glittering dreams of fame), regular income for ten years to come or more. In return he was to produce two albums for them and license his Rings of Saturn independent label to them, with all the obscure young producers he had painstakingly discovered and nurtured on it.

He signed on the dotted line. "Let's drink," urged Wanstall and produced a bottle of champagne from a mini refrigerator. Cajmere loved champagne, there was often a bottle of vintage chilling in his fridge in Detroit, specifically for entertaining girls, and he drank enthusiastically, thinking he could have downed several more.

Daniel Cajmere stepped out of the glass and steel monolith that was the record label's home with a multimillion-pound contract folded and stuffed into his black Levis pocket. Light rain was falling, flecking his clothes with cool ardour. He didn't have an umbrella, but it didn't seem to matter. Suddenly London's streets seemed full of infinite possibility, he trod a thousand dreams underfoot on each paving stone. He had accepted his reward, he mused, and now, at this very moment in time the whole world seemed to be spread out before him. The freedom to do what he wanted; from that tiny warehouse studio in Detroit he could soundtrack the globe.

He wasn't quite sure where he was going but he wanted to walk. Past the imperious stucco terraces of Kensington grand immaculate houses, tall, reaching upwards, that looked like they were coated in thick white royal icing. He decided to indulge himself in his favourite activity as a reward for the deal and hailed a black cab to Notting Hill Record and Tape exchange.

The independent record store specialising in dance music was a relatively new phenomena in the early 90s. It had evolved from the indie record shops of the post punk and eighties to offer the latest 12" vinyl from the house and techno diaspora. These were new sub-genres of music that had evolved from the late seventies explosion of disco – Donna Summer, Chic, Sister Sledge. House hailed from the (mid eighties) gay clubs of Chicago and had its genesis in the mid eighties. It had shucked off the stardust glitter of disco and was characterised by the ticking metronomic beats of rudimentary drum machines, clunking piano refrains and baritone vocals importuning you to 'jack', the favoured dance of the house acolyte, a sort of jerking locomotion.

The warm chemical odour of black vinyl greeted him as he walked through the doors. He often pondered the processes of record production: the mechanical production lines, the backstory of each disc that bore his name. He'd seen a documentary once on the TV about how the glossy melted plastic, like coils of lucent liquorice was formed into plates and inscribed with those fine lines capable of emitting the strings of life.

The shop was busy, as usual there were clusters of twenty something guys with bobbed hair and puffa jackets on hanging our around the counter, jostling to get the attention of the head nodders behind the counter. Studious figures dotted around the store fingered through the racks with expert attentiveness, like archaeologists sifting for precious remains. Cajmere recognised the sound permeating the air as an insistent, ebullient, minor key opus called Kinetic from a new Belgian techno imprint called R and S.

"Dan, Dan, mate, you're back" gestured a slightly chubby bespectacled figure in a Warp record label t-shirt who stood behind the counter. Cajmere hustled to front of the melee. "Mark, wassup" he reciprocated with a triumphal air, "meet the new dark prince of global techno."

"We knew you were that anyway," replied Mark warmly, "tell me something I don't know."

"You're looking at one major label's latest hottest property, the cheque's right here," he patted his denim jacket pocket proudly.

Mark raised his eyebrows, and with a hint of mischief he couldn't resist said "you've sold out then. When are the rinky dink rave hits coming out?"

Daniel felt slighted, his humour (not to mention ego) didn't stretch to this rather over-familiar form of ribbing the English seemed to like to indulge in. "Ha ha," he laughed. A laugh that rang hollow in his own head. More like taking it to the next level he thought to himself irascibly. He tried not to display his annoyance. "Next step global domination with rave hits."

Okay mate, we're right behind you, you rule" nodded Mark, sensing Cajmere's pride had been pricked and that he needed a bit of stroking.

Cajmere was hungry for the latest white labels, test pressings and rareties that had come into the Exchange in recent days. Mark winked and dived behind the counter to the stash he kept for the coterie of top DJs he counted as friends.

"Some interesting stuff coming out of Glasgow right now on the Tropicalia label," he ventured.

"Yeah I heard about that," mused Cajmere in his melted chocolate North American intonation. "I dunno there's like a real affinity with Detroit in Scotland. Every time I play there its kinda magical."

"You know what," interjected Mark, suddenly excited. Forget about Scotland. We've got a new person called Rachael coming to work here next month and she really knows about music. I've never met a girl like her. I mean like the most serious female trainspotter I've ever encountered. She really knows her stuff."

"Oh really," remarked Cajmere, raising his eyebrows with a touch of ennui. "that good huh. She know my tracks?"

"Oh crikey and some," said Mark emphatically, "I bet you she can identify all your samples and even some of your studio kit from listening to your back catalogue. She's blown us all away."

"Hmm" Cajmere remained unconvinced. "What colour hair she got." He hoped blonde. He liked white girls, preferably with blonde hair and a thick paste of terracotta make up, eyelashes clotted with mascara like spiders legs and ersatz pink shimmering lipstick. He was not one for subtlety or androgynous charm. He was a connoisseur of a certain type of woman, a woman who he perceived to have indulged in the thoughtless brash objectification of herself, he was seeking a female who had abnegated the threat of all intellect, creativity and individuality from her appearance. A woman who would adorn him, accessorise him: an adjunct to his infallible self-image.

"Red, auburn, natural auburn. She's not really your usual clubbing girl. Dresses casual, not interested in fashion. No make up. Lumberjack shirts. Stonewash jeans. Clompy shoes."

And for some reason this information lodged itself in Cajmere's consciousness like a little chip of ice or a glinting shard of glass.

Days later and Cajmere was in Liverpool in a club called Colourbox. It was housed in a huge dank warehouse. As he walked in through the fire escape doors the yowling cat leitmotif of The Prodigy's Charly inveigled his ears. Spread out in front of him was a vast dancefloor peopled with hundreds, even thousands of ravers, an undulating sea of bobbing heads, long sleeved t shirts, girls in neon, glazed eyes, fixed stares, water bottles, sweat dripping off walls; blackness, blackness enveloping blackness.

A dense, warm vapour had risen off the top of the crowd. Cajmere identified the smell, it was a mixture of cool, glacial dry ice billowing from the stage area and the soapy freshness of fabric conditioner, the unmistakable odour of suburbia – the glimpse of a thought of a thousand mothers washing the sweat saturated clothes of this thousand lost children.

Cajmere mused upon the origins of the spectacle before him. Four DJs had brought the phenomenon, known as 'Balearic' or 'Acid House', from Ibiza to London in the summer of 1988. It coincided with an explosion of new electronic music tailored towards dancing and the arrival of a new drug ecstasy from the US gay and disco scenes - this small white pill engendered ersatz feelings of love and goodwill towards the world in an age where religious faith was dwindling and it spurred users into a state of kinetic perpetuity. They would want to embrace each other in a temperate woozy haze of innocence, without the electric frission of sexuality and be liberated, or was it enslaved? to dance all night to repetitive machine music. And now this, five years on, an empire of the night, clubs and raves and kids who wanted to dance in dervish-like Somatic abandon, all over the UK, then Europe, then the world.

He glanced to see who was up on stage in the DJ booth. It was Gareth Goldberg. He smiled to himself. Goldberg was a big name rave DJ in the UK who was notorious amongst other DJs for having taken 24 ecstasy tablets in 24 hours. After this he had allegedly passed out and died for several minutes, been rushed to hospital and successfully resuscitated. But famously, this hadn't stopped him and he continued to neck doves (ecstasy tablets) at every available opportunity. Cajmere felt a surge of anticipation – he knew he'd have a good night with Goldberg about – there would be girls - Goldberg was party central. Cajmere hauled his record box to the DJ booth. Goldberg looked up from the white label he was carefully cueing up and smiled at him – a smile full of mischievous hedonism - a smile that said 'wait till I get back to the stash at my hotel room.'

"Yo Gareth" winked Cajmere cheekily. "Awright matey. Get on one. Lawwge!" exclaimed Goldberg and Cajmere could just glimpse a gold tooth in his splay of drug-yellowed teeth.

Cajmere waited next to the DJ booth, attentive to the tracks Goldberg was seguing together. His heart sank. Goldberg was playing what might be termed a 'rave hits' set, or if you were going to be less generous, 'cheese' – brash, commercial, lowest- common-denominator music. Crowd pleasers were prime Gorgonzola according to the DJ lexicon. Cajmere took a deep breath in loaded with resignation. It was going to be hard to win over this crowd who were currently sucking on a saccharine teat of 'chipmunk' ardkore, music with the vocals so speeded up they sounded like the helium entrails of words, chattering squiggles of cartoon reverie scampering over a resolute battalion of militaristic breakbeats. Cajmere knew this music was out of date and dreadfully provincial, the last hurrah of rave pop before the diaspora of jungle, Detroit techno, ambient, trance, house and garage took over – as they had in London already.

He brooded on what he perceived to be the sheer saccharine inferiority of what Goldman was playing, irritated. How could he follow what was essentially pop ephemera, a sugar hit, with the subliminal sublime of his Detroit requiems. But then, he figured, this crowd was probably too far-gone to notice if he played them classical music over a kick drum. And perhaps, just perhaps, they were ripe for educating. Edutainment, that was what he liked to call it, after the KRS One LP. The subtle injection of innovation and avant garde sonic modulation into a broadly populist genre or oeuvre. He figured he could start with some anthems – his mentor Carter Kings' 'Euphoric Strings' and then gradually seep insidiously, imperceptibly into the new Rings of Saturn plates in his box.

He glanced at Goldberg who was punching the air with an ebullient triumphalism with one hand and had another arm curved around a voluptuous bleach blonde who looked a like a porn star – all bubblegum pink bra top and black lycra leggings. Cajmere felt a twinge of jealousy, although he knew, thanks to Goldberg there would be plenty of women when they got back to the hotel. Cajmere felt himself cringe inwardly as Guru Josh's Infinity inveigled his ears, the synthetic arpeggios cruising through the air into nothingness, admittedly there was something spine tingling about this little chapter of chart flotsam and yet it was so dated, in an electronic music scene that was now moving at lightspeed even something from 2 or three years ago had somehow faded into obscurity, or become remotely undesirable. Goldberg seemed to have lost his grip on the nuances of fashionability, of the fleeting temporality of their calling as DJs, of the continual need to thrust a vector into the future. Cajmere felt an implicit weakness, a misty-eyed sentimentality that repelled him about nostalgia. The early nineties was a time for vision and visionaries – in music at least. And that is exactly how Cajmere viewed himself – here was here to evangelise, to convert, to preach from a pulpit of sound and below him the populace would yield to his coruscating light.

Goldberg was halfway through his last track, a shameless Italo piano anthem and Cajmere stood impatiently beside him, moving the cross fader gradually into Strings of Life. He inhaled deeply and felt a surge of imperious anticipation as he deftly manipulated the Technics 1210s. A glance down into the crowd – the DJ booth was at the side of a stage – revealed a forest of arms reaching up, like bronchioles splaying in a lung mass, all enveloped in the darkness of night. Down the walls ran rivulets of the condensed steam rising from kinetic bodies. Lasers scythed the Cimmerian gloom. Here they were, thousands of them, the losing it, the lost, locked into the music. He imagined their souls had migrated from their bodies and dwelt in the space between the straining hands and the ceiling. Someone had once told him that ecstasy did that – an apocryphal story – the spirit left the body and the body was left empty, devoid, yet in perpetual motion, a soft fleshy automaton surrendering to the thrill and prickle of sensation and all our corporeal Dionysian desires.

Cajmere was confident he could manipulate this crowd to enjoy something more esoteric than Goldberg's plastic and carnivalesque merry go round of rave hits. He sifted through his white labels with a calculated air, planning to move through melodic reverie to transcendental string washes – all underscored by rigid and unyielding kick drums. In a sense he had been right – it did not matter what he played this was a crowd so effervescent with serotonin that they would have danced to bagpipes or a Theremin had he been so inclined or indeed perverse.

Goldberg returned to the DJ booth some half an hour later to collect his record bag and leered at Cajmere with a quite unsettling rictus grin. He tugged his headphone away from his ear 'see you back at the hotel matey' he bellowed and Cajmere nodded and smiled. Goldberg was a Neanderthal but he did know how to party, he gave him that and somehow, God only knows how, he attracted, in Cajmere's opinion at least, a very hot sort of women – half dressed, breasts, buttocks, thickly anointed with make up, vivacious yet low on intellect and crucially eager to please any superannuated DJ whose name appeared on a flyer.

He announced his arrival with Strings of Life. Yes, perhaps he was as culpable as Goldberg of being dated here but he needed to bridge from what was, sonically speaking a regressive crayon scribble to his own self-perceived Sistine Chapel of sonic 'artchitecture'. Cajmere took a moment to wonder about Strings of Life as the emphatic pianos of the track engendered a kinetic ripple through the mesmerised crowd, had it's ubiquity and classic status in some way de-libidinised it's potency? Had over play and the reverential screeds devoted to it somehow rendered it dull and void, ascribing it a bizarre tasteless neutrality, a default setting of 'good taste', the more people hailed it as the ur-track, the year zero of Detroit techno, the more he wanted to take refuge in some halcyon test pressing that was only in his possession and no one elses, the more his obscurist and obscurant defiance was roused. He was obsessed with the dialectic between the underground and the commercial vectors that were beginning to be so apparent in this relatively nascent rave and dance music scene. Of course his record deal was symptomatic of this, as he cued up the next record Cajmere was aware he stood on the shifting tectonic plates that comprised Detroit techno, if not all electronic music at that golden moment in time.

And oh how his music soared that night, taking flight on gilded strings, an orchestral opus writ to pluck teardrops from your soul and floated over kick drums. White labels by all his Rings of Saturn protégées: among them gifted young studio heads like Eddie Frowk and Tony Silkin. This was not just a linear progression of 808 drumbeats like many of his fellow Detroit DJs. Cajmere was the master of manipulating temporality in the form of tempo and texture alike. He would build, build, build: tiny spatial increments, like staccato breaths would characterise one track. Gently, imperceptibly, faster, harder, climbing a mountain until he segued into a hyperventilating pitch of panic attack extremity with alarm bells ringing and hammering synth stabs. He played with atonalities, dissonance a dazzling lexicon of modern classical techniques embodied imperceptibly in those white labels of his and disguised, absorbed into tracks that were predicated on the axis between avant-garde and mass distraction.

As the crowd rippled and convulsed, a perspiring battalion of bodies in motion, time itself was bending, invisible currents of this dazzling music were thick vapour in the air, very magic was being conjured out of the void with his deft and magisterial dexterity on the 1210s.

His set surged towards the end and he felt as though he had all those thousand odd malign children in the crowd suspended on a golden thread, he was bobbing them up and down quite masterful, filtering sounds through the atmosphere that might fleck their lunar consciousness's with specks of platinum bright.

In the midst of this reverie he was vaguely aware of an anorak clad form nudging next to him. It was the Manucunian DJ Graham Price 'okay I'm ready to go mate.' Cajmere left his last track spinning and crouched down to sort out his record box. He was in a daze. He was spent. He couldn't focus. Adrenalin. Abstracted. He walked off the side of the stage, desperate to get o the hotel and start partying with Goldberg, the effervescence of being young and reckless permeating his consciousness. The unstoppable testosterone of a twentysomething male. Suddenly he heard voices "Daniel, Daniel, I've wanted to meet you for so long." He felt himself rolling his eyes inwardly. A fan. He hated fans. It was a tall blonde boy with bobbed hair, dank, clammy skin and almost almond eyes in an R and S records black t-shirt. He forced a grin. "Well here I am," he heaved a sigh.

"Wow the dexterity of your mixing tonight was incredible," Cajmere could tell by the articulacy of this sincere young man that he was not spaced out like the rest of them. "Was that really the Simon Twist that samples Pierre Boulez that you played?" He was just the kind of enthusiast that Cajmere felt a kind of imperious disdain for. "Yeah, yeah, personally I don't feel it's as good as Roger Goten's new Astral mix," "Oh I don't know that one," the boy looked slightly crestfallen. "Yeah, said Cajmere with an air of casual superiority, "I guess it's because there are only 15 test press issues right now circulating amongst us DJs." "So when…." The boy started. Excuse me I've gotta go" said Cajmere, the urgency of the hedonism that awaited him taking over. He cut the boy off mid sentence, leaving him ashamed, humiliated and cast adrift in the crowd, hoping desperately his friends hadn't witnessed the snub. Cajmere shoved his way through the human traffic towards the exit.

Cajmere surveyed the morose façade of the hotel he was being put up in. 19th century and singed with sooty urbanity. A sorrowful demeanour, rows of windows, glazed eyes glinting in the darkness. He dropped his record box in his room. The light didn't work properly and in the dimness the dated burgundy flock wallpaper was vaguely visible.

Goldberg flung his arms around him as he entered his room. There were a couple of male ravers there, his driver and two record company girls, one brunette in tight leather trousers and a white vest top and one blonde in flesh and black lycra leggings, smoking Silk Cuts. "Oh mate I heard about your deal, you're amazing," he enthused, his face slightly too close for comfort, Cajmere noticed his pupils, black as the void, were generously dilated, Goldberg's thirst for oblivion was seemingly insatiable.

"Have you met Anya and Pippa," he gestured towards the women who were sprawled on a puce colour draylon settee.

"Er, no, hi there," he grinned knowingly, wondering where Goldberg had put his stash.

"We need to get you sorted out gorgeous man," corralled Goldberg the full pusillanimous spectrum of his teeth visible in a rather unnerving smile. He grubbed dirty fingernails in a fluorescent nylon bum bag, which, Cajmere noted, was stuffed with a scroll of wrinkled banknotes.

'E's, whizz, Charlie," he snorted, " I've even got a few acid tabs if you're feeling really adventurous."

"You know what I'll skip the drugs," smirked Cajmere. Acid was for students, tie dye t-shirt wearers, freaks and weirdos. He wondered why it was in Goldberg's stash, then quickly remembered that Goldberg guzzled up anything remotely mindbending with a similar zeal to a sea lion gulping fish in a marine park, or a Pac man gobbling up pixelated biscuits, each with a staccato bleep. "But women, now that's another matter."

"That's my boy," chuckled Goldberg and proceeded to remove a dated teasmaid from a melamine tray and chop out a fat line of white powder on it. Goldberg fished out a note from the bum bag, rolled it up expertly and snorted up the drug in a quick, almost violent inhalation.

The blonde, Anya, who Cajmere knew from Eternal records, a small hardcore imprint, proceeded to drape her arms around Goldberg. "Gareth doll, she said stroking his sandpapery stubbly cheek," give us another eccy will ya."

He went and sat down beside Pippa on the sofa. She had a pleasing face, slightly downcast blue eyes, like Diane Keaton he thought, vaguely bronzed dry looking skin and centre parted dark hair with a slight halo of frizz that licked her shoulders sensually. She was drawing on a cigarette and grinding her teeth noticeably.

"So you're the PA to Simon Wanstall," he raised his eyebrows, waiting for her to impress him, he was staring upon her thin form condescendingly, those cheap chain store clothes tight vest and squeaking leatherette trousers, almost like he was scrutinising a very small speck from a very high mountain. He felt, even more so than usual, on the verge of greatness, on the cusp of some insightful breakthrough that would change things irrevocably. DJing served to extrapolate his existing hubris into an invincible carapace of ego. Here, in this slightly down at heel hotel room, he ruled imperious. And they would sink, they would sink at his feet and worship his innate brilliance.

" Oh yeah yeah, she said in a suburban estuarine accent, "he's such a sweetie. Doesn't touch the naughty stuff of course" - giggle – "but still a lovely guy. He was so excited to sign you," she smiled billowing smoke and oozing empathogens, a halo of friendly innocence about her that Cajmere, in his exalted state, almost deemed slightly pathetic.

'Youaregorgeousandamazingandmadeintheimageofperfection' ran Pippas interior monologue, absolutely inured to any condescension or arrogance that was emanating from Cajmere. She saw a purity and goodness and immeasurable genius in him and she searched for meaning in his large mahogany eyes. All she wanted was to tell him how much he meant to the world right now, to share with him this bliss. But it was a strange bliss, like a bubble, devoid of a centre or a core apart from the chemicals coursing through her veins. And it was insubstantial, it seemed to burst upon contact with any other solid. Was it really bliss? Or was it nothing and nothing and nothing.

Pippa's slightly drooping, curved shoulders were a giveaway that insecurity may have belied the emotional sunbeams effervescing from every pore. Cajmere noted this staring at her dispassionately whilst making rather offhand smalltalk.

Divorced parents. Broken home. Absent father. 'Hit on the ones with low self esteem first.' As his Detroit DJ mentor Carter had joked once. That joke, or was it a truth disguised as a joke, had lodged in his mind.

"Wanna come back to my room?" he shrugged nonchalantly. He couldn't be bothered to talk for hours. Strangely DJing made him not only invincible, but mute. Not for him the airborne chatter of the champagne bubble high. He became abstracted, silent; curiously pure and resolute after playing a set. Chit chat was for airheads – he imagined there was a brooding profundity in his aphonic superiority. As for this girl beside him, he figured she was far gone enough to be compliant to his wishes. Gazing upon her sunbed tanned skin, he felt his groin harden. Quite suddenly, he had a flashback to being at a gig with Carter who suddenly demanded of the promoter 'bring me woman', with a Neanderthal grunt. He felt he could merely click his fingers and she'd be on her knees, ready to please him.

Back in his room Pippa flung herself back on the bed, a quilted burgundy bedspread with burnished gold Fleur De Lys motifs was the backdrop to her skinny silhouette. All she wanted was to caress him in her arms, flesh upon flesh, warm skin on warm skin. But Cajmere, staring down at her, had other ideas. She began to remove her clothes, she did it in the manner of a child getting ready for bed, struggling to get her vest top over her head. There was no artfulness in her journey from clothed to deshabille. And she ended up laying there topless and he surveyed her coolly: small breasts flat to her chest nipples pricked up and erect. There was an abstracted look in her eye and a beatific guileless smile spread across her mouth.

"Stay there" commanded Cajmere and rummaged for his stash. He shook up a bottle of champagne, uncorked it and started pouring it on her sternum. His arousal was growing as he licked up the liquid. "Ooh you are naughty" giggled Pippa as he stared at her body, thinking that he'd like to jerk one out with an edge of contempt over those paltry breasts. He was an emperor, imperious. He was a rock star. He was carved of granite and impervious to assault.

"Suck me," he said like Nero issuing an edict to minions. He needed release but he couldn't be bothered with the body to body intimacy of fucking, the feign of a caress, the entanglement of limbs and potentially emotions. She took him in her mouth and he closed his eyes. Frankly it could have been any woman there, pleasuring him, another girl, another groupie, worshipping his magnificence and pulchritude. It was a soft wet mouth with gripping teeth, almost completely disconnected from a personality, a brain, a body.

All was priapic.

She swallowed him gratefully.

She wanted to talk. How tedious thought Cajmere. "I need to sleep now," he explained. "Oh okay," she seemed slightly crestfallen, yet the continuing flush of MDMA, her radiant, undinted consciousness, prevented her from feeling the stinging empty rejection, the cold hard transactional cruelty this situation would have elicited in one fully cognisant of all its unforgiving ramifications. The half-life of the dove was still swimming through her platelets and sensation was all. A billion snowflakes alighted upon her epidermis. A million flakes of glitter descended before her eyes. A thousand molecules of the finest rose petal perfume inveigled her nostrils. A hundred atoms of sugar-spun ice cream were upon her tongue (rather than the crude reality of Cajmere's sour, salty emission) and a shimmering arpeggio from an Aeolian harp was in her ears.

That was the low glow of beauty she felt around her as she walked out of that rather dingy burgundy room.

Cajmere was left alone in a dark room. He swallowed a sleeping pill and clambered into bed, glazed eyes contemplating a small dated flickering TV set. There was a 1970s film with Jack Nicholson on Channel 4. He started to watch it before sinking into sleep.

London, days later. There was still drizzle. Cajmere found himself rolling nonchalantly into the record store once again. It was a social scene for him. Arrive in most European cities by the early to mid nineties and there would be an independent record store where you could hang out and talk music. Mostly guys. But that didn't bother him particularly. He didn't expect a woman to tell him something he didn't know about music. It was a male dominated scene. Cajmere and his mentor Carter King didn't question this; in fact they revelled in their omnipotent status.

As he walked through the aisles of glassy black records in their start white and black cardboard sleeves he could hear the floating euphony of Art of Noise's Moments in Love coming out of the speakers. This ephemeral consonance of synthesisers happened to be one of his favourite pop records of the eighties, a foggy rumination of electronics with a sublime sweetness about it. The very breath of amorousness, he thought as it floated through him that day. He thought of playing it in his teenage bedroom, the anticipation of pulling it from the sleeve, the intermittent scratches and jumps a reminder of his youthful ham fistedness with vinyl.

It led Cajmere to muse for a number of minutes, as he stopped to leaf through the record racks on the way to the counter, upon the waves of nostalgia that intermittently lapped the shore of pop culture. The nineties was shaping up to be a decade of resolute futurism in music – the rise of new digital technologies and the sounds produced by them. But how long before a lapse into the comforting haze of nostalgia again he wondered. The seventies had enjoyed –

and were still enjoying – some popularity in clubs. The late eighties had seen a boom of rare groove (obscure seventies funk and soul records) in London and rare groove and disco clubs had continued to proliferate in student venues. The eighties were ripe for reinvention he prophesised, and indeed he had already started going to record fairs and stocking up on eighties street soul. The sounds were already dated enough to have a quaint appeal to them, although not yet old enough to be fashionable. Although, he thought it was only a matter of time. Was it the case that youth culture simply seized upon its least fashionable forebear in a kind of rudimentary reflex action and anointed it with the status of Avant-garde. Or did what was truly Avant-garde and experimental transcend the about turns of fashionability. He found himself attracted by twin urges: firstly to create some kind of Avant-garde classicism in the music he produced and played and secondly, to pre-empt fashion, to conquer its momentum and prefigure what was to come. This second urge would necessitate constant reinvention, continual instinctive manoeuvring to stay ahead of the crowd. But this proved to be second nature. Cajmere, was, something of a seer and a visionary where pop culture was concerned. And despite his considerable opinion of himself, he only had a vague grasp that he might be different in this respect.

"Heya Daniel," he heard Mark shout above the dissolving strains of Moments in Love, "come and have a cuppa behind the counter." He knew that cuppa in English parlance meant cup of tea, a strange drink he'd never got his head around. It was always coffee in Detroit, fresh from the filter machine. He'd tried making tea in various English hotel rooms and ended up with tiny flakes of tea leaf scattered everywhere and a strange grainy milky mess. But he did like it when it was made for him.

He found himself in a back room cluttered with big steel shelving units full of 12" records. There was a table in one corner with a number of white plastic chairs arranged about it and a sink with a kettle and a fridge. Chubby Mark, owl-like eyes behind round framed spectacles and a small twentysomething female with dirty auburn hair sat at the table. He guessed this girl was Rachael. He gave her a quick glance – white powdery skin and a large forehead like a baby's, pellucid watery greeny eyes, centre parted hair dyed coppery red with an inch of brown roots visible and pencilled eyebrows, a funny reddish colour overlaying a few sparse dark hairs. She was wearing a cobalt blue fleece, zipped up, faded mannish jeans and on her feet the ugliest shoes he had ever seen a female wear (he liked women stuffed into cruel high heels, feet arched almost vertical at an angle that looked painful) scuffed earth-hued brown lace ups with chunky soled heels. They reminded him of the built up shoes that disabled and elderly people wore. He dismissed her right there and then on the basis of those hideous shoes.

"Tea?" proffered Mark perkily. "Yeah, four sugars please," drawled Cajmere kinda pissed that a woman might be intruding on a potentially in depth conversation with Mark about music. Although he did vaguely remember that she was meant to be informed.

"So Mark tells me you've just been at Colourbox with Gareth Goldberg and Graham Price," offered the girl. She was friendly with no airs and a clear bell like voice.

"Yeah, sheez heavy night," said Cajmere remembering the debauchery with a smug smile.

"Never mind that," continued the girl earnestly, "what about Goldberg's set. I heard he's become very commercial recently."

"Oh yeah, for sure," he shook his head, "I mean I had to follow The Prodigy's Charly and Guru Josh's Infinity, it was hard to bring around a crowd like that, weaned on very obvious music."

"I'm conflicted though," said Rachael, "its true that hardcore breakbeat (speeded up hip hop beats and squiggly helium vocals) has become a very mass phenomenon. But don't you think there are redeeming aspects in that it's a very very progressive music in terms of sonic innovation. I mean one day we might look back on this music, as we will no doubt do on Detroit techno and think of it not only as something original, but as something very totemic of its time, Isn't it just snobbery to dismiss it as the music of the lumpen proletariat."

Cajmere was slightly taken aback at this interjection, firstly, a woman had contradicted him on the topic of music. Secondly, he hated to concede it but she did have a point. And thirdly *this was a woman using the term lumpen proletariat*. He could hardly believe his ears. He'd read Marx, naturally, and even recently Frederic Jameson as a riposte to post-modernism and what he perceived to be the realpolitik of Fukayama. But a woman. And for a woman to politicise music and youth culture in this way. *He could hardly believe his ears.*

He was so shocked he momentarily lost his thread of thought and was unable to formulate an immediate reply.

"Yeah I mean, I don't really know about the class system in the UK," he demurred, quite uncharacteristically. "Yes it is a rough music in terms of the sound. But what I don't like is that it's infantilising, those helium vocals remind me of baby talk and all those ravers with dummies in their mouths. There's something regressive about it all. Detroit is about advancement, evolvement, humanity moving forward into a machine like state. It's for grown ups."

"Look I'm on your side," continued the girl warmly – he had to admit there was something kind radiating from her, as well as honest, she wasn't just being contrary for the sake of it. "I love Detroit too, in fact alongwith New York garage and Chicago house, it's my favourite genre. I'm just as guilty of purism as the next record shop head nodder," she laughed at herself – endearing he thought. "But I'm just saying we shouldn't dismiss the whole hardcore thing. It's coming from quite a gritty urban multicultural place in Britain and there's almost a subliminal racism about some of the people who are dismissing it as crude and backward. And there are undeniably new sounds, some of them exciting. People are starting to play with the programming of breakbeats, not just speed them up to 160BPM but actually splinter them and reassemble them, almost into freeform jazz and those helium vocals, yes I agree there's something eerily childlike and cartoonish about them, like a malign disembodied spirit incanting venom in a horror movie but who ever thought of doing that before, but its new, its fresh, its taking the pitch of vocals new places."

"Yeah yeah, you've got a point." He was frankly dumbstruck, he'd never heard a woman utter the acronym BPM (beats per minute) in his life before and suddenly, this small unassuming redhead, never mind the shoes, had walked in and lit a string of lightbulbs in his head. And of course, yes, he'd thought about the socio-economic backdrop to all of this music, especially coming from a city so ostensibly sliding into a state of ruin and decay - how did that relate to the admittedly anomalous music he was making in that environment? But he'd never heard anyone articulate it before. Even the more intelligent and studious heads of his acquaintance in Detroit, the book readers, the introverts.

"What's going on with Rings of Saturn," quizzed Mark, quite unaware of the epiphany about womankind that Cajmere was currently undergoing and bringing him his tooth rotting tea.

"Well I discovered this new kid called Brian, he's from the suburbs," he explained. "He hasn't got much equipment, makes stuff in his bedroom but he's got these strange dolorous melodies, its all very minor key, but beautiful, melancholy beautiful, that sorta feeling you have on a rainy Sunday afternoon. I've let him loose in my studio whilst I'm in Europe this time to see what he comes up with. He's fond of analogue sounds, I've got a feeling there's going to be quite a fetish for analogue in the next few years. People trying to turn the clock back."

"You never get the same warmth with digital," mused Rachael. "Some of the digital stuff I hear now, especially the new trance sound coming out of Germany and Europe almost sounds like all evidence of humanity has been erased from the studio. It's ruthlessly efficient but also cold and clinical."

God she's put it better than I ever could, thought Cajmere, still somewhat dumbstruck.

"Have you heard this Dan, it's from Belgium?" said Mark cueing up a disc on the Technics 1210 stacked on boxes next to the sink.

"Yeah, Kinetic, on that brilliant new label from Joachim Toop. "It's going to be massive," pronounced Cajmere gaining back some of his customary ebullience.

The chords, thick wedges of minor key bombast, filled the room. *'Cmon and get you some more'* urged the commanding, dominant diva vocal.

"I'm gonna play that on Saturday," considered Cajmere. "It's quite a good midpoint between stripped back beats and more instrumental tracks and straight up tuneful. "It's going to be an anthem, no two ways about it."

"Where are you playing?" asked Rachael.

"Small club called Milk in Birmingham,"

"Oh yeah I know that one, Turntable mag just ran a feature on it. Resident DJs are very much Chicago and Detroit purists."

This girl was on it.

"Yeah could be as difficult as playing Colourbox with cheese head Goldberg - for different reasons," he reckoned. "They might have all the same records in their boxes as me!" he laughed to himself, his superiority complex knowing they wouldn't. "Time to get some one off test pressings and rarities out, pre-release stuff from the label I think."

The green rushing past the windows seemed infinite to Daniel Cajmere as he sat on the Inter City train to Birmingham, record box at his feet. He gulped on a whisky and coke, it was one of those generic whiskies with a slightly synthetic taste that had been dispensed from an unmarked bottle behind the bar. Cajmere liked something branded and fairly obscure, or Jack Daniels, the rock'n'roll drink of choice, but he would make do with this for now. Nothing more than malted water and alcohol he thought disparagingly. He popped an SSRI in his mouth, without people around him or the adrenalin of the club set, the gloom tended to set in. These days, heady, speeding past like the train as youth so often does. Yet strangely devoid of profundity and, for all his intelligence, true insight. He lived for the night.

The English countryside distracted him. The sky was dark today, leaden, a piece of metal alloy sheeting. No light. There was slight drizzle and somehow the chlorophyll green of the grass and the trees was thrown into sharper focus. Cows dotted the fields, their soft bovine forms becoming sculpted and solid from a distance. For all his readings of

Jameson, he had barely seen a real cow was until his late teens (although he had had some on a toy farm as a child), so landlocked was he in the sprawling metropolis of his home city Detroit.

He cast his mind back to the encounter in the record shop with the red haired girl, Rachael. It's true she had irritated him – those repellent shoes – so devoid of glamour and femininity – what a waste of a potentially nubile young chick. He tried to imagine her done up like a porn star or a stripper – she could be hot with some make up and a catsuit.

Yet she had shocked him. There was, undeniably, something so sweet about her, so honest, so guileless that even a hardened operator like Cajmere had to admit his heart had been softened. She didn't try to impress with her thoughts, or to gain some kind of superior status with him or Mark, she was merely offering, quite earnestly a very considered opinion. And he had never entered into such an intelligent debate about music and politics like this with a young woman his age. Sure the record company babes could just about string a chatty, unthinking sentence together about a track being 'four to the floor' or having a 'banging kick drum' but this was a whole nother league. A woman who was thinking quite deeply and sentiently about what was going on right now with clubs, music, politics. He didn't feel lustful towards her, as was usually the case with an attractive young woman who had crossed his path. But he wanted to talk to her again. He wanted to hear her opinions. He'd even like her to stand and listen to his set and be honest, he thought. He wanted to impress her, he wanted to show her he could keep up and he thought about things too. She'd awakened something in him too. It's just that Daniel Cajmere didn't know it just yet.

Birmingham was the drabbest UK city he had encountered yet. The architecture: pebbledashed concrete rotundas, shopping centres and tower blocks spoke of 1960s and 70s bleakness, without some of the redeeming features of this eras bolder brutalist works. Cajmere had a nascent love of architecture. Some clear blue mornings in Detroit he would stand on the pavement and look up at Albert Khan's Fisher Building, breathing in its camel beige magnificence, stepping up, incrementally, in Art Deco splendour to scrape the cerulean sky. But as he sped through Birmingham in a taxi all he could see were looping ring roads, sooty grey underpasses, a bleak vision of cityscape devoid of all but the disfigured cement caked breeze blocks that passed as characterless grey edifices, piled high in recent decades.

Another gig, another hotel. This time a Holiday Inn. More corporate blandness. Cajmere sighed internally as he perused the dusty pink carpet of his room and matching curtains, the magnolia walls and plastic beige fixtures. The studied inoffensiveness of it, designed to traverse days, months, years, decades even and please the unquestioning majority of people thought Cajmere, with a placating subtext of harmless recreation rather than whole hearted fun or, dare it be said, raucous hedonism.

The phone rang. It was Phil the promoter of Milk. "Hello mate," he said in a crooning accent Cajmere hadn't heard before. Must be native to Birmingham he thought. "Do you want to come over for a drink before kick off?"

"Yeah sure" replied Cajmere. In truth he was desperate for company in this blighted metropolis.

Half an hour later he found himself chatting with the convivial promoters and DJs Phil and Matt in a bar that was straight out of the seventies. The seating was brown buttoned velvet with chrome tubing around the edges, it had definitely seen better days. The air was filled with the choke of old men's cigarettes, Capstan Full Strength. A lone barmaid ranged behind the mirrored bar in a black sweater with a glittering gold tiger intarsia design. A chalkboard trumpeted 'chicken in the basket - £4.50'.

Whilst Cajmere was glad of the company, it was certainly better than the anodyne purgatory of the hotel, again, he was enervated by the surroundings. He was desperate to reach for another SSRI but Phil (short blonde bob and pale eyes) and Matt (grown out crew cut and Italianate complexion), who were at least friendly and jovial managed to rouse him out of his funk.

"We're nuts for Detroit," said Phil in his strange curvilinear accent. "What's it like?" I've always wanted to go there."

"Gee it's kinda falling apart the last decade to be honest," replied Cajmere with a note of sadness. "The music is the great hope. It's all we got. The car factories closed down, neighbourhoods struck by unemployment and crime, buildings falling into disrepair, derelict. The myth, the romance to you guys is nothing but a castle in the sky."

"Well just look at Birmingham, tell me about it," shrugged Phil raising his eyebrows.

Cajmere didn't want to talk about Detroit, or techno. He was bored. His heart was sinking at the thought of a night of debauchery hosted by these two earnest guys.

"Will there be ,err, any partying at the club tonight." He meant girls. Hot girls

"You might gerra glass of warm white wine if you're lucky," laughed Matt. "No but seriously we're not really big ones for the eccies. They give me panic attacks. There's a good bar and we'll sort you out with a tab."

"I don't like drugs either," agreed Cajmere. A night of boozy oblivion did have a certain appeal. Alcohol was messy though, it made for uncontrolled sentimentalism, sobbing into drinks over loves you had lost. He preferred sex, given the choice.

"Many girls at Milk?" he tried to sound casual about it. He had low hopes though, it would be techno trainspotters like these guys and their tomboy girlfriends – all puffa jackets and trainers. That was if they had girlfriends at all. Not the sort of 'disco dollies' as he jokingly referred to them in his mind, that he liked, with their pneumatic figures, porn star demeanour, thickly applied orange foundation and bubblegum pink lips.

"We gerra few, yeah," Matt sounded uncertain. "We tend to find they are the ones who come for the music rather than your flitty glamour puss rave babes though. Ha you know the sort of girls in neon bra tops!" Cajmere sighed inwardly. He was saying this as though it were a *good thing*? Although he supposed at least he might get the serious intellectual appreciation he deserved he reckoned, but did he want it off a woman? He thought of Rachael suddenly. Well perhaps he did.

Milk was held in a small black box of a club, you had to descend a flight of stairs, walk through a basement bar and then ascend another flight to get to the main room. That familiar smells of dry ice, metal, the rubber of trainers and senescent perspiration greeted him as he walked in. It was a small crowd, as he'd anticipated mostly late teenage boys in long sleeved red or grey t shirts with flashes of fluoro. Rather tedious. He dropped his record box in at the DJ box and sought refuge at the bar at the back of the room.

He ordered a Jack Daniels and coke and assessed what the resident DJs - who were Phil and Matt the promoters – were playing. It was fairly pedestrian, if not boring. He wasn't sure where the records came from but it was not Detroit, probably the UK, Germany, Holland or Belgium, producers churning out rather wooden Detroit homages. Too reverential, thought Cajmere. They were so preoccupied with paying homage to the generic tenets of Detroit techno they had lost all the verve and flair that had gone into the original records. Oh if only they had known some of the pop flotsam the Detroit heads had listened to in the studio before making some of those supposedly 'seminal' tracks. He remembered one day when he and Carter King had been listening and messing around to Kid Creole and the Coconuts, August Darnell, of all things. But then posited within the multifarious post punk landscape there was actually something quite radical about the ersatz exotica of Kid Creole. And, of course, Darnell had been behind one of the most coruscating, politicised disco tracks ever made – Machine's There But For The Grace of God.

He was saddened in a way by the lack of imagination in their sets. The music sounded like a car or an aeroplane on cruise control, gliding machinery, seamlessly blended, drums in forward motion, motorik synthesisers, but curiously mono emotional, safe, the volatility of humanity seemingly expunged from the sonic architecture. A polite and respectful interpretation intent on mastering the rules. It made Cajmere vaguely irritated, as did any paean to his oeuvre or personality.

He sank another Jack Daniels before gearing up to take the decks. Tonight he was going to make this crowd fly, he thought to himself. No more dull, polite, obeisance. He would show them the genius of the real Detroit.

Within half an hour, Daniel Cajmere was sprinkling stardust into the air. He decided to construct his set like an opera – he had been to see an opera for the first time in the last year – Carmen. Recitative tracts – sparse beat backdrops overlaid with spoken word from The Last Poets, Gil Scott Heron and other proto hip hop heads – interspersed with fluttering arias. He had made a test pressing of Elizabeth Fraser's vocal culled from The Cocteau Twins Carolyn's Fingers and he played this over one a very simple and sparse four to the floor percussive track. There was an apocryphal story in the music industry at the time that Fraser was a reclusive heroin addict – he thought he might have read it in the NME or something. Smackhead, he thought contemptuously; the worst drug to get sucked in by. Scummy. But it didn't detract from the fact that her music was still unspeakably lovely and he thought he could almost see and touch her voice as atoms of it fizzled in the air around him, a trilling, hiccupping, rivulet of treble clarity and sweetness. The crowd, who were, he sensed quite musically literate and educated could be coaxed from the whole lukewarm sub-Detroit thing that had been going on and enlightened further. Besides he was in the situation where, as the new prince of the genre, anything he touched turned to gold as far as these promoters and their club were concerned. He could have *almost* played some execrable MOR anthem by Journey and they'd have been lapping it up. *Almost*. He laughed inside his head.

By now the club was full. Kids were standing on the stage, on chairs at the side of the room locked into the groove with the robotic fervour of automatons charged up with a high voltage electric current. Cajmere's limbic machine music with its flight of fancy arias and spoken word narrative had ignited the room. The crowd were engaging on a cerebral and a corporeal level. Steam was rising up off them, perspiration condensed and tricked down the walls; it was humid like a hothouse. One or two ravers took their tops off to reveal chalky white torsos, skinny, with the feint ripple of musculature visible. They would talk about this night for weeks and months to come. How Daniel Cajmere re-wrote the rulebook of Detroit.

Of course there were pedants who would have called Cajmere's set that night Balearic rather than Detroit – Balearic being the patchwork of house and indie rock and random pop that had originated in Ibiza in the late eighties. But Cajmere's mix was more refined and the bedrock of each track was the silvery glide of Detroit chords and 808 beats. He was improvising, playing with the borders of the genre, as only one who was at the very epicentre of its creation was allowed to. And this crowd loved it. True they would have loved whatever he had played. But there was a certain breed of Detroit devotee whose musical trajectory included eighties indie rock of the Cocteau Twins or New Order/Smiths strain and also hip-hop. Even though many house and techno fans proclaimed it as a kind of baseline, a springboard for their musical tastes, love of Detroit, particularly by those who read the music papers, did not exist in isolation. Many of these kids had record collections that ran the gamut of late 20th century pop and rock; Cajmere knew that, which is why as a DJ, controversially perhaps, he viewed purism with derision. You had to know the rules of the genre to break them however. Which is where he had a privileged position, he was making them and smashing them up almost simultaneously.

His set was coming to an end and he glanced around the room in the hope of some after-hours hedonism. Phil and Matt were at the bar – no hope of them introducing him to some girls – he thought to himself dolefully. Most of the girls on the dancefloor were clad in t-shirts and sweatpants or jeans and trainers with a studied mousy look about them. Out of the corner of his eye he clocked a girl hanging near to the DJ booth. After he had cued his last record up he took the chance to have a closer look at her. She was probably about 16 or 17 with dirty blonde lank hair, a crumpled grubby white t-shirt and the hollowed gaunt look he knew too well – too many ecstasy tablets each and every weekend. A nameless guy in black jeans started to mix a new record into his last track and he got himself ready to go.

"My God you're amazing!" the girl beseeched him as he left the DJ box. She put her face very close to his so that, even in the flickering strobe light he could see the inherent emptiness in her engorged pupils and the clamminess of sweat on her greying skin. The odour of cigarettes was on her breath. *Gone, gone, gone* he thought. A desperate specimen. But he was high, charged, unstoppable and indestructible after rousing the crowd with his virtuoso set and he breathed in her admiration like the very oxygen of life. Even though there was an underlying suspicion she had no idea what Detroit techno was

"Wanna drink?" He knew he shouldn't be asking her, but he was strangely drawn to this pitiful girl. He wanted to take her and shake her, overpower her and do other things to her too. Things that his mind said were wrong, but his body was overpoweringly surging towards.

"Oh yeah," she spoke in with the same elongated vowel sounds as Matt and Phil he noted. "Luvvit"

"Who are yew again?"

She didn't even know who he was. Only that he was the DJ and he was important. He could tell conversation would be limited, in part due to this girl's palpable delirium. *But lets be honest, he thought, was he really in the mood to discuss astrophysics with a woman right now?*

" I don't usually come here," she offered, "I like the big raves at the NEC. I can get me glow sticks out and go really nuts," she beamed urgently. "I love a bit of hardcore."

"I'll have what you're having," she continued. "Shouldn't really drink on an eccy though. Alcohol makes me comedown really messy."

She gulped her drink down. Kids were always urging each other to rehydrate on e, he remembered, especially with that fervid bonhomie the drug engendered. *Smothering others with their love, he thought. What a fallacy.*

She chatted away about what her mates were doing that night, they had gone somewhere else, cheap booze. She told him she was working on her GSCE coursework. He didn't know what that was but assumed it was something to do with school. He was bored. He vaguely feigned a bare minimum of interest.

"Wanna come back to my hotel?" he finally urged after what he deemed to be a reasonable amount of time had elapsed listening to her drivelling on.

"Gorr yeah – where are you staying?"

"Holiday Inn – not the greatest but you know, it'll do."

Back at the hotel she stripped off her clothes almost as soon as they'd got in the door.

"Can I have a shower?"

"Yeah sure," he knew it was all about sensation for e heads. The warm gush of water on skin like sequins falling upon velvet.

But her body wasn't velvet, it was emaciated, angular, he could see nodular outcrops of bone, her clavicle, her hipbones, what was the word people used: *jutting*.

He put MTV on, some Eurotrash pop to distract him.

She was running around the room, smothering herself with unguents from the bathroom, plundering the mini bar and dancing to Culture Beat, probably the most execrable pap ever to have been made into vinyl he thought.
It occurred to him then and there that she might never have been in a hotel before.

"Come here" he beckoned and patted the bed. She suddenly stopped, flopped next to him like a rag doll and yielded up her thin lips to the damp kiss of his full mouth. Within minutes he was prostrated on those acute-angled hip bones and was forcefully thrusting away with nary a thought for the poor limp creature that lay underneath him. She must have been all of eight stone.

He was vaguely aware of her shifting underneath him and what he thought was moaning or sighing. He was still surging with the adrenalin of what he'd achieved in the club and he also felt that tangible taint of aggression catalysing his desire for this broken girl.

He stopped for a minute – he suddenly realised she hadn't moved or responded under him for at least a minute. He took a sharp intake of breath and felt himself go cold. She was lying there unconscious. He quickly withdrew himself from her in shock. A horrific thought crossed his mind. Had he been locked in sexual congress with – a corpse? He quickly put his face near hers to discern if she was breathing. She was. Thank God for that. He thought about slapping her to make her come to, but that might be a step too far. He tried to take her pulse and could feel something throbbing under her skinny wrist. Phew.

He sat on the side of the bed with his head in his hands, massaging his forehead and tried to work out what to do. He hadn't got a clue what she had ingested prior to meeting him. A couple of ecstasy tablets probably, maybe some amphetamines and then alcohol on top of that. Not a good combination. He decided it would be safest to call an ambulance. Lying like that she could choke on her own vomit. But he was scared too – would they think that he had raped her? A young girl naked and prone like that in his hotel room. Whatever the lead up to this sorry situation, he would fall under suspicion. He quickly pulled on her knickers and grey tracksuit bottoms and her crumpled t-shirt, which she'd discarded in a heap at the bottom of the bed. Then he rang down to reception and asked them to call an ambulance.

Within half an hour two paramedics had come to his room and removed the girl. They'd asked a few questions with a hint of disapproval. He explained he was a DJ and she'd come back to his room for a party and then collapsed. She'd been drinking, and he suspected taking drugs. No he didn't know her next of kin. Her name was Louise. He thought.

There were a few nights in London before he headed back to Detroit. Once back he intended to get into his studio, sort it out, mentor some of the kids producing new tracks for the label and buy himself a flat or house with the proceeds of his record company advance.

One last visit to the record shop, he thought before going back. He wanted to see Rachael, although he was trying to deny to himself that there was anything in it.

"Yo wassup," he called to Mark and Tom as he stepped into the shop.

"Hey prince of techno come back and avva cuppa with us again," retorted Mark warmly, "Rachael's in the back." He had hoped she would be.

"Back again!" she exclaimed as she put the kettle on for another cup of tea. "Where've you been DJing"?

"Oh just at Milk, lotta homage to Deet-roit going on," he chuckled to himself. "Hmm earnest head nodding boys," she observed. "Makes me long for a bit of Eightball or Strictly Rhythm vocal house and garage at times."

"Traitor!" he countered. And it suddenly occurred to him that he was flirting with her.

Actually she looked a bit better today. He thought he could discern a feint trace of eye make up and she had trainers on and a hooded top rather than those hideous built up shoes.

True she wasn't a disco bunny, but there was a delicate prettiness to her features and her pallid skin and auburn hair had a sepia toned charm to them that made him think of recent black and white photo shoots in The Face and i-D magazine, girls with scrubbed faces and windswept hair in rural locations.

Although it was all a bit too near to junkie chic for his liking. One step away from squalid bedsits, floors strewn with dirty spoons and tin foil. No, he liked his women voluptuous and heavily anointed with Max Factor, or whatever it was they called that stuff.

"So what do you think about the new stuff on Electric records," she handed him a cup of tea and went to the stereo to put a 12" on."

"Gotta be honest, I haven't heard it."

"Woah. You. Haven't. Heard the new Electric stuff.? I can't believe it!"

Cajmere couldn't believe it either - a woman was going to introduce him to some new music before he had managed to get his hands on it.

Dense, analogue balmy chords floated out of the speaker. This was something new. The aerated electronics of the new ambient movement that had kicked off around 1990 with The Orb, married to looping staccato beats. It was good. Really good.

"Where is it from," he asked, gulping back his pride to admit she had superior knowledge.

"Sfrom London," she explained.

He wanted to know more about her, this wan girl who knew about music.

How old are you?

"23" she replied. Same age as him.

"What did you do before you worked in the record store?" he quizzed.

"I was at Uni," she replied matter of fact. "In Manchester. Great place to be at University in the late 80s. I didn't do much work. Went to the Hacienda most nights, just to soak up the tunes."

"Ah yes," the Hacienda. Even Cajmere, far away in Detroit had heard about this crucible of youth insurrection. It was a legendary club. Like Chicago's Warehouse or New York's Paradise Garage. Despite her awful shoes and her stubborn lack of glamour and geeky demeanour, this girl knew what was groovy. *She had been there.*

He wanted to know everything about her. He found himself gazing at her. *I could talk to you forever.* But it wouldn't be the done thing to hit on a girl in front of Tom and Mark. Especially one who would do so little for his impenetrable aura of cool, or at least the aura of cool he perceived himself as having.

"What are you doing next?" she asked in the course of general conversation. Although he found himself wanting to read into it as a sign she was interested in him.

"Going back to Deetroit. Yeah. Gotta a lot to do there. Sort out my studio and the kids who are making tracks for me. See my folks. The record company want an album and a compilation of the Rings of Saturn stuff. So there's that to do too."

He had a heartbeat of anxiety and felt himself sinking slightly at the volume of work the massive advance demanded. Was it insurmountable? Could he manage it all alone? As well as his hectic DJing schedule?

Of course he could. Self doubt didn't weigh heavily upon him. There were only occasions where he felt unable to cope and even they were few and far between.

Tom and Mark were out the front now. It was just the two of them. He had to have her number but he was simultaneously trying to deny it to himself even as he thought it. She was plain. She was smart. It was possible she knew more about music than he did. She was everything he had historically found a turn off in a woman.

"Can I get your number? I mean, you know, its good to have people I can call on in the UK to find out what's going down in Europe,"

"Yeah sure" she said casually as though she thought nothing of it. DJs and record company people were constantly asking for her number to phone up and chat about music. It was a sociable industry, although women were few and far between. But she enjoyed chatting to blokes, a lot of the time they were easier than women she found, despite her feminist principles.

Within days Daniel Cajmere was back on the red eye to Detroit, drinking Bordeaux that was reminiscent of blackcurrant juice and trying to read Nietzsche. As he exited the airport with his rucksack and his record box the sky was periwinkle blue and high above and the air was crisp. He was high on hope.

He took a cab to his mother's house in Rosedale Park , a suburb in the North West of the city. He still had a room there although he spent more and more time in his studio on Service Street, often sleeping on the sofa there. Rosedale

Park was not falling into decay as fast as some of the other neighbourhoods in the suburbs. But a few months ago his mother told him that a man had pulled a gun on a guy down the street as he was washing his car one day.

"I'm back Mom," he swung into the hallway, there was the smell of baking permeating the air. "Honey its great to see you," she embraced him. "We're so so proud of you with this record deal, we need to celebrate." Cajmere's mother had spent her life building up her son, massaging his ego, telling him he was unstoppable, invincible. She felt her greatest achievement was producing a child with high self esteem in this broken down world.

"Mom, I'm thinking of moving out and buying a Mies Van Der Rohe town house in Lafayette Park." He announced.

"That's a great idea," she agreed. "You need your own place now and it's a wise thing to do with the record company money. I heard its quite a creative community there – architects and designers, writers and artists."

"I've been reading about modernist architecture and those buildings are iconic,' mused Cajmere. "I can't stay here all my life and I figured it would be a good investment."

"You're so smart," he felt his feelings of self-importance swell in his mother's presence. He felt she more than anyone had the clarity to see his brilliance, the light that radiated from every pore.

"Your father was here," she revealed.

"Oh no – really. What did he want?" he frowned

"Money - as usual."

Cajmere hated his father as much as he loved and also pitied his mother (mainly for the beaten down life she'd had with his father). His father was a wastrel who had walked out when he was seven. His mother had spent the rest of his childhood working two and three jobs to give Cajmere the best upbringing she could.

"It'll be one happy day for me when he passes." rued Cajmere bitterly.

"Don't say that about anyone, even your father, whatever hell he's put us through in the past. We have to forgive."

Christ his mother was a soft touch. It riled him.

The next day he was back in his studio. Housed in a loft space above a Chinese restaurant it was a draughty space cluttered with equipment – a large black mixing desk, keyboards old and new, samplers, drum machines, a beige Apple computer and a pair of Technics 1210 decks. The walls were matt black and the floor was greying splintering and splitting wood floorboards. There was also a row of metal shelving with all of Cajmere's 12" records stacked neatly – he'd got some kid from the neighbourhood to help him do this one day. He liked everything ordered and under control.

It was a month since Cajmere had been in the studio last and some of his protégées from his Rings of Saturn label; Eddie Fowke and Tony Silkin had had keys in his absence. He sighed at the crumpled empty coke cans and slimy take away cartons they'd left strewn on the floor, picking them up with irritation at the desecration of his carefully tended environment. *Didn't they have any respect?* Tapes and records were scattered about out of their sleeves and cases. He could feel himself getting infuriated at the lack of organisation.

Eventually he settled, with the coffee he'd got from the deli round the block, to work on some of the material he'd started laying down for an album six weeks previously. He listened to the drumbeats he had chosen – a simple syncopated handclap – perhaps not quintessential Detroit but then he was veering to something more jazz inspired. He switched on the keyboard and played some chords. He struck a few notes. A surge of warmth, like balmy water, emanated from his Roland 808. He put some records on to inspire him: Terry Riley and Steve Reich and Miles Davis and Herbie Hancock. It was coming easily today, not just tracks looping samples of other records, but whole melodies, fully formed, swirled around his head, building and building until they urgently entreated the listener to move, to submit.

Some hours later and the doorbell went. He answered it and there stood a formidable presence – a six foot tall black guy, slightly bulbous eyes, broad nose, thinnish mouth, imposing but not conventionally handsome like Cajmere was, with a baseball cap and black anorak on. It was Carter King, his mentor and friend and one of the founding fathers of the Detroit sound.

"Wassup man," he exclaimed.

"I heard there was some guy here with a multimillion pound record deal," Carter congratulated.

"You. Are. Looking. At. The. Prince." retorted Cajmere emphatically. "Come in Carter and hang out. I'm just laying down some tracks for the album. You gotta hear these, gonna blow you away."

He played back what he'd been working on. Gentle washes of synth and some jazz inspired meandering that spiralled into a whirl of melody.

"Yeah not bad not bad," King was not generally one for effusive praise – he reserved that for his own efforts. "Reminds me I must get that 12" out I've been working on." He always liked to bring the conversation back to his own work – if at all possible.

"By the way have you heard this?" he pulled a record out of his bag and handed it to Cajmere.

"A Walk Across The Rooftops by The Blue Nile, hmm sounds interesting," he concurred, putting it on one of the 1210s.

"Tinseltown in the Rain is the track," advised King and the record began - cinematic, exquisite soundscaping, twinkling piano embellishments. The sound of rain lashed streets in downtown Glasgow, Saturday night; the sound of the moon low in the sky; of a lone crooner in a piano bar and of the inherent melancholy emptiness of the culture of postmodern surfaces and simulacra.

'Why did we ever come so far/I knew I'd seen it all before'

"Oh my God I love this, it's poetic," nodded Cajmere "When was it released?"

"1983, I found it in a second hand store. Good find huh?" nodded King.

His first thought was that he wanted to play it to Rachael. Because here in one record was all he had to say to her. *'love was so exciting'* coursed the vocal dramatically, like an elegy for a fleeting amour glimpsed in a matinee showing. *'Do I love you? Yes I love you"* Sometimes the words in the air were running away before his eyes and he felt like he was admitting to things that had barely formed and swelled in his consciousness. Yet. But something had stirred. Something in him *was* excited.

He swallowed the thought before it had actualised as words on the tip of his tongue. This was not something for sharing with King – which he was increasingly thinking about a girl who worked in a record store. King who frequented strip clubs, who had advised him once upon a time 'spin the tracks - never get involved'. King the eternal bachelor with his string of casual babes dotted in every city. For he had followed King like a disciple for these last three or four years they'd known each other. It would be seen as a betrayal of the male bond between them. Getting emotional. Emotions were something for the records, for your set, not to be kindled with or dispensed freely for a female. It was an unwritten rule.

"You gonna buy somewhere to live, then, finally move out from your folks?" quizzed King.

"Yeah, I'm going to see somewhere tomorrow in Lafayette Park."

"Not very er, fitting for a prince, you know that place used to be a slum full of us negroidians called Black Bottom don't you?" King was unimpressed, he liked high-rise penthouses, mirrored edifices, deluxe executive homes with neoclassical porticos, BMW's and Mercs, Italian leather jackets, branded clothes -Armani and Calvin Klein.

Cajmere liked cars too, but he had a nascent interest in architecture and although Mies Van Der Rohe's International Style was yet to experience a full revival, it was already of interest to a small cognoscenti. Particularly those who felt the pastiche-ridden postmodernism of 1980s architecture – Venturi et al - had left them cold. He felt slighted by Carter's dismissal of it, he was always keen to impress him somehow.

Carter had to go, he announced he was taking one of his casual girlfriends out for a meal. He left the record and Cajmere found himself playing it over and over again, head full of thoughts of a girl he barely knew.

He decided to loop some of The Blue Nile and build something abstract, ambient and atmospheric for the album from it. Why had no one remixed this record and revived it yet, he wondered? Who were these guys, The Blue Nile and why did they call themselves that? He knew a peripatetic, minor Detroit techno producer, Alexis Drake who was obsessed with Egyptology. He would scratch hieroglyphics on the run out grooves of his records. It was kinda a cult thing.

The very next day he was looking around a town house in Lafayette Park. The whole place had been built between 1958 and 1960 and perfectly exemplified the architectural aesthetic of mid century modernism. There was a living room, one wall all windows, the whole space whiteness - beautifully illuminated by the crystalline natural light of the morning. He ambled around the house, imagining it with a few choice pieces of low-key furniture – he liked simple things – not ornate – in natural fabrics. The kitchen was small but neat and there were three bedrooms, all with big windows and fulgent – flooded with light. An artist had lived there before and it was all freshly painted, still quite pristine, noted Cajmere. The community was one of architects, designers, writers and professionals. He thought he would feel at home here. He decided to put in an offer for it.

Back in the studio that afternoon and his protégée Eddie had phoned to say he was coming in. Cajmere was playing around on his treasured Rhodes piano, he wanted to make a Rhodes track for the album using that thermal clarity of the keyboard, something gently upbeat, with all the early seventies reference points the use of the Rhodes implied.

That afternoon, once Eddie had left he decided to phone Rachael.

"Oh hi Daniel, how are you?" She said in a friendly and casual but not especially excited manner. She didn't sound surprised, she was used to getting phone calls from DJs and producers and record company contacts all the time he supposed. It meant nothing to her apart from the chance to dissect the current state of music, which was, after all her livelihood and passion.

She had no idea.

"How is your album coming along?

"Good, all good," he did feel rather pressurised with the album but he could barely admit it to himself let alone anyone else. "Just laying down a Rhodes piano track today actually."

"Wow I do love the Rhodes, I only know of one or two people who've started collecting them in the last year or so," she recounted, "mainly ambient producers who are veering towards easy listening and kitsch at times. But I think it's going to be an important sound texturally in years to come."

He noted her voice on the phone, it's clarity and softness and friendliness. There was no guile in her.

She can save me.

"Yeah I picked mine up for a few hundred bucks in a junk store, it's got a beautiful tone, how could anyone throw it out?"

"The fast obsolescence of technology is a very interesting subject. I suspect one day in music we're going to fetishize out-dated technology even more than we do now and yearn for its clunky forms and less polished timbres. Even as we speak the crackle and the fizz of flawed humanity are being erased with the new digital technology," she sighed.

"You're right, all around me I see people debating whether they should keep their 808s because they really epitomise the 80s, but I say keep them, you just never know what's around the corner. I've got an old 80s Apple Mac in my studio that I use to play computer games. Its actually a really beautifully designed object for its period, cream moulded plastic, cuboid but also curvilinear. I suspect one day it might be worth a lot of money."

He was wondering if she had a boyfriend.

To ask would be too blatant. Not yet anyway. It was odd, usually picking up women was second nature to him. But now, when it really mattered it was the hardest thing in the world. But an inner dialogue overruled these doubts. He was Daniel Cajmere. He was handsome. He had a multimillion-pound record contract. He could have any woman he so desired – swooning over him and worshipping him. Why would he let an uncool chick like this rock his world. He wasn't going to let these feelings get the better of him.

"So when are you back in London next?" she didn't mean anything by it, he could tell.

"I've got another two weeks in the studio here, and then some DJ dates in Europe so I'll be back next month. I'm buying a house here and I need to sort out some of the legal stuff around that before I come too. Where do you live."

"Oh I live in Notting Hill, I can walk to the shop from here."

"Where's that?"

"West London. A lot of West Indian immigrants came and settled in Notting Hill in the 50s. Quite a few DJs live around here. I suspect that depressingly, its ripe for what we Londoners call 'gentrification'."

"What's that"

"It meant that it will become fashionable and the real estate prices will soar and penniless musos like me and my housemates will be forced out for finance workers and wealthy types."

"Oh, that sucks. We got the opposite going on here. Whole cities sliding into ruin and no one seems to give a damn."

"Why's that?"

It started when the motor industry started shutting down. Rising unemployment. Crime. Neighbourhoods burning down. Derelict buildings. Detroit is on a downward incline."

"Really? But all we seem to hear about over here is the music, how Detroit techno is saving the world." Said Rachel, sounding naïve for the first time in the conversation.

"It's ironic. It can't even save its own city."

"A phoenix from the ashes."

"Right. Look I gotta go now. How about if I call you again? Are you around next week?"

"Sure," now she sounded vaguely surprised. Perhaps the slow dawning that there was some ulterior motive to his call. "But you'll see me in a few weeks anyway."

"Yeah I know," he said trying to sound casual. "But it's good to check in. " He quickly thought of an excuse for calling. "Remember I've got to answer to the tastes of the record company in London, I need you to help me stay ahead of the game."

"Course, I understand. Bye then. Good luck in the studio."

He felt high after speaking to her. The rest of the day was fruitless. He played a stack of his favourite tracks and then went on home to go to sleep.

When he wasn't in the studio, Cajmere liked to perambulate around the city with his camera, photographing ruined buildings and derelict houses. In his meditative moments he saw himself as a kind of 21st century flaneur, observing and documenting the life of Detroit around him, or was it the destruction of life, the end of community, devastation, entropy. And whilst his music was often sleek and metallic in its timbre, he was simultaneously saddened by the cities downfall and entranced by the aesthetics of decay: birds nesting in crumbling chimney stacks, trees growing out of tiled roofs, blocks of concrete cracked, dislodged and weatherbeaten.

Carter, like many black Detroitians was perturbed by the broken down place his home city was becoming. "We need to raise these ruins to the ground," he told Cajmere irritably. "We need projects, investment, new blood – not to be reminded of wreckage all around us." And to some extent Cajmere agreed. But whilst the ruins were here, and they may only be temporary, there was some vestige of melancholy beauty about them – they spoke of time passing - *tiempe passate*, the transience of existence, the gradual and slow falling into disrepair of all of our corporeal reality; despite our futile attempts to render shiny new edifices and creations at every turn.

On day that winter, he had found an abandoned dentists on the first floor of an old house in a neighbourhood to the North East of the city. There were crusts of plaster scattered on the linoleum floor – the walls were pitted where plaster had just fallen off. In the centre of the room was an old 1950s dentists chair, still with its chrome exoskeleton and armrests, but padded seating ripped, stuffing haemorrhaging out of the leather upholstery. It almost looked as though it had been in the middle of rotating and then had just eerily stopped.

Snap.

Cream paint was peeling off the walls like patches of psoriasis, revealing stark white plasterboard underneath.

Next to the chair stood a buttermilk hued enamel pedestal with a small moulded rinse and spit bowl at its upper end. Black grime was smeared around the once white bowl, Cajmere felt vaguely repelled by the thought of all that saliva. Next door there was an anteroom with a receptionists desk and several old filing cabinets. They were dusty but out of curiosity he found himself opening one and leafing through the browned and furling sheaves of paper within. He pulled one out; it was someone's dental records from the sixties replete with lines of scrolling handwriting in blue and black ink recording the dates of their various visits and a diagram of their teeth. There were crosses over some of the teeth, for cavities or extractions or fillings he guessed. He felt remotely furtive looking at these old irrelevant documents, like someone was about to come up behind him and tap him on the shoulder and tell him to get out. He noticed that his shoes were covered in debris and plaster dust from trudging through the dilapidated building. He spent a few minutes brushing them off meticulously.

Back in the studio he placed his treasured camera on a high shelf. He would take more pictures in a few days and then get the film developed.

Suddenly the phone rang. "Hey kid its Carter," a corralling voice announced on the other end. "Whattur you doing?"

"Um not much," demurred Cajmere. "I was planning on spending the evening in the studio and maybe laying down a few more tracks."

"No you're not. I'm coming round with a few beers and some rekkids. And then we're going out."

"Uh huh"

"So get yourself together, we're gonna hit some bars."

Cajmere brightened noticeably. Music. Women. The two motivating forces in his life beckoned him like sirens on the rocks.

Half an hour later Carter arrived. By then Cajmere had hidden away his camera and his photo albums of ruin photography. Carter wouldn't understand and he might think him weird. It was strange, he had a slight feeling that he was growing incrementally apart from Carter. There were increasingly things in his life that he couldn't share with him. This had never been the case before. "I'm the king and he's the prince," he remembered the words Carter had used to introduced them to a visiting Dutch techno DJ called Joachim. "He's like the son I never had."

They wound up in a bar on the end of Service Street. Cajmere, disappointed, noted there were no women in there, only guys who'd rolled in after work in jeans and lumberjack work. They sat at the bar of varnished blonde wood.

"So you pleased with the album so far?" quizzed King. Sometimes he liked to test Cajmere a little. See if he could get beyond the bluster to his insecurities. He knew Cajmere was on a tight deadline and likely to be tetchy or defensive about progress.

"Yeah yeah its all great. Laying down a little Rhodes track for a single, sampling the Blue Nile."

He paused and swirled his Jack Daniels and coke around. He had to admit it. He was feeling stressed. Carter knew just how to play him.

"I gotta admit, there's a lot to do and not much time," he conceded.

"These record companies not as friendly as they make out huh," wheedled King.

"Nothing comes for free."

"That's why I stay independent," replied King with a note of smugness. "Not having anything to do with those money men." Of course there was a slight note of disingenuousness about this. King had not been offered a deal as he had only put out one or two tracks and didn't have his own label as Cajmere did. But King was making large amounts of cash DJing in Europe, enough to put down a deposit on a house and buy a top of the range Mercedes. He didn't say this entirely out of bitterness. If the record companies had come calling, he could have chosen not to sell out and still been a wealthy man.

"There ain't no women here," noted Cajmere rather glumly, staring again into his drink, which was having the usual, predictable softening, woozy effect on his consciousness, especially on top of the SSRI he had faithfully swallowed that morning with juice.

They repaired to another bar near the derelict Michigan Station. There were a few women here, noted Cajmere, but mostly with men. Guns and Roses' November Rain was pounding out of the speakers - an aural stream of pomp.

"God this is bad shit music" noted King. "If there's one kinda music I cannot stand its big hair heavy metal. Who likes this shit? Poor rednecks who don't know any better, white trash from trailer parks. Pah!"

"The sorta people who ain't never gonna know who Kraftwerk or Faust are," said Cajmere, his speech often descended into Detroit vernacular with King. "But there is a certain cynicism about it, Guns and Roses are writing for blue collar guys who just got their wage check and just wanna down a beer in a bar just like this. People for whom music is just wallpaper to their hopes and dreams and ups and downs. Not people for whom music is life and death.

But listen to this track though Carter, the strings are really beautiful. There's something redemptive about it. I like this track despite myself."

"You gotta be kidding Prince Daniel. You are so wrong on this one." Interjected King. They laughed as they downed their drinks.

Actually, pondered Cajmere, despite the fact that he was immersed in music day and night, there was nothing he liked better than to dissect the socio economic milieu of a certain music. He wondered if it was coming from Detroit. Detroit with its two great factories: Ford for automobiles and Motown for black pop. Motown, now that was another interesting one. How had Berry Gordy, during that era when Civil Rights was on the rise, fashioned a black pop music so easily digestible and loved by white teenagers – even those ones who were racists! He and King had had this conversation many times. The Motown formula – had it in some way made black music tame and bubblegum and digestible for a white audience. Or should they never question the mythos of one of the greatest black pop production lines of all time. Because it was revolutionary in that the music became so successful at all.

But then music was complicated. He pondered the influence of Kraftwerk and modern classical – white musics – on Detroit techno. You couldn't say that Detroit techno was a radical black statement. It was a hybrid, taking as much from white electronic music (possibly more even) than it did from the black funk of George Clinton, Bootsy Collins and Sly Stone. Talking of Sly Stone and his stalled career was one of Cajmere's favourite topics.

"You think Sly Stone ever gonna make a comeback?" he asked King earnestly.

"Why is it once we've had a few drinks you always ask me that question?" said King slightly exasperated by Cajmere's various musical obsessions. Which he knew only too well by now.

"He's a coke head," King didn't approve of drugs either. He was hard on anyone who got hooked, particularly if they were a black man, seeing it as a sign of weakness. "He walks out of his own gigs. What do *you* think? Be a miracle if that man resurrects his career."

"Yeah but so many rappers sampling him now, he's having a renaissance."

"He's probably too wired in some dive somewhere to take advantage of it," countered King sagely. "Can't get his ass into a studio, get his shit together."

You know he was in Detroit in the early 80s, recording with Bootsy Collins," Cajmere tried to persevere with the line of conversation.

"Yeah yeah," replied King wearily, "You told me that a million times. You're like a broken rekkid."

Cajmere felt pricked, stung by King's dismissal of his line of conversation. He was virtually dismissing him as a bore. Dare he rebuke King, the strongest man in the universe? Never.

"But there is a point to this," continued Cajmere now slightly rebuked and crestfallen. If you were listening very closely to him you might have determined a slightly cracked, broken, *hurt* tenor to his voice. He was almost wheedling King like a child now seeking favour. "See he's just been inducted into the rock and roll hall of fame."

"Really?" said King his interest faintly revived. "Well it's about time. Why does it take us niggas so much longer to get into that? Twenty years too late if you ask me."

"I'm sick of this music," Cajmere knew he was on safer territory with this line of conversation, playing to King's earlier dismissal of it. Guns'n'Roses Sweet Child Of Mine was blasting, machismo out of the stereo and Cajmere, like King, could find no redemption in Axl Rose's almost caustic and screeching snarl of a vocal. It offended his aural sensibility to the very core.

"Yeah this place sucks man," agreed King. Neither mentioned the fact they were the only black faces in the bar for the duration of their stay, but it had registered with them even if subconsciously. It was late now and both men felt the puffed up bravado of the alcohol swimming within them. They could go anywhere. They could do anything. "Hey lemme take you to this after hours place I know," announced King.

"Is it jumping?" said Cajmere expectant.

"Have I ever failed you?" retorted King slightly affronted that his junior would even question his taste in bars.

"Let's go"

It was a few blocks away. Due to the alcohol Cajmere was losing sense of all space and time and he wasn't quite sure where they were headed. King had a prodigious appetite for alcohol and Cajmere, despite being fairly robust compared to most people, under the effects of alcohol, was feeling ever so slightly destabilised. Not that he would admit it to King. Beyond a door with peeling paint on it – looked like it had been kicked in a few too many times. Down some pitch black stairs – thick cigarette smoke drifted up to greet them. And there they were in a smallish room, walls painted black with a bar at one end and a makeshift dancefloor at another. The lighting was low, save for a red light bulb dangled from the ceiling on a desultory electric cable. For some reason it reminded Cajmere of a William Eggleston photograph of the deep south he had seen in an exhibition in Paris some months ago.

The music was 80s soul, Luther Vandross, in fact the whole place seemed to be stuck in a time warp of five even ten years previously. It was busy, nearly every chair and table was taken, mainly black teens and twentysomethings, a few white. A black couple smooched enthusiastically on the dancefloor. All around was the intoxicating smell of cheap perfume, whisky, cigarettes (a melange of stale and fresh smoke) and sweat. Dingy as it was it was certainly a lot closer to the edge than the last place. There was a feeling of untrammelled hedonism as bodies crowded the bar with an urgent desire to dive into oblivion.

"This place is major," shouted Cajmere to King above the strains of Vandross. His body and mind was now so saturated with alcohol he craved the seedy embrace of such a mise en scene. They headed to the bar and stood next to two black women in their thirties. Cajmere observed the one closest to him. She was dark skinned, almost that purple bluey black that signified straight from Africa. She had large almond eyes and a broad nose. Her ringleted weave had been applied roughly and at her hairline he witnessed a black fuzz of Afro wool where it had been badly attached. She wore high sandals, white but slightly scuffed at the heel. He couldn't help noticing, in his drink sodden state, that she had enormous breasts filling out a dated stretchy metallic vest dress she was wearing. He found himself staring at her breasts hypnotised by their burgeoning voluptuous perfection.

"Wanna picture *boy friend*," she fronted up to him, eyes mock challenging, lips smirking.

"Photographs are extra by the way, but if you wanna good start you can buy me and girlfriend here a drink."

"Sure" said Cajmere "what do you want?". He decided he needed to urinate first leaving King at the bar to sort out drinks for the girls.

The toilet was insanitary, floor flooded with murky brown liquid, seat ripped off and discarded in a corner. Brown liquid overflowing in the small white sink. But Cajmere – who would have usually been disgusted by this unhygienic scenario - barely noticed as he relieved himself. The cistern too had been removed and the inner plumbing of the toilet was starkly visible.

Back at the bar the girl was offering him a smoke. "No thanks," Cajmere thought it was foul, dirty, made him feel sick. She clamped a long thin white menthol Sobranie between her plump lips. Her fulsome lips beckoned to him, moist and pneumatic.

"You come here much?" he felt the familiar feelings of imperviousness and imperiousness.

"Sometimes" she sipped her cocktail provocatively though a straw. The liquid was luminous algae green in the black light.

"I've been warned about women like you," cajoled Cajmere, slightly turned on by the fact she was at least ten years older than him.

"Oh yeah, and what's a woman like me then?"

"I dunno, a fast kinda girl, sassy, dangle a young man on the end of a string."

"How dare you imply I am loose. I'm the most high moral girl in this whole city," smirking again, the whites of her eyes were glinting naughtily and the straw was tantalising on her lips. He was sure it was deliberate.

"You can call me Leonie,"

She turned to talk to her friend.

"You know they is hoes brother, don't you?" King advised in his ear. "The thought had crossed my mind," said Cajmere. It hadn't, he was too inebriated, but he couldn't let King think he had missed a trick.

Time passed quickly as they indulged in a hormone-fuelled repartee that tripped lightly through the air, vacant as it was of all but desire itself. Cajmere had to admit, she was as much of a smooth operator as he was, bright and quick and very dextrous in flirtation. A double helix rather than yin and yang – separate but intertwined, mirroring each other with their twists and turns. She was feisty, for sure and the challenge grated on him slightly. He had to be in control. He felt a powerful compulsion to master this woman who was perhaps ten years his senior, to teach her a lesson and make her bend to his iron will.

He could toy with her. He could make her compliant. He could crush her just like that.

'Wanna come back to mine?"

Finally she had said it, the words he had been mouthing in his mind. He was vaguely cognisant that this was a transaction and that he would need money. He reached in his puffa jacket pocket and fingered a thin wad of notes. Must be $150 there. Surely that was enough?

He nodded and winked at King, who barely acknowledged him and was about to head out into the night anyway. Even King drew the line at whores. He paid for a taxi and they sped through the streets to some black-silhouetted street that he didn't recognise. He had lived in Detroit all his life but he was lost now. Completely lost.

Her room was on the second floor. The door opened and the light went on. Oh the smell. He could never forget that smell. It smelled like the windows had not been opened in ten years. Stale menthol tinged smoke. Cheap perfume bought discounted from a pharmacy – acrid – but the acridity had mellowed somewhat. The almost palpable smell of the bodies' excretions and exhalations. Mouth. Armpit. Vagina.

Mess and dirt. The brown carpet needed a good hoover – hairballs, broken biscuits, ground in dirt. There was a black sheet hung makeshift at the window. And on the large king size bed there were red satin sheets – rumpled – it had not been made. Cajmere touched them as he sat on it. They were nylon, synthetic and almost gave off an electric charge. The walls were a sickly pepto bismol pink. At least there was a lampshade here, some small semblance of civilisation – it was an anaemic pink with synthetic brocade fringing.

"I didn't plan on bringing anyone back tonight," she said gesturing to the bed. This was the nearest she was going to get to an excuse or an apology. Like Cajmere, she was a seasoned operator. Like Cajmere, she felt no shame.

"What you want honey?" she slipped off her dress expertly to reveal a black lace basque and thong

"Suck you off is twenty"

"Full sex is forty"

He couldn't bring himself to lie down naked on those sweat suffused and stained sheets.

"Suck me" he demanded feeling impatient. "Quickly," he unzipped his fly.

God she was good at this. He felt the impulses in his tumescent groin build and build until he wanted to thrust away mindlessly into an oblivion where fireworks shot off his skin. He felt an overweening potency as the older woman crumpled under him submissively – or at least he imagined she did. She certainly put all those amateur groupies in hotel rooms with their teenage fumblings to shame. Although black women weren't usually his thing.

"You smoke rock?" She retrieved a little glass pipe from a battered melamine chest of drawers.

"I don't take drugs."

"Time to get high honey," she urged taking a rock from a little plastic bag, put it in the pipe, lit the end and took a deep inhalation.

He watched her.

They sat there, on the rumpled red satin bed: she high, he post-coital. He lay back on the buttoned velveteen headboard.

Time passed. Due to the alcohol and hormones rushing through his bloodstream it was unclear whether it was passing very quickly or very slowly and it just seemed to be quick. All seemed fast. A bullet train into the future. Timestretch, that was what he did in the studio and now he was doing it with his lifestyle too. He was prince of his own reality, speeding up and speeding up and driving very very fast and oh, he was never going to crash ever – the breakneck velocity of his consciousness streaked into the ether. *Fuck civilisation. This was living. Really living.*

Suddenly his momentum was derailed

"Oh honey I spilled my baggie on the floor," she screeched, panicking. Walking to the door she had scattered little white rocks and powder all over the dirty brown carpet. "Help me look for them would you?" Cajmere was slow to react, so abstracted he was by the alcohol and the sex. Gradually he roused himself and soon they were both on their hands and knees, scrabbling on the soiled carpet for small specks of white. It was the last thing he wanted to be doing. He could feel the synthetic fur of the carpet under his fingers very acutely, it pinged with static, he could feel hairs, grease between his fingers, his skin was hyper sensitive after the drug, it was almost too much to bear. He sighed loudly and she must have heard him. "Sokay honey, I think I got all of it."

An hour passed and he was feeling an increasing sense of spaciousness and floatation and wooziness from drinking. Still he wanted to hang there with her a while more, their body chemistry had bonded them for a short time and, hate it as he did, he felt slightly vulnerable. He wanted someone to hold his hand..

"You gotta go now, I gotta regular." He zipped up his trousers and, very slowly, made for the door.

"Aren't you forgetting something honey? Where's my 20 bucks?"

"Oh God yes" he rummaged in his trousers and for a split second he couldn't find his cash. Panic. Suddenly his fingers grasped it.

"Here you go"

He called another cab and sped back to the studio. A bleary morning light was dawning. He called in a 7-11 to buy some juice. His mouth was dry and all he could smell was that room and stale smoke. His throat was sore, in fact it felt as though he had swallowed razor blades. He felt dirty and irascible. He had just slept with a whore, *this was as low as it got.*

He dived into the couch in the studio and pulled a blanket over himself.

He longed for a hot shower. For his mother to put her arms around him and accept him. For someone to tell him they loved him.

But there was no one. Emptiness.

The phone rang. It was Eddie Fowke one of the kids signed to his label.

"Hey Daniel Wassup," he sounded upbeat.

"Why you calling me this early?" he boomed, his voice unusually loud.

"I'm sorry Daniel, I didn't realise," said Eddie, taken aback at the blatant aggression in Cajmere's voice.

"What is it anyway, be quick, I've got a lot on today."

"Well I was wondering if those test presses were ready yet that Tony and I laid down the other day."

"What test presses were those? I can't remember" Cajmere was getting more and more riled. "You need to take more responsibility for your own work. I can't be doing mothering you like this any more."

"Yeah but I have to lay down stuff in your studio, I don't have the equipment in my bedroom" Charlie continued trying to stay calm and strong despite Cajmere's continued attacks.

" Don't go calling me like this about some Goddamn test pressing. Don't you think I've got enough on my mind without you pestering me. I've got an album to produce and all you can think about is some Goddamn white label. You need to realise there are more important things that you on this planet. Besides you're lucky to be on my label. I've got hundreds of teenagers out there hungry for the chance that you've got. What makes you think you're so special."?

He was becoming personal now and Eddie, who was confused and hurt by his behaviour decided to bring the conversation to a close.

"Okay Daniel," he said his voice cracked after this onslaught, "I can see I caught you at a bad time. I'm really sorry I annoyed you. I'll drop by next week."

"You do that. We'll talk then." No remorse as he slammed the phone down on his hopeful protégée.

Meanwhile Eddie was left in his suburban house on the other side of town, worried and wondering where his future lay with Rings of Saturn.

He was used to vaguely bad moods coming down after an a few drinks the morning after. But nothing like this. This was like the gates of hell and he felt like it was everyone else's fault

He felt depleted but not guilty after his outburst. Wanted a hug.

A second later he slapped himself back into reality. He felt annoyed with himself for being so Goddamn sentimental and needy. A hug? When did Daniel Cajmere ever need a hug like some pathetic five year old. He knew how to handle himself.

He was a Nietschean superman and he would overcome these fleeting weaknesses. He would beat them down, pugilist that he was and run them out of his consciousness. This was just a bad alcohol and sex comedown talking and he had no Valium on him to quell the neurosis.

King wasn't the kind to call and see if his friend was okay. But he did come round to the studio that day, more out of curiosity. King, for all his love of material wealth and egotism, drew the line when it came to whores. His strict church upbringing had instilled quite a strong sense of morality in him. But he was wondering how low it was possible for his protégée to sink.

""You didn't? Did you?" He questioned as they put a master tape by a new producer Alton Miller in the deck.

Cajmere looked furtive. "Oh we just got off, nothing serious, " he shrugged.

"You know those girls are crack hoes, they're not for toying with."

"Sure, sure," Cajmere nodded, wary of his mentor's wrath.

 "Let's listen to Alton's new stuff," he changed the subject quickly, "I think he's laying down some interesting drum programming."

Alton Miller's jazz- inflected improvisations filled the air, it epitomised the mellower side of Detroit techno that some of the youngsters were making now in the wake of the British ambient explosion. They'd been listening to producers like Balil (also known as Black Dog), Aphex Twin and Global Communications (or Reload). Cajmere loved the sound but he didn't know what had become of these young black guys, some of them were really nerdy, most of them had day jobs in offices and sat in their bedrooms of an evening making music. He couldn't think of one of the younger generation who took drugs. He wondered what they got off on.

"Alton's a cool young guy" agreed King, gonna go a long way. "You should license a track for your compilation."

He turned to go

"But no more messing with the crack whores, I'm telling you now."

He knew what he had done. There was no escaping Carter King. He knew.

Some weeks passed and Cajmere was in the studio every day, building the album. Friends and fellow producers came and went, including Carter King, although nothing more was said about the night of Cajmere's perceived fall from grace. The young coterie of producers Cajmere was nurturing for Rings Of Saturn often joined him. And the music, the music went on and on and on, a looping electronic glide through galaxies and universes, the pure electronic expanse, constantly grasping at the future, reaching towards something, was there really something there? just glimpsed and better, much better than what had gone before.

There he was, in the sky again, heading back to London. This time he was reading J G Ballard. The same combination of his green and white SSRI and glass of warm, if rather acidic for his liking, red wine in a plastic cup was, once again, melting his calcified heart. He was vaguely aware of the middle-aged woman next to him with her coarse short masculine grey hair. He wondered indignantly why he never had any honeys sitting next to him on the plane, it was always the same, businessman, families, tourists but never a glamorous girl. He remembered Carter King telling him a brief tale about picking up a girl off a plane and taking her straight to the hotel room. He sighed wistfully at the thought of this. Right now he was sinking into the pale plasticised grey of his surroundings, surrendering to the somnambulistic blandness of the aircraft interior, feelings

uncharacteristically warm and soft flooded through his body like the red and white cells floating in his bloodstream.
The very next day he decided to visit the record store again.

"Yo guys" he hailed as he walked through the door.
Everyone – the usual shuffling coterie of puffa jacket and trainer clad boys by the counter - turned to look at him. He loved that.

The Orb was on the turntables, Little Fluffy Clouds, the ghostly poetry of Rickie Lee Jones' narration filtered into his ears. Much as he was an evangelist for the sound of his hometown, the Brits sure were making some good music these days, he had to admit. This ambient thing, post Brian Eno, it was fresh and interesting in terms of the tempo and the textures. He'd played at plenty of raves with chill out rooms, and Melkweg in Amsterdam was famous for hosting nights of film and lounge music, but was eager to know if Rachel had been to any of the ambient clubs that were now springing up in London.

He slipped behind the counter. Rachael and Mark were out the back. "We can't chat for long today, we're really busy and we've got a delivery and a stock take," she explained. Mark disappeared for a moment. Now was his chance.

"Hey I'm playing a gig in Brixton this weekend, he offered casually, "wanna come out with me, hear me play?"

"Sure thing" she said half taking notice half concentrating on unwrapping a fresh box of 12 inch records.

"Where are you staying this time?"

"Shoreditch, with Kevin Richards who promotes the Space Odyssey raves," he explained.

"Yeah heard of him, don't know him," again she was cutting through masking tape on a box.

"Wanna come and have a drink with us first?" he was expert at the insouciant pick up. Unutterably devoid of any kind of self consciousness or shame. He made it seem so easy, so casual, so effortless. There was never any notion of him putting himself on the line.

They never said no.

He smiled to himself.

You smooth operator.

"I'm not being rude but I gotta get on," she was engrossed in the boxes. He slipped her a piece of paper with the address and phone number.

"See you," he swung out.

It was done.

Friday came. He was slightly dreading what she might be wearing. That pellucid skin of hers needed a thorough coating with make up and blusher. Her appearance needed a rethink. Never mind, once he'd cracked her he would work on her, take her shopping with one of the record company girls and, mould her into his type. He'd make all his DJ friends jealous. He'd be the once whose girl knew about music, I mean, really knew.

She arrived at Kevin's warehouse,as he'd expected wearing a sleeveless navy puffa, red long sleeved record company t shirt and nubuck timbaland boots. He looked her up and down, his eyes gliding over her form with intent, making a mental look of every detail. Even in this scrubbed bare tomboy state there was something unconsciously beautiful about her. Yes, he would have preferred high heels and a taut stretchy mini skirt, for his eyes to alight upon curves that he would later manipulate with his fingers; but those grey green eyes were as pure as the hue of sage leaves and her hair, falling down her back, a burnished strawberry blonde, was freshly washed and abundant.

"Wanna drink?", he took a step closer to her. He wanted to smell her. She was clean, unperfumed, freshly washed and ironed clothes. No clinging odour of cigarettes (which repulsed him) as you so often found in the UK.

"Well get a cab down there, it's all arranged." Cajmere liked to have complete control over proceedings with women and his DJ gigs were also planned with a military precision. Unlike some flaky DJs he had never missed a flight or showed up late for a set and he prided himself on his meticulous time keeping.

"Who else is playing?" she was still, as far as he could tell, unaware of his intentions. She seemed to think it was just another night out with industry friends. He liked her innocence, her purity, her straightforwardness. She was devoid of artifice in every sense. She had none of the faux mateyness of the record company girls or rave promotion chicks with their seasoned, lugubrious chit chat, "awright darling" the ultimate meaninglessness of their every utterance.

This one was special.

 She was studied, maybe a bit serious, but entirely earnest. With her there was no 'patter', there was conversation and thoughtfulness without the seduction of the schmooze. Oh yes he could spot those whose over familiar, over confidence bubbled over into hubris, if only because they were kindred spirits to him.

"Who else is playing?" she would certainly have an opinion on this, he thought.

"Well it's a bit of a mixture really, quite odd for London, you know how the scene has fragmented here."

In the late seventies it had been disco and in the mid eighties it was just Chicago house. In the late eighties Detroit techno and Chicago house and in London acid house and in Ibiza Balearic. But by the early nineties there were increasingly fractures and fissures in this nascent scene – Balearic, progressive house (which had more of a synthetic digitised Euro feel to it) hardcore – which was rapidly mutating into jungle (a music of speeded up hip hop breakbeats) piano dominated Italo house, soulful and vocal New York garage, Detroit techno, European techno, ambient…. It was now a fragmented and highly specialised group of musics which may have seemed impenetrable and cryptic to the casual observer. But to the aficionado these were serious schisms to be debated and dissected at length. Where did one genre begin and another end? Were there racial divisions to these musics too and within Britain were there class divisions. And there most certainly were both of these. The secret subtexts of sound were an oft debated topic amongst the more cerebral DJs, journalists and record company bosses on the circuit. For a rare few music was not just music, it was a tribal motif representing your ethical, moral and even political stance. It was a lifestyle, a set of values to aspire to, it was all encompassing. And, drug like, it was all consuming.

So there they were, stood, in the dark together high up in the DJ box with hundreds of bobbing heads panning out beyond them on the dancefloor. Strobe lights cut the air like sabres of luminescence and the music, the music Daniel Cajmere played that night felt like the celestial heavens had been brought low and compressed through the speakers of that pulsing black box of a nightclub. That night he played for his life, a summation of all his talents broadcast to the assembled throng. A series of white labels from his Rings of Saturn record label that danced on the line between melancholy and beautiful, sheeny silver motor music hymning an elegy to the car production lines that had deserted his native city. The ghosts of cars were in that music, a dream of gliding along in a metal carcass, a glissando paeon to a lost world of industrial production. And for his very last track he had sampled the waterfall cascades of Gillian Gilbert's synth from New Order's Bizarre Love Triangle and run them over a four to the floor beat and the kids below on the dancefloor were holding their hands aloft and the words were mapping through Daniel Cajmeres brain like a mantra – he had always loved this song.

"Wow that was magical," Rachael looked genuinely impressed. "Great denouement."

"Yeah, that's my favourite New Order record of all time," he nodded packing up his box. "Speaks to me, not sure why, I think its the synths. Coming for a drink?"

They were standing at the bar. He was drinking Jack Daniels and coke and she was drinking gin and tonic. He'd half expected her to have a can of beer or a cider – she was surprisingly sophisticated in her choice.

"Strange line up tonight," she observed. It was true, someone had booked a very odd mix of DJs indeed crossing genres and tempos with abandon. "Strange for London which is becoming so tribal and fragmented."

"Yeah you don't really see progressive house or that Euro sound and hardcore and Detroit in the same places any more," he agreed.

Forget this music stuff, he wanted to push her freshly washed hair with its synthesised chemical rendition of herb smells behind her ears and gaze into her grey green eyes and tell her how beautiful she was, even in her unadorned paleness and with her boyish clothes and clumpy boots. He checked himself for being so sentimental, he must be going soft after one Jack Daniels and coke. Get over it, its only a woman, his ego urged, she can be managed.

And so they talked. And then they drank. And then they talked some more. But they did not dance. Because girls who worked in record shops did not dance, they just marshalled the songs that would become the hits on the dancefloor. Because superstar DJs such as Cajmere did not dance along with the regular punters. They watched imperiously from the sidelines as the kids danced and sweated and became more wasted yet.

He could feel her looking at him as they talked, gazing upon his clear tan coloured epidermis, scanning the laminated mahogany orbs of his irises that melded into full black pupils imperceptibly, taking in his tall yet perfectly taut frame. *His face looked kind*, she thought, *it was those brown eyes*.

 There was an efflorescence, a flowering of her perception of him after that majestic DJ set. He was the whole package she thought, the very picture of male pulchritude and also possessed of a coruscating talent. This wasn't just a guy who frequented the record store, like all the others, bustling about in their puffas jostling to get their hands on the latest test pressing, this was a prince among men. She found herself cringing against these fairy tale clichés that were fomenting in her mind, she had always dismissed princess delusions of pink ballgowns and glittering diamonds and handsome male protagonists who showed up and swept you off your feet. But she felt like she had discovered a secret, only she could see this brilliance, she felt like a schoolgirl with a crush on her art teacher.

I'm waiting for that final moment, he thought. Except, unlike the song, they would both be able to declare their love in the months that were to come.

"Do you want to come back to Kevin's for a final drink?"

"Yeah sure" she smiled woozily.

He reached and slipped his arm round her as they walked outside to the cab. There, it was easy. The deal was done

She felt so completely awestruck by the white light of his set that she felt she wanted to hang out with him… *for the rest of her life*. She felt teenage again, awestruck, dizzy, discombobulated – this man was a genius. And she came into contact with great DJs every day. But this one. *He was the one.*

The taxi sped to East London and they sat together talking in mutual blissfulness, bodies effervescent next to each other. They talked of music, of test pressing and new signings to his label, but they were far beyond music now, apart from a mutual music playing in their heads as their bodies synchronised and purred to some invisible vibrato. Somewhere crossing the Thames with the reflections of the sodium streetlights glinting, refracted in the water their lips touched plush together on the back seat. And suddenly, her body was alight like a glow stick and Gillian Gilbert's synths were cascading through her head again and again and again in arpeggios of ecstasy.

The events of that night replayed itself again and again in Rachael's head for days afterwards. She went into the record shop in a trance like state, the events of each day burred into the background. In the foreground, was Daniel Cajmere, she was full of him, he coursed through every vein, he jumped, electrical, from every synapse.

"I went out with Daniel Cajmere on Friday night," she finally confessed to Mark as they unpacked a box in the back one day.

"Good grief he's awesome, he's a savant," she was trying to suppress an urgent need to confess her burgeoning love for him.

"Yeah I heard that," sighed Mark with a hint of resignation. "But you do know that he knows it too don't you?" he warned.

"Yes, he's a genius, but he's a cruel genius." Mark was thinking: *have you got any idea what he gets up to?* He knew the stories.

"I don't really know him that well," she demurred.

But despite the visceral swell of emotion that had taken over like a tsunami, his words stayed with her.

Exactly a week after that night in Brixton, Cajmere phoned the record shop. He knew exactly how to manipulate a woman, despite his youth, plant the seeds of nascent romance and then absent yourself for a while, let her dream and let her yearn. It was calculated to the very last minute. By this point she was on the cusp of insanity with longing for him.

"Wassup,: he intoned casually.

"Hey there Daniel," what she wanted to say was 'why have you taken so long,' but she knew this would seem needy and be offputting to him.

"Wanna come for dinner with me this weekend Rachael?"

Her heart was singing. She urgently wanted to ask where have you been? What have you been doing? But she knew you couldn't question a man in this way, you had to play it cool. She also knew in theory that she shouldn't just drop everything for this man, but oh, how he had taken her unawares and deranged her moral compass and made her drop her principles and made them shatter on the floor in a million tiny pieces.

"I've booked a table at The Dorchester for tomorrow night, ever been before?" He knew she would say no.

"I've never been before, no,"

"Meet me in reception at 7pm, dress up."

Her first thought was panic: what am I going to wear. She just didn't have the kind of clothes to go to these places. She did have a dress that might be serviceable but she didn't own one pair of high-heeled shoes, they were just irrelevant for the life she led in the record shop and going out clubbing. You couldn't exactly wear trainers to dine in The Dorchester.

She wanted to tell someone. She decided against Mark and Tom. But her flatmates were all male, she needed a woman to advise her on what to wear and how to comport herself. She'd had boyfriends before but this formal concept of 'a date' somewhere grand and forbidding and opulent was completely alien to her. She got home that night and phoned her friend Claire from university – Claire was the most feminine girl she knew, she had worked on the Estee Lauder counter, she had shiny hair, she smelled nice, she was always on a diet.

"Crikey who is this guy – some kind of millionaire?" she gasped when Rachael told her the news of the assignation.

"I don't know how much money he's got but he's got a big record deal so I guess yeah he must be rich. You gotta help me out though, I've never been to a posh hotel with a very talented handsome guy like this before. What do I wear? What do I do? I can't afford expensive clothes and make up. I'm just a girl who works in a record store."

"Don't worry, I'm here for you, come round," Claire knew about these things. She'd had a boyfriend for four years now and was positively sage in those matters of men and femininity.

Claire lived in a basement flat in Mile End which meant a significant trip east the next afternoon. As soon as Emma walked through the door she knew she had come to the right place. Claire's flat even smelled sumptuous, like an odalisque's boudoir as a dense oriental wood and vanilla note fragrance drifted through the air. Despite having once been a damp cellar in a Victorian terrace on the road to Limehouse, she had created an impeccable interior replicated in every detail from expensive interiors magazines: everything was white or cream. It felt like an upmarket hair salon, overstuffed sofas, junk shop furniture painted with distressed white paint, a vast gilt framed Victorian mirror hung over the fireplace.

"Are you going to wave your magic wand?" sighed Rachael with a faint laugh. "I hope so because I need all the help I can get."

"Don't worry," said Claire, a statuesque blond with ironed albino white hair and very precisely executed sophisticated 'heavy natural' griege make up that she had copied painstakingly from a page in Vogue. "I'm taking care of this. We need to put some work into this but you're not a total lost cause – even if you do work in a record shop and wear promotional t shirts and Timbalands seven days a week."

"Do I need to change for this guy?" Rachael was worried.

"Not necessarily but you need to work on yourself if he's taking you somewhere expensive, you can't just roll up in your trainers."

She sat Rachael down and wiped her face clean with a cotton pad.

"You need to sort out your make up Rach,"

"Oh really?"

"Yeah and your hair. Look if this date is a winner, I'll take you round the shops and we'll get new make up, new clothes, new shoes. I can help you with all of that. For starters you need to start getting your hair done in a salon. Don't dye it at home, it'll mess up your bathroom and the colour won't be as professional. As for your make up - there are shades of indie goth about it from your student days. You need a change. Something more sophisticated and grown up. You can't mooch around looking like you are still in a C86 shambling band or you're a sixth former modelling yourself on a Pre Raphaelite painting. This is the nineties, times have changed. It's all about natural make up now, or that wonderful 1930s via Biba look with venomous purple lipgloss and Marlene Dietrich eyebrows."

"Oh I just don't have a clue," sighted Rachael resignedly after her friend's impassioned monologue.

"Look the bottom line is, a man isn't going to know or care whether purple lipgloss is in or not, He just wants to see that you've made an effort. But you're not going to attract a proper grown up boyfriend the way you were looking, you'll only have record shop boys and indie student types mooning over you. If you're going for the big league, someone successful who you're going to be serious about you've got to prepare yourself accordingly."

Rachael admitted she did know what she was talking about. Claire's boyfriend was a big name art director at an ad agency. He was successful, a high earner and they didn't go clubbing any more, they went to restaurants like Quaglinos (somewhere she had barely heard of – but it sounded sophisticated) and hotels, he took her to Provence and Tuscany on holiday, they were talking about moving in and marriage and children. It was all so, so adult, a world away from packing records in boxes and discussing 303 frequencies with other kidult twentysomethings. She had dismissed it, but perhaps there was more outside her world than she was aware of.

Two hours later her hair and make up were finished. Gone was the blanched complexion and the amateur liquid eyeliner, she sat and looked at her new self – golden apricot skin, lightly flushing cheeks, Clinique black honey lips (the shade du jour) and hair in soft ringlets bouncing around her face.

"I think you should wear this," said Claire holding up a little pale blue bias cut satin slip dress that looked like lingerie. "It's a total high street rip off of G--- (she named a designer) but it'll look gorgeous with your hair and your figure, you can wear a pair of my flatmates heels with it – they're your size. Borrow my coat too. You can't wear that beaten up biker jacket to The Dorchester. You need faux fur or something movie starry."

And thus with an hour to spare before she met Daniel Cajmere, Rachael's transformation was complete.

She walked through the Dorchester feeling vaguely intimidated. It wasn't like her to feel nervous, she tended to feel capable wherever she was, but the combination of wandering through such a gleaming palace of luxury (everything was lucent in this place, polished to a mirrored sheen) and the fact that she had butterflies at the thought of meeting the man who had riven through her mind, a constant thread since that fateful Friday.
He was sat at the bar. He wasn't wearing a suit just black shirt and trousers, but he looked debonair. She was determined not to be phased by it all. She would not be

cowed by all this money and glamour and romance. It was just a façade she told herself.

"Wow I never knew a record shop girl could look like a movie queen," gasped Cajmere, taken aback by her transformation. His eyes alighted upon her eyes, her lips succulent and their impeccable made up embellishment and her perfect hourglass figure in the satin gown snaking down her body suggestively, all voluptuous, S bend fulsome breasts and hips, swooping curves. He breathed in and her perfume inveigled his nostrils. It smelled like honeyed roses – a plisse of petals that had been macerated in ambrosial fluid and from which the sweetest pink molecules of plump floralcy had been extracted. Never mind those record company girls: here was the full package: looks and brain. You only bumped into this kinda female once in a lifetime he reckoned.

"You certainly know what to say to a girl Mr Cajmere," she smiled knowingly. But that was the thing, he really did know what to say. Despite her cynicism he was truly a prince.

And so they drank cocktails. Then they repaired to the restaurant which was housed ina capacious ballroom. Vast chandeliers of frozen crystal raindrops dripped from the ceiling. The proportions of the room were grandiose, all Robert Adam plasterwork and neo classical drama. The furnishings were discreet dusky pink and sage green. She was reminded of the ballroom scene in Anna Karenina, a book she had just read. This room could have been full of Tolstoy's gilded but doomed denizens, dancing in their rusting taffeta crinolines and tail coats.

They dined. They talked. And for a few gilded hours they were no longer a girl who lived in a shared flat and knew why XL records was different from R and S and a boy from a single parent family in the suburbs of Detroit who had just got lucky with a lottery figure record contract. They were

Fred and Ginger, gliding together on a dancefloor of witty and erudite repartee. They talked about all the things that mattered and all the things they said you should never talk about at a dinner party or on a first date: politics in the post-Reagan, post-Thatcher and post-Cold War era, religion - both were unsure and music. Although less about music because they talked about that every day.

She couldn't help but wonder, weren't there loads of other women out there chasing after this man. *The one thing she wanted to ask him but couldn't what went on when he DJed? Did he go home with a girl every night?*

He was so charming though, so attentive, so intelligent and so well read, she managed to put this right out of her mind. How could someone so smart also be a dog who ill treated women. Surely that would be impossible? He read books, he must know about feminism. General intelligence meant emotional intelligence – right?

"So you've no longer got Mrs Thatcher in power here in the UK – right" he questioned her lightly, without force or aggression.

"Yeah we've got Major now. Britain was very polarised under Thatcher. It's become a very selfish society after her reign. It's all about money grabbing, making sure you're okay, never mind the poor, the oppressed minority groups."

"You're a socialist then," he teased her "a real live socialist? We don't really have those in the States,"

"I guess so, for want of a better word. If the question is: do you want the world to be a more equal and less iniquitous place? The answer is most definitely yes."

You gotta admit though, it doesn't work in practice, I just read The End Of History,"

"Well Fukuyama's pretty right wing…."

"He's a pragmatist"

Oh its all about pragmatism with you American lot isn't it," she was flirting now as well as gently arguing her point.

"All I'm saying is that sure, communism doesn't work, or at leas the totalitarian versions we've seen of it doesn't. But surely redistribution of wealth can't be a bad thing"

Ah so you're coming at me with that Marxism has never been properly realised schtick are you now," he was flirting too.

She sighed and smiled "I can't win with you can I? You've got what is known as an overarching worldview."

"In all honesty I've started losing interest in politics anyway. Music interests me more now. Although I'm interested in the socio-economic origins of the music too. Like Detroit – it's black and working class – right?"

"Not necessarily working class blue collar in that sense," considered Cajmere. "More suburban. A lot of the producers came out of the burbs. Lower middle class I guess. Respectable homes but not much money to spare."

They wound up having a drink at the bar. He was drinking Jack Daniels which she thought was ineffably rock and roll and rugged.

He leaned in to kiss her. It was atomic. Two force fields meeting and sparks dancing and invisible bubbles of oxygen effervescing in the air all around them. And there, in this decorous, rather stuffy, grand old hotel were two kids from the burbs and they were young and amorous and the very epitome of pulchritude. If you had wanted a picture plate of nineteen nineties elegance and romance and exquisite grace, here it was for all to see.

Or so it seemed.

He knew now, now that they had spoken, now that they knew each other albeit in a cursory way, that she was a woman he wanted to make his own. He was decisive like that.

" So I've got a DJ tour of the UK coming up to promote my new single," he chanced. "How about you come with me? You can help me organising my sets and stuff. Hotels are free and transports paid for. Can you get the time off work?"

She was taken aback.

"That's a rather forward thing to ask a girl on her first night out!" she gasped, shocked and delighted all at once. I suppose I'd have to see about getting the time off work. But yes, hell yes. So what, throw caution to the wind."

He thought the deal was signed and sealed, surely she would sleep with him now. "You wanna stay here tonight," he said as though dangling a shimmering set of diamond encrusted keys before her very eyes."

Er no, the meal was lovely but I don't think I'll stay."

She demurred, she stood firm. Despite his being a prince she had fortitude, she resisted, she didnt come cheap. And he could see this. He respected her more for it.

The record shop on Monday seemed impossibly dull in comparison to this glittering world that had suddenly opened up to her.

"So you're going on tour with Daniel Cajmere?" asked Mark. He seemed solemn. Are you sure that's a good idea? I mean *really* sure?

"Yeah, I mean what the heck. I'm young. To paraphrase Peter Fonda in Wild Angels via Primal Scream I wanna get loaded, I wanna have a good time."

"I can tell you now you don't wanna get loaded because you told me you don't take drugs."

"No that's true I don't. I meant it metaphorically not literally."

"So hotels travel, Daniel's taking care of it all?"

"Yup he's sorting it all out"

"Wow, some guy huh." Mark went quiet as though he was re-reading the irony in his own exclamation. "Okay so no problem you having the time off but please don't come back and tell me you're having his baby as well will you now?"

They both laughed. It was a relief. She sensed there was reservation on the part of Mark, if not full on disapproval. She wasn't quite sure why. Ultimately she didn't care what anyone else thought, only she could know this magic, to her it was tangible, it was dream made real.

The first date, Edinburgh was two weeks away. All she could think about was that she needed to go shopping with Claire and remodel herself in the glamorous mould of their evening at the hotel. She got on the phone.

"So he's asked you to go on tour with him, oh wow, it worked, we did it, well you did it, I just did a bit of polishing. I'm so pleased for you. You found yourself a really gorgeous man. Or rather he found you. Now we need to make sure you look the part. DJ girlfriend is kinda like the new rock star girlfriend really isn't it? you've gotta get the clothes, the hair the make up honey."

"But I haven't got much money"

" Don't worry, I'm going to help you out."

And so they convened in central London shortly afterwards to shop and to discuss the etiquette of dating a DJ. As they cruised through the bright lights and carnivalesque chromatic displays of department stores and high street shops Rachael felt herself rebelling internally. She had no interest in clothes at all. She loved music, why couldnt her taste in music do the talking, what did it matter what she looked like? Claire, in mentor mode, led her by the hand into various shops and they spent a day assessing and supplementing Rachael's wardrobe – which currently consisted of puffa jackets, record company t-shirts, lumberjack shirts, hiking boots and jeans. Claire coaxed her to buy lingerie-like satiny slip camisoles and dresses in jewel colours (seams exposed as was the 'deconstructed' fashion of the time), the softest fluffiest teal hued faux fur coat, a Peptmo Bismol pink catsuit and metallic leather hot pants. "It's all very Jean Harlow I feel, or early 70s Biba, but you can dress it down with trainers so it's not too dressed up for a techno club" said Claire triumphantly surveying Rachael in the mirror in one of her slip dresses and her faux fur. The rest she would loan her from her own wardrobe. They visited make up counters and perfumeries and Rachael felt somewhat intoxicated and heady after spending an afternoon under harsh strip lights testing waxy carmine lipsticks and smelling lush resinous perfumes.

"What you've gotta remember is that if Daniel's got a big deal – and people know about it - every two bit record company and PR girl is going to be launching themselves at him. It's a meat market and a little bit more glamour won't do you any harm."

"Isn't that rather cynical Claire," Rachael looked worried, "I mean applying the tenets of free market capitalism to modern relationships feels rather harsh."

"Look of course you're special and of course he's falling in love with you. You're my friend how could he not fall in love with you. But you've got to be realistic. This is a DJ you're seeing not a priest."

"Hmm I suppose so," said Rachael looking crestfallen. "But you know what if I can handle myself with the guys in the record shop surely I can deal with this?"

"Yes but you're falling in love. That involves making yourself vulnerable. It's all very well being the tough girl hanging out with muso boys but this is a whole nother level you're going to now."

"But he's smart, surely he wouldn't fall prey to those vacuous girls you see on rave videos? Surely he wants a woman who's an equal, who can think for herself?"

" I honestly don't know," said Claire, "I know it sounds harsh but I'm just being the devils' advocate. It's tough love. You know him better than I do. I guess you've just gotta follow your gut instinct and hope for the best."

Hope for the best. It was so much more than hope for the best, thought Rachael. This was it, the summation of all she had achieved and hoped for in her life thus far, a soulmate, someone she could commune with on a purely cerebral level and someone worthy of her love. When finally, she met him at the airport to fly up to Edinburgh for the first night of the DJ tour, she was consumed with starry-eyed admiration.

As for Cajmere, he was certainly rapt too, but his overriding certainty in his own magnificence served to obfuscate any misty-eyed romanticism. Yes, she was surely special, but he could have anyone he wanted, he was the catch, he believed firmly in this. He gave her his DJ box to carry as they walked to check in at Heathrow, it was admittedly nice to have someone to travel with he thought. Boarding planes alone had become a depressing ritual. He hated being cooped up in a grey seat for hours on end with no one to talk to apart from dumb tourists and corporate middle managers. Although it was a chance to read, at least, he thought to himself.

He looked at her with her carefully applied make up and glossy lipstick. He had carefully noted her transformation from the girl behind the counter in the record store wearing a lumberjack shirt to this newly made up and polished Rachael with her silvery tops and her sumptuous fluffy coat. It was impressive. She really looked the part of a DJ girlfriend, but in this case she was a DJ girlfriend with a mind of her own, which was nothing short of a miracle in his eyes; something he had never encountered before.

They sped to a hotel in a taxi. Cajmere contented himself with the thought they would be checking into a double room, she would have to succumb to him tonight. It was the usual middle market business hotel – The Sheraton - a bleak office block in a concrete square – could almost be Eastern block – he'd been to Berlin recently and there were similarities.

He took her for dinner in the vaguely depressing hotel restaurant before they hit the club, noting its fading beige textured wallpaper and faux Italianate wrought iron seating. She was charming company, so thoughtful and meditative and sensitive to everything around and so smart in her dissection of people and things. She wanted to know what he was going to play tonight.

"You'll have to wait and see. A few test pressings for you to contemplate."

The air was bitter cold as they jumped into a taxi to go to the venue, which was, appropriately enough called The Venue. Inside, the small club, was hot as a sauna, packed with bodies in motion, alive with the kinetic energy of wide eyed dancing, arms reaching, ritualistically for the sky above. Daniel had heard so much about this club, it was meant to be the nearest thing to Detroit in the UK. Certainly the resident DJs had got the groove right, the sound was all gleaming machine music, vaguely melancholy, gliding to a mythic destination, no one knew where. The kids were tuned into this, not expecting rinky dink rave hits, but locked to the sound of wistful electronica, that felt like it was veering into the future. Cajmere and Rachael dropped his record box in the DJ booth and went with the promoter Julie for a drink.

"It's unusual but refreshing to meet a female promoter," said Rachael to Julie, a small black haired Scottish girl dressed in a long sleeved burgundy t shirt and leggings.

"Yeah we like to do things differently up here," said Julie, "although admittedly the Scottish techno scene does have its macho elements."

"I can imagine," Rachael smiled.

"We've been waiting so long for Daniel," said Julie.

"He's having what you might call a peak," said Rachael.

"You must have heard the album he's been signed to make? Questioned Julie.

"A few test pressings of potential singles but no, not really," explained Rachael.

Cajmere finshed his drink and exited the conversation, he was gearing up to go on stage and play. And oh how he played that night. He played for Rachael, he wanted to her to swoon with his paeon of longing for her. He built from very sparse, clear four to the floor rhythms to more complex stuttering breakbeats and hip swinginig syncopations. Above the beats soared chords evocative in their chiascuro renderings from dark to light, storm and gloom, sturm and drang to the brightest most lucent, effulgent sunshine. The general movement in his set went from minimal and empty through mournful and disconsolate to a denouement that was pure optimism and radiance. He was carrying that crowd and he was playing the heartstrings of these kids with the ease and intuition of a virtuoso violinist. By the time he had finished the crowd were stamping cheering his name 'Dan-yell Cash – myear! Dan-yell Cash-myear!" The lights went up and he kept on playing. The kids looked pale and shell-shocked yet they kept on dancing until the cheering and the clapping even drowned out those few major key chords at the end. He finished up, there was a sizeable crowd around the DJ booth, sweat drenched, paper white skinned teenagers clamouring for a handshake with their techno DJ saviour.

"Wow he sure rocked it," gasped Julie, "I've never seen anything like that in this club, even when Carter King played here last year."

Each time I hear him play I am more amazed, thought Rachael attuned to the subtle modulation of emotion that had carried his set from steel skied dolefulness to brilliant and hopeful exhilaration. He truly was a master, not just of the technicalities, the beat mixing, the invisible segue, but of calibrating the way music transmitted emotions and the way those emotions manipulated the human heart. It was undoubtedly genius.

He finally wrested himself free from the well wishers and made his way to the back of the club where Rachael and Julie were waiting at the bar.

"Very good set," said Rachael looking straight into those liquid mahogany eyes. "But also, it has to be said, without detracting from your efforts an unbelievably receptive crowd."

"Yeah, they sure 'get' Detroit," he agreed, "they're nuts for it."

"Lots of the DJs we have from Detroit have commented on the affinities between Scotland and Detroit," nodded Julie. "Personally I think its to do with the weather, a general air of gloom!"

The sped back to the hotel in a taxi. "Of course the best bit of the night is that I get to go home with you," he whispered in her ear.

"You are SO cheesy and such a charmer Daniel Cajmere, I shouldn't really entertain your smooth talking, my feminist principles don't allow it."

Although deep down of course she felt he was saying words she'd been waiting all her life to hear.

When they got back to the hotel they sat on the edge of the bed talking, drinking shorts from the mini bar. Woozy from drinking she looked into his eyes and murmured "I think I'm falling in love with you."

"Love is a dangerous place to be you know," he teased, although of course there was a nagging element of truth to this.

'I'm prepared to take the risk," she laughed, making light of it.

And as they fell into each other's arms he noted her glistening lipstick and smudged charcoal eyeliner and her perfume, how enveloping and sumptuous the roses were now. Her pale skin felt like satin and the plumpness of her lips and her breasts and buttocks and how he wanted to possess her in her voluptuous entirety and not just work her like his sexual ho. Although he wanted to do that too. He always wanted to do that.

He guessed this too, might be a kind of love. Something he had never felt before. Was he softening? Perhaps he was.

The next day was free before they took the train to Glasgow and Julie had promised to take them around the city before they left. They walked up a street called The Royal Mile to the castle, which was crowned upon a craggy outcrop of rock in the very centre of the city and they ate lunch at a small restaurant on a winding street called Candlemaker Row.

"And now we're going for a real walk,' announced Julie, as they approached what was a small mountain growing out of the land near to Holyrood House. They progressed up the hill with its scrubby grass. Rachel loved this sort of thing and often thought that she would like to go on a walking holiday; Cajmere was more at home in clubs and recording studios but he could see the beauty of the vista as they started to gain height and the city was panning out beneath then with its tenements and church steeples and grid of streets.

"Bit of a curve ball eh? Laughed Julie. I often bring guest DJs up here just to see how they are going to react to a bit of the outdoors. But the view is so incredible at the top they always feel its been worth it. Even if there's a bit of resistance on the way up!"

The three of them sat at the top and, with all Edinburgh spread out below it felt like they were on the very roof of the world. The wind was blowing them about as they sat down, but the cold had abated. The sky was that very high very clear blue that you sometimes get in Scotland in springtime.

"Amazing huh," confirmed Julie as they drank some small cartons of juice they'd brought from a newsagent.

"So what's your take on the whole rave phenomenon then?" she continued, " is ecstasy in general a good or a bad thing."

"We just don't have it in the states so I can't really comment." Said Cajmere "Maybe we will in ten, 20 years time but for now the likes of me and Carter are unknown in our own country."

"Sure, it's a strange state of affairs," agreed Julie.

"But what about you Rachael, you work in a record store, what do you make of it all?"

"Well," she considered with a pause, "me personally, I love the music, I am lost in the music, but I've got a downer on ecstasy and drug culture. I think combined with the general political drift towards the centre its produced voter and political apathy amongst a whole generation. It's just what the Thatcher government wanted in a way, a mass of young people silenced by sucking at a teat of sensorial bliss."

"But you can't say it's a plot to quell discontent, it's just a bunch of young people having a good time," sighed Cajmere. "You can't stop people enjoying themselves."

"Yes but what I'm saying is the long term ramification of that enjoyment is that they are sucked into a subculture that's not really questioning or fighting against the system in any way. The bliss is an end in itself. There's no rage at the inequalities that over a decade of far right government has produced. Just a kind of acquiescence."

"But what about the police raids on all the acid house raves in the late 80s down south? " interjected Julie, "surely there was some threat to the status quo?"

"Yeah but there will always be a moral panic when young people get together to enjoy themselves," countered Rachael, "just look at the history - mods, rockers, hippies, punks. What I'm pointing out is that we're not talking about May 1968 here or Vietnam where there was a genuine battle against the establishment. This drug creates a temporary comfort blanket that placates youth discontent rather than stokes the fire of rebellion. I'm very sceptical about ecstasy, even though I suppose in the record store I'm right in the epicentre of the culture."

"I think you're wrong. What's so bad about a drug experience as an end in itself? Widening the doors of perception?" mused Cajmere playing devil's advocate. 'Besides the alchemy with the music, people hearing music in a whole new way, sounds in 3 D from the speakers. I wouldn't take ecstasy myself, I don't fancy being a sweaty mess and I've got to be together to DJ, but there's certainly a place for it."

"Yes I don't dispute that the sensory experience is all consuming, even though I've never had it myself. But I'm just saying is that a good thing? What does it mean for society that a whole generation are caught up in this. Besides you would defend it, those kids that are taking it, in our world you're their God, their saviour, they feel you're talking to them through the speakers."

"Ha ha you're right in that I like the adulation, who wouldn't?" laughed Cajmere.

"But seriously though," said Julie, what about the argument that it's brought out a kind of Thatcherite entrepreneurial spirit in terms of the people organising the clubs and raves?"

"Yeah but that's only a very small minority, really ecstasy culture isn't about the promoters at all but the communing between the DJs and the crowd," considered Rachael. "And quite a lot of those promoters from what I've read were either wide boys or public school boys who had that swagger and confidence anyway, they'd have ended up working in the city if they hadn't been organising raves."

But don't you think there's been a slide towards political apathy in the UK anyway," interjected Julie, 'when power changed hands from Thatcher to Major we went from hard right to soft right. Young people were exhausted after the polarised battles of the eighties. They were losing interest anyway as politics became more centrist. A whole generation with political ennui.

Rachael paused, the wind on the top of the hill was buffeting her about now and her hair was sticking to her lipgloss. " That's possibly true. I suppose if there is anything positive to be gained from rave culture it was the sense of social cohesion. Remember Thatcher said 'there is no such thing as society' well I guess this was the retort of our generation. But crucially the society it created was temporary and illusory – something that lasted for a couple of chemically fuelled hours in the corner of a field. Can that really replace all those working class communities Thatcher destroyed by closing the pits and by devastating British manufacturing?"

"I'm not sure I agree with you. I mean the drug/music experience is virtually free," said Cajmere. "Surely that's as political as you get, people getting blissed out and you don't have to have a mortgage or material wealth to do it. Isn't that as good as life gets?"

"I think that's a fairly simplistic approach," countered Rachael.

Cajmere swallowed. No one had ever called him simplistic. He was taken aback.

"I guess I don't know British politics well enough but you're good when you talk about this stuff," said Cajmere his voice a little broken, slightly piqued but admiring her intelligence and analysis nevertheless.

"I know," she said smiling back at him. "You're one lucky guy."

They took a train to Glasgow next. After the theme park, fairy tale castles and cobbles of Edinburgh they were soon aware that this city was grittier, harder, more urban, as the train passed through outcrops of austere looking grey tower blocks on the outskirts.

"Now this reminds me of Detroit. The projects," Cajmere seemed solemn and distracted as they stared out of the window of the train.

That night they were in a nightclub called The Tunnel. It was quite a glamorous crowd compared to a lot of techno clubs they'd both been in: girls wearing sequinned tops, boys in leather trousers.

"I wonder why they booked you here?" questioned Rachel above the din as they stood behind the DJ box. "It's not really your scene."

"No its not a real techno crowd, more glitzy house and garage."

"Progressive house and trance," observed Rachael. "Don't ask me why but I always think of progressive house when I see leather trousers."

"Ha ha, its that kind of poseur Euro sound isn't it? Pseudo tough, pseudo serious. They've taken the soul and funk out.

White boy dance music. I've got no time for it myself," surmised Cajmere. "I think they just booked me because of the big record deal. I'm getting a lot of press, I'm a hot name, it's the surface coolness of it isn't it."

Rachael stood at the bar as he played, watching the crowd with interest. A girl caught her eye, she was wearing head to toe white, gleaming white, a white long sleeved t shirt and slightly baggy white pants also cotton jersey and a sort of blue turban or African head wrap on her head. She had a kind face that reminded Rachael of Sarah Cracknell of St Etienne, well disposed, friendly seeming. She was dancing in a sort of old fashioned way 'jacking' they called it jerking her elbows back and forth like the dancers did in those old house videos of the 80s. The girl, who must have been all of twenty, wasn't aware of Rachael watching her. In turn, she was watching a boy. He had shoulder length, slightly lank dark brown hair parted in the middle and olive skin with large brown sunken eyes. He was dressed in a long sleeved cobalt blue t shirt and baggy khaki combat trousers. Both the girl and the boy seemed mesmerised, she assumed both had taken Ecstasy. Initially they were several metres apart on the dancefloor. The girl had caught the boys gaze and gradually there was a slow process whereby they were moving through the crowd towards each other. An incremental edging closer, acknowledging each other, looking at each other with the glassy eyed stare of those who were rapt, both with each other and in their general state. Finally the girl went up to the boy and whispered in his ear for a few minutes. And then finally, they kissed, a long languorous embrace. Rachael imagined their wet tongues twisting, slithering and dancing inside each other's mouths as their cheeks made that sucking motion of those whose faces were locked in ecstasy together.

She realised because she was in love she was willing the whole world to be in love.

It briefly reminded her of a story one of her flatmates had told her about a couple who had met when they were both high on ecstasy. They had spend a few blurry months together, going out every weekend and taking pills, coming down together, drifting in and out of each other's arms. And then, finally, realising there was nothing in their relationship but the highs and lows of the pills themselves, a couple of months later they had split up, again high on an ecstasy pill. What a strange little tale of how lives could surf on the waves of chemical excess and how dipping back into reality could crack their brittle dream.

And so the tour continued, they took trains to Manchester and Leeds and Bristol and Exeter and Southhampton. Different nights, different clubs, darkness, music, dancing. They fell into a pattern, after Cajmere's set they would retire to the hotel bar for a few drinks and Rachael would dissect his set, offering thoughts on how it could be improved, which records worked and which didn't. She was the first person he let comment on his work. Prior to their relationship, it had been a private thing. He wouldn't have discussed his set with anyone, perhaps Carter or some of the guys signed to Rings of Saturn, but it was largely interior, something he worked out himself without any interference from anyone else. But he welcomed her commentary. In fact she was really the only person he wanted to comment. Every night he was playing for her, it was a musical paean to her from him through the decks and through the speakers. That first night in Edinburgh, the torment, the tempest the sturm and drang giving way to light. Light breaking through the clouds. That was the emotional narrative of his life before and after they met. A journey from bleakness and ennui through to hope and enlightenment. One day he would tell her this.

In Bristol he was playing on a boat. They went back to the hotel with the promoters afterwards and drank vodka shots. Obliterated, Rachael went to bed without being aware of where Daniel was, but she trusted him. Hours later she heard a banging at her hotel room door. "Let me in I'm naked!" It was Daniel. "What the hell have you been doing!" she doubled up with laughter. "We took all our clothes off and they chased me down the corridor,"

"You are crazy." She threw his trousers at him.

"Let me into the bed, I'm freezing"

"No"

"Oh please"

"oh go on when you say it like that."

And when they made love, he swore it was like white doves falling from the sky and their wings caressing him gently. His skin sparkled to her touch, the cells in his epidermis were dancing as those gentle finger pads pressed his skin softly. If he could have envisaged a perfect female corporeality before meeting Rachel it would have been hers: cushioned curves - the boom and bust and boom again of breast to waist to hip; tenuous sylphlike limbs; small childlike hands and feet. Everything that had gone before had been merely *fucking*, he decided, an almost mechanical desire to conquer and subdue, but this, this was sublime. He could never have foreseen under that greying lumberjack shirt how sinuously she would move when he penetrated her, the arch of her back, the dangerous choreography of her mobile hips. But strangely he didn't just feel the titanium vector of testosterone surging. Once he even felt himself welling up with tears as they had sex. And as he climaxed, there was a fleeting thought, fleeting but registered nevertheless, he wanted to be one with her, he wanted to impregnate her and make her his own, he wanted to give her a child.

"Let's get married" he said to her on impulse as they sat in a particularly dreary hotel room - all cream plastic fittings and stained kettle - in Southampton after his gig.

"Really, are you sure you haven't taken something?!" she laughed and rocked on the bed. He had certainly taken her aback with this one.

"No I'm serious, I want to marry you. My life is better with you. You make me a better person," this last cliche wasn't entirely true, he wasn't completely reformed as he still cast his eye upon other women. But he wasn't going to tell her that.

"I guess, standing outside myself and looking in, I'm saying yes"

Marriage had never crossed her mind, not once in 23 years. It was certainly not what she'd been expecting. She didn't think a DJ like this would want to settle down and commit himself for years yet. It was enough that he'd invited her to go on tour with him but a wedding. He'd certainly hit her with something unexpected this time. She immediately thought of the practicalities.

"Where are we going to do it? Don't these things take a lot of organisation? I mean like years and a lot of money? Who do we invite?"

"We'll do it in Vegas. I'll book the flights. No one there just you and me and we'll get some witness off the street. Someone I know in Detroit did it a few years ago."

"It's slightly nuts," she said quizzically. 'But hell yeah, why not!"

She was coming round to the idea.

"What do I wear?" an afterthought but it seemed like a crucial one.

"I dunno what do brides wear? A white dress. I guess any old white dress will do. You can wear whatever you like in Vegas, anything goes. I'll just hire a suit."

When they got back to London he phoned Carter King from the flat he was staying in.

"You're wha aaaa!!!???," the voice on the other end of the line was incredulous.

"Yeah I'm getting married," he tried to play it down and make it sound as though it was something bland and prosaic he did every day.

"You fool Cajmere, have you got any idea what you're getting yourself into. She's gonna get half of your money to start with. Any ho with half a brain gonna marry you, wait a few years and then clean you out for all you're worth."

"She's not cynical like that. She wouldn't do that. I know her," Cajmere responded quietly.

But do you? Do you really know her?" hectored King. "You haven't got a clue. And what about all the other women, the wild nights in hotel rooms, the hoes. I know you Daniel Cajmere and you're not ready to give all that up for one woman. You're still young. For crying out loud. I feel like I've lost you. Next thing it will be a baby and nappies and a house in the burbs. Sheez!"

"King, I'm still gonna be me. I just happen to like her and I want to make it official."

"You're a traitor to the cause Cajmere and I'm not really following you. What I'm guessing is that on the one hand you wanna get married, you want to take solemn vows and commit to one woman. But on the other you're still gonna live like a playboy and horse around with whoever you want? You've really really lost me now. You are certified crazy."

"Do you have to make it so explicit? I mean I haven't really thought it through. It was impulsive – you know – a flash of inspiration – spur of the moment. All I want to say is essentially I'm getting married but I'm still going to be me. I like her King, she's cute and smart and unlike any woman I've ever met before. This one is different. I guess getting all dressed up and taking the vows is a bit of fun for us really. We're gonna go to Vegas."

"Vegas – woo. You know what my advice is, take her on holiday to Vegas. Gamble, get loaded. Have a lot of sex in your palatial suite hotel room. But skip the marriage vows. You're not cut out for it. I know you too well." Back in her flat, Rachael phoned her friend Claire.

"Claire, you'll never guess what…"

"What?"

"Daniel has asked me to marry him. And I said yes,"

"Oh my gosh! When? Where? I can't quite believe it. I guess the hair and make up and clothes worked then!" She squeaked with delight.

"We were in a really dingy hotel room in Southampton on the DJ tour, he just took me by the hand and looked me in the eye and asked me."

"Are you sure he was serious? It wasn't just some drunken prank."

Honestly, he was serious. He's off out shopping today getting me a ring."

"You really have shocked me now. I never expected you to tell me that."

"Yeah I mean it took me by surprise too. It's weird I'm overjoyed. It's not even like marriage is fashionable these days. No one gets married these days. In fact I vowed in my Spare Rib reading teenage years that I would never get married. I wanted to rebel and live in sin. I used to see marriage as the shackles of patriarchy, an institution designed to keep women subordinate. Part of me just doesn't know what I am doing any more."

"I guess you fell in love, " Claire sighed wistfully.

"I guess I did. We're doing it in Vegas. Next month. Just flying out there and getting hitched."

"What are you going to wear?"

"Well that's partly why I'm phoning you. Daniel gave me £600 and told me to buy what I want."

"Some Prince Charming huh. I'm still flabbergasted. I didn't think millionaire techno DJs plighted their troth for just one woman, I thought they were footloose and fancy-free. I thought wrong huh."

"I spose I changed his mind."

"You sure did. That's my girl. Now, when are we going shopping?"

A week later, a clear bright spring day they met at South Kensington tube station. Rachael felt rather cast adrift in this part of London. It was alien to her, pristine white terraces, gleaming shop windows, brasseries, expensive boutiques.

"C'mon lets go and spend find something show stopping" exhorted Claire. There was nothing she liked more than the opportunity to shop.

They entered a vast white shop with a concrete floor. Rachel noticed there were barely any clothes in the shop; it was like some kind of avant-garde theatre space, with odd garments displayed minimally on wires. The shop assistants were angularly thin and clad all in black and they stared down their noses imperiously. She had never been anywhere like this before. It was frightening. She felt like a small inconspicuous speck. She was an imposter in her lumberjack shirt and her scuffed up trainers.

"Where's your W----?" Sarah confidently approached an assistant.

It's at the back, on the far rail," said the assistant with cool indifference. There was nothing servile about these shop workers; they were the arbiters of a particular type of glacial hauteur.

"Okay so, how about a white satin corset with silver foiled embellishment," Sarah had seized upon an item.

"I mean I don't know. It seems nice enough," Rachael wanted to flee the shop more than anything else.

"You know these corsets are a little bit late eighties now, I think but, Daniel won't know that and it will show off your figure wonderfully. I think they are still fabulously glamorous and glamour is coming back in clubs anyway, that's what it says in i-D and The Face."

"Isn't white just for virgins though?"

It's the nineties Rachael, you can wear what you want. And you *are* pure – in your own way."

She picked outa long draped white silk bias-cut silk skirt with a bustle to accompany the corset and some marabou trimmed high-heeled white mules.

"Try these on, you are going to look so gorgeous!"

Rachael still felt like an imposter as she disrobed in the changing room. She was petrified they would think she was stealing something. She looked in the mirror. Her skin looked grey and her hair was all fuzzy. No wonder they had looked at her as though she was a farmyard animal. But Claire was right, her embonpoint bosom spilled over the top of the corset like a bountiful promise of infinite sensuality and the skirt encased and augmented her comely derriere, skimming over her slender long legs. With her blanched skin and gently rosy cheeks she looked not unlike a painting by Watteau.

"Oh my gosh he is going to love you!" exclaimed Claire as she walked out of the changing room to show her.

"You angel. Oh sublime!"

Rachael felt herself welling up with excitement. She was going to be married. It. Was,. Crazy. She thought of an old 80s feminist slogan she had on a postcard 'first you sink into his arms and then you end up with your arms in his sink' She identified herself as a feminist who wasn't going to end up with her arms in anyone else's kitchen sink. But she was in love. And she was discovering that life could be complex – cognitive dissonance – divergent urges housed in one expansive consciousness. Perhaps I am stupid, she thought. Perhaps I have let myself be duped. Perhaps I want to be duped, perhaps I am so drunk, so far gone on romance that all reason has departed me.

It was drizzling lightly as Rachael and Daniel boarded the flight that spring day at Heathrow.

"It will be sunny and balmy in Vegas. Say goodbye to grey," mused Cajmere. Rachael, who'd never flown long haul before was trying to imagine what it might be like. All she could think of was Blackpool, where she'd been once with her parents for a damp holiday in a static caravan. Daniel was opening up a whole new world to her. It was frightening – she felt as though she were stepping off the edge of a cliff – but exhilarating too. They were flying business class. Rachael noted the heavy cutlery and the stiff napkin on her table. "Making an educated guess I'd say to order the South African Sauvignon Blanc," said Daniel as they contemplated their meals. *So you know about wine too* she thought to herself. Cajmere the debonair prince had swept her off her feet. She laughed to herself. What a dreadful cliché that was.

As they travelled, in that curious seemingly motionless suspension that constitutes the experience of a long hail flight; she was engrossed in a book. She was reading Naomi Wolf's The Beauty Myth. She thoroughly concurred with Wolf's thesis about the beauty industry and magazines being conduits for patriarchal oppression, although she wondered whether this book was really the ground-breaking thesis it had been hyped up to be and more just common sense. She sighed at the thought of her own conscientious preparations for the wedding, the vanity case full of make up and perfume that was in the hold, the expensive clothes, the hair curlers, the lotions. The Iron Maiden certainly had her in its intractable grip, or rather it had Claire, who was nevertheless an intelligent girl, and Claire had the key to what Daniel Cajmere liked. Rachael's favourite author was Angela Carter, she liked the vivacity of her prose and her postmodern take on fairy tales – albeit cracked ones.

. She glanced across at Daniel, he was reading Burroughs. She had this sense that there was a sizeable area of his life that he had never told her about. The lifestyle the boys in the record shop were referring to. She couldn't ask him about it. Would it break the spell? In her love for him, she was fascinated by it, compelled by it, even though she had never taken a drug stronger than paracetamol. Increasingly, as he possessed her, she wanted to inhabit him and to experience his drives.

And suddenly, here was Vegas…… they were speeding in a taxi past vast white multi storey hotels and skyscraper casinos and flashing lights blurring into a rainbow of electric fizz. She stared out of the car window rapt at the strangeness and the massive scale of the States. It made London seem like toy town, these widescreen edifices, monuments to capitalism, of glass and concrete and steel.

The hotel lobby had a gleaming cream-hued marble floor and there were faux Egyptian statuettes and everything shone and was polished and effulgent.

"Isn't Vegas magnificent," beamed Daniel, he'd never been before. "I am awestruck by the grandiosity of its kitsch visions. It's a world of gleaming surfaces and facsimile, of vulgarity and architectural folly and when you breathe in even the air smells of candy. We are gonna have such a blast here. Let's go to our room and then lets go jump in the pool and swim."

Cajmere had booked them into the penthouse suite. They shot up to it in a glass walled elevator and as they walked through the doors inside she couldn't help but gasp. It was huge, probably three or four times the size of her shared flat in Notting Hill: a sitting room, with wood panelled walls and capacious sage green chesterfield sofas and a large television. A bedroom, again in a very low-key, expensive pink and pale green decor with a bed that you could fit at least five people in. A massive marble bathroom – replete with two or three person corner bath and a walk in shower and very expensive unguents. She couldn't help but wonder how much he had spent on all this, it was paradise. They were on top of the world.

"Come and look out here" Cajmere had opened French doors in the sitting room and was outside on a deck "there's a Jacuzzi!"

"Oh my gosh," she covered her mouth with her hands and looked at him with a mixture of shock and excitement.

There was a bottle of Moet chilling in the mini bar. He opened it and poured them each a glass and they went and sat in the Jacuzzi completely naked. The water swirled and bubbled and frothed around them and the sky was blue and below them all Vegas was stretched out with its lights and amusements and man-made fantasy.

The next morning Cajmere went out to book the chapel. Rachel decided to go for a walk in this strange adult Disneyland. She idled away a few hours walking in the vicinity of the hotel, stopping by a diner for coffee, looking in a boutique, even though she had no real interest in clothes. There were rails and rails of sparkly kaftans, she didn't even know whether these were in fashion or not, she supposed someone must like them, she was drawn to the glittery patina of a pair of ruby red shoes with high heels, Daniel would like those. She decided to have her nails done, that is the sort of thing that DJ fiancés do, she thought to herself. It was almost as though she was toying with a different identity to adopt once she was married. As the Korean girl pushed back her cuticles she found herself chatting abstractly.

Why are you in Vegas? Having a holiday? Asked the girl breezily.

"I'm getting married to my boyfriend."

"Married – wow – you need special nails then."

"I probably do," she sighed, the whole ritual of wedding preparation felt so alien to her. She felt like some other woman should be in her shoes, someone who gloried in the vacant preening that was required to play the part. Some women obsessed over this stuff. She felt fraudulent, like some kind of drag act. She could hardly tell Daniel "erm, excuse me, I'm having a problem with the accoutrements and trappings of femininity. I feel like a fake." He wanted a woman to be fully engrossed with the artifices of femininity; he wanted a hyper femininity, a living Barbie doll to compliment his alpha male.

That night before they married he took her for dinner in another 5 star hotel and to a Casino. They didn't really know what they were doing, and some of the time they were just watching anyway. To Rachael it was crazy, she was watching a film of her own life, the life of someone glamorous and carefree and rich. She was way out of her comfort zone now, the back room of the record shop thinking about 303s and four to the floor, but this new life was exhilarating and dizzying and all she wanted was to be with Daniel, wherever that might take her.

And so, the very next day, there they stood, about to become man and wife in a little chapel on the outskirts of Vegas. It was all painted white, quite pristine in the noonday sun. As the priest solemnly intoned she stood there tightly encased in her white satin corset, it was digging into her bottom rib, her breathing was shallow as a result. She was holding a fresh bunch of white roses he'd bought her from a roadside garage, still in their cellophane casing. He was in a dark grey hired suit, which fitted him surprisingly well. She had only ever seen him before in jeans or combats or trainers and he looked dashingly handsome she thought. What was going through his mind? He was about to possess this woman and she was by far the most knowledgeable and fascinating and voluptuously gorgeous woman he had ever met. There could be no doubt about it, he was entranced, he wanted her body every single minute of the day, and he wanted her mind too. He had surprised himself with this. Together they could be the first couple of techno – beautiful and invincible and intelligent and talented.

He carefully slotted the diamond ring he had bought onto her slender pale finger and she looked into his eyes, light poured in through the high chapel window and the moment was endless, or at least there was an infinity to the way they were feeling as well as a gut viscerality. But all around them was the backdrop of Vegas, of gaudy flashing lights and venal transactions in dodgy casinos and immediate impulse gratification – the lure of cold hard cash and hot sweaty flesh and the momentary thrill surmounting the sort of love and grace that was hard won but enduring.

When she said her vows she said them with a gravitas that was palpable; she had never meant anything quite as much as this; she was concentrating so hard her mind had gone blank. She was naturally disposed to sincerity anyway, she was not one for platitudes and chitchat and unconsidered small talk. It was always always the semantic over the gloss of the semiotic for her. And she vaguely sensed this might become old fashioned in a decade where the old certainties of political left and right and, on their scene at least, commercial and underground were being eroded all around them. But she clung to her sense of morality and to her sense of always wanting meaning, profundity, and thoughtfulness. Even at her young age she had a preternatural assurance and a conviction about the right way to do things and the right way to say things.

He looked at her all in white, her breasts pleasingly rotund and quivering in the sculptural surround of the corset, it was as though she were one of the graces carved from white marble. His eyes alighted for a moment upon the succulent gloss of her lips. It flashed through his mind for a split second that this woman was far too good for him. But he quickly resumed his customary hubris and decided he was the prize. Despite this arrogance, in that moment he did mean the vows too. They weren't just empty profferings falling from his lips. He felt himself evolving in her presence. She plucked out some innate purity, some decency, some honour and augmented it. He genuinely did want to be a better man. For now at least.

"What are we going to do now, husband?" she asked as they walked out of the chapel as man and wife.

"I suggest we go to a really good old fashioned American diner and eat and drink as much as humanly possible. And then we go to bed because I want your body."

They found a little 1950s diner that looked a little like an airstream caravan, all gleaming metal and they sat in a booth over pancakes syrup and bacon, gazing at each other blissfully, almost barely aware of the sobriety of the commitment they'd just made to each other. She was still rather entranced by the size of the plates in American restaurants – she wasn't the kind of girl who dieted, she had never needed to and it just wasn't the kind of neurotic behaviour she indulged in.

" So what happens now, I mean the next six months?" It was the first time that day she'd really contemplated their future together and what it would mean. Even though the whole axis of romance is often looking forward and looking forward and dreaming of when you'll be together and what you're going to do.

"Well" said Cajmere, he'd thought about this. "You're going to phone the record store and tell them you're quitting for good and you're going to come with me and live in Detroit. And I'm going to make an album, an album that's going to blow the world away and put Detroit techno on the map for once and for all."

"Well you're certainly not beset by the self doubt that dogs many creative people."

"There is no room for doubt, I'm a Nietschean superman," he responded without the slightest trace of irony.

"Do you really really think that Detroit can parlay into an album format though?" she wasn't sure. Everyone said that dance music was a 12 inch single format. She'd bought far too many so-called dance albums that were predicated on one or two singles; those albums had proved to be disappointing and a complete waste of money.

"I mean how are you going to inject a narrative into it? How are you going to make it continuous without just seguing a whole bunch of singles."

"Excuse me lady," he joked "you've just vowed to have the ultimate faith in me, to love honour and obey me, don't start questioning me now"

She raised her eyebrows "someone's gotta keep that prodigious ego in check and I reckon that's my full time job now."

"Ego?!, what ego" She spluttered with laughter over her half finished plate.

He was blissful – they had just gotten married and now they could talk together forever about music. It was perfection. He had found perfection in female form.

That night they slipped into the Jacuzzi and toasted their future with more champagne. And he immersed in the deliciousness of her flesh, burying himself deep between her thighs in a slow ritualistic worshipping lovemaking. Lovemaking where the self dissolved into ripples of ecstasy. Smooth young skin on smooth young skin. Cradled together on this vast ocean liner of a bed. They made love until they were sick and oozing and then sleepy with desire. A blur of limbs, the glow of the epidermis aroused, the slippery merging of bodily emissions. As dawn broke and light fizzled in they were wrapped around each other and drifting into unconsciousness.

'You are going to love my house – well from now on it's our house," he told her the next morning as they sat having room service breakfast on the deck. "It's like a little white cube. It's a classic design by Mies Van Der Rohe. He was a famous modernist architect and the last director of the Bauhaus school. He emigrated to the US in the thirties and lived in Chicago, he designed Lafayette Park, where my house is, in the early sixties. I haven't got around to furnishing it yet, but you can help me with that when we go back to Detroit."

"How do you know all of this?"

"Oh just some books I read – about Mies Van Der Rohe and Bauhaus. It's not really fashionable in our era of postmodern architectural pastiche but I reckon it'll make a comeback."

She was constantly learning in his company. Having worked in a record shop she knew all about men's passions and obsessions, their yen to collect objects, accumulate knowledge and categorise things. She understood because she shared this love of imbibing information, of defining yourself and expressing yourself through music or films or art or books. In some ways she was like an honorary boy – she had often mused upon her own anomalous gender identity. Yet for the first time in her life Daniel Cajmere had made her feel like a proper girl. He was such an unreconstructed alpha male it was impossible to feel anything other than slight and feminine and fragile in his company. He made you feel safe, protected; such was his confidence and his aura of capability.

They stayed in Vegas for another few days, lying in bed gazing at each other, eating, drinking and making brief forays into the casinos. "The music in these places is really beyond," mused Cajmere as they listened to some lounge music whilst witnessing a poker game in a vast casino with a lurid yellow and brown checked carpet and glowing sodium strip lighting. "Perhaps one day they'll get proper dance clubs here," wondered Rachael. "its unreconstructed cheese right now. The days of Liberace and DJ clad crooners don't feel so long ago."

It's funny how things that seem very far away from what constitutes good taste can very quickly be assimilated into fashion again," pondered Cajmere.

" In the late eighties the rare groove thing in London," she remembered, "suddenly it seemed everyone was wearing flared trousers – and I'm not even really interested in fashion."

"This lounge music, it's ripe for reinvention," he observed. But I don't think country will ever be reclaimed, it's just far too redneck."

Within the month she had vacated her small room in Notting Hill, shipped her small crate of belongings to the US and moved in with Daniel Cajmere in Lafayette Park.

"I still think you've completely taken leave of your senses," said Mark as she bid Thom and Mark goodbye in the record and tape exchange.

"But you know there's a place for you here if you ever want to come back."

"I'm not coming back Mark, I'm very decisive and I know my own mind, you must know me by now. I'm with Daniel now and we're making a new start in Detroit."

"You'll have to write the book one day – my marriage to a top techno DJ."

"I'm no writer Mark, there won't be any book. The only thing I know about is music."

" Don't change too much for him Rachael, you're better than that."

"I won't. Or at least I'll try not to."

After several weeks of living in Detroit Rachael quickly became aware that this was a city in decay. There were certain no-go areas that Daniel advised her not to visit. But she loved Lafayette Park, which turned out to be a friendly community of creative types and professionals – artists, architects, teachers and lawyers numbered its residents. Daniel set about making his duplex inhabitable for two. Together they painted the rooms in white and colours, the living room was a blancmange pink, despite his alpha male tendencies Daniel loved pink, and the kitchen an optimistic lemon yellow. They selected modern furniture from an upmarket department store and some replica Barcelona chairs. Daniel found some industrial metal shelving in a junkyard to house all his records which stretched across one whole wall of their living room – he also stored some in his studio.

He took her out driving in his car. He wanted to go to Highland Park, where the old car factories had been. As they drove she looked out of the window of the car and all she could see was block after block of derelict buildings. Some of them had been subsumed by foliage and wildlife – trees poked out of the older ruins, grass and weeds pushed up around piles of bricks and through cracks in concrete flooring. They stopped near an old car factory and got out.

"I like photographing this stuff," noted Cajmere.

"But why, it's so unbelievably sad. Where are the people? Where is the life? Where has the industry gone? This is a city dying and decaying. It's a post-industrial wasteland." She mused.

"It is but there is beauty in this desolation."

They roamed into a factory building itself. It was dark, once electric lights would have illuminated it. Tens of tiny windows had all been smashed. Shards of glass lay on the floor. The window frames had rusted a deep terracotta. The concrete walls were blackened from fire damage.

"You brought me here half way across the world...... for this? I feel like I climbed to the top of a mountain and there's nothing there."

"But we're what's going to change this, don't you see," he implored "The machines died here, but we're alive and we're making a new music from machines. Something beautiful has risen from the dust."

He ventured into an old office with his camera and took a close up of a sheaf of yellowing papers splayed across a desk. She kicked through the flaking plaster on the floor in her boots. It was so empty..... so bereft. Once, people had worked here, it had all been alive with chatter and activity. And now just echoes. Hauntings of life.

"Detroit is an ending and a beginning," he was good at gnomic statements.

"And we have each other." He turned and looked at her and in the middle of this huge hangar of destruction he cradled her in his arms.

"Look, in the midst of all this. Here we are." He was talking to himself more than anyone else now.

He held her close.

"*It was meant.*"

Daniel tried hard to integrate Rachael into his world. He took her to the studio, although there was little she could do there apart from watch him, painstakingly, fiddle about with Cubase, his keyboards and his record decks. Together they went on forays to investigate and photograph the ruins. She spent her days shopping for food, cooking for him and cleaning up the house, just like a traditional wife. It was something of a novelty for her at first and for a while she quite enjoyed pushing a trolley around the endless American supermarket, with it's varied and exotic selection of breakfast cereals and convenience foods. She imagined herself fleetingly as a Stepford wife, loyally living out her days servicing her executive husband in their white picket home. But there was limited mileage in this little role-play for her, she needed mental stimulation and he too became quickly aware that she needed some kind of focus.

"I do feel a bit purposeless," she admitted one night as they sat together on the sofa watching cable TV together.

"You wanna get a job?" asked Cajmere. "We don't need the money. But I don't want you to go crazy either. And I can sense you are lonely when I'm not around."

"I am, and I don't know the city well enough to know where to go or what to do. Thinking about it, what I'd like is a part time job, something to do with music, maybe in a record store and I would also like to do some voluntary work. Surely there are some youth groups, some kids that I could work with and mentor."

"Are you sure you wanna do that?" he was somewhat incredulous. "Don't martyr yourself, there are some rough kids in this city. I wouldn't do it."

"I'll think about it, I toyed with the idea of teacher training after university and looking around me, I see a city that desperately needs educated people to work with the underprivileged and to help build back communities decimated by the ravages of capitalism."

"Phew – you gonna run for mayor too are you once you've fixed all Detroit's socio economic ills." He was sceptical. "Honestly why be so hard on yourself, why not kick back and enjoy being a rich man's wife!"

"Have you got any idea how empty and meaningless a life like that might be?" she was getting angry now. "I mean what was the point of me going through University, of bettering myself to be no more than someone's chattel."

"I don't even know what a chattel is but I'm sensing it's not good."

"Oh it's an old English term – more uni stuff. But seriously Daniel. I *am* going insane here. Help me out. Do you know of a record shop I might be able to do some hours in?"

"You know what, as a matter of fact I do."

Some days later he took her to a small, rather dilapidated shop down a side street in one of the quieter parts of downtown Detroit. The frontage bore the legend Reeves Records and it looked fairly unprepossessing and as they opened the door and entered there was that familiar slightly chemical smell – of warmed black vinyl mingled with cigarette smoke. It was a small, dingy cuboid space with racks from wall to wall, all filled with albums some of them in scuffed plastic sleeves and someone had pinned album covers up on the wall, mostly classical and jazz, everything from Herbie Hancock to Bobby Womack, penguin suit clad orchestras and various Wagner operas. Up at the far end there was a counter, where a wizened black man with round sunglasses and a seventies rare groove leather cap sat, smoking a cigarette. "Yo Marvin, wassup," greeted Cajmere.

"Hey Daniel, my best customer, replied the man in a growly low voice.

"This is where I come for my jazz samples," explained Cajmere to Rachel. "No one knows fusion music like Marvin."

"You like jazz too?" Marvin asked Rachel.

"I'm conversant with be bop," she replied "and seventies fusion and some Latin stuff. I love the female vocalists best: Billie Holliday, Ella Fitzgerald, Nina Simone, Flora Purim,"

"Good girl. Flora Purim, now that's a name I don't hear very often," he chuckled. "Daniel says you need a job. You any good at sorting out rekkids, making coffee and doing stocktakes? It sounds awful boring but there'll be a lot of music talk along with it too."

"I can do all of that. Especially if there's music talk!"

Daniel noted that she sounded brighter than she had done for weeks.

Very quickly Rachael's weeks assumed a kind of rhythm. She went into Reeves records, Monday Tuesday and Wednesday and she planned to start helping in a community centre on Thursday and Friday.

Meanwhile, Daniel was in his studio struggling to work on his album. One day he found himself sitting with Carter there clasping a warm beer for comfort.

"You've run out of ideas haven't you Cajmere," Daniel Cajmere found it almost impossible to admit, but Carter had successfully identified the truth.

"Do you think I should make a 1970s concept album Carter?"

"Well you gotta have an idea to do that. And I don't think you got any ideas left."

" A lot of producers talking about space travel and science and quantum physics right now."

"That's true, I heard that some writer had called it Afrofuturism. I suppose that comes from (Sun) Ra and George Clinton. And that would tie in with your Rings of Saturn imprint. But your sound is very warm, very human, isn't that the antithesis of sci-fi themes and fantasies?"

"Maybe, but the dialectic, the essential tension of Detroit techno is that it's a voyage into the unknown with futuristic effects but you're carried by melodies and textures that pull on the human soul. There is an intrinsic divergence in this music between the drive towards science fiction and the yearning melancholy, the feelings we all experience."

"But are we meant to have faith in these machines and this technology or are they what killed Detroit? Mused Carter. One of my relatives told me that machines had been used to take over from people in the car factories in the 80s. A planet run by machines would be a tragedy. Perhaps that's what we're expressing in our music."

"Well there's no point in just being good, or just being talented. I'm not content with that. I've gotta be original. I've gotta be the genius. I am the genius."

"Well if you're so high on your own self belief I don't know what the problem is," shrugged Carter and picked up his record bag and bid Daniel goodbye.

Reeves Records was mostly quiet early in the week and Rachael often found herself in the back room, sifting through old stock and making coffee for Marvin. Refreshingly she found there were no dance music records in this shop, the stock comprised of classical, opera, modern classical and jazz, rare groove, funk and soul. The occasional young music producer or DJ would come in hunting for jazz or funk samples and, when the shop was empty, Marvin began to teach her about jazz, it's evolution since the 1920s, it's significance as a black cultural art-form, the great virtuosos and the important developments in the sound.

"You won't find any of that Detroit techno rubbish in Reeves!" proclaimed Marvin with pride. He was traditional in his tastes. But Rachael was relieved, to some extent she'd had enough of the incremental nuances of late 80s and early 90s house and techno, she wanted a new challenge and she wanted to further her knowledge. She even had some vague ideas that she might like to DJ or produce a record herself.

"What did you get up to today," Daniel asked her one evening as they sat in front of the cable eating chicken fajitas that she had made.

"Well I had an interesting discussion with Marvin about Miles Davis. We talked about his defining albums and his influence."

"Did you listen to Kind of Blue?"

"Yeah I mean I knew a bit about it before. But where his sound became really interesting for me was when he got into Stockhausen in 1972. The space-jazz music that resulted from that was pretty interesting."

"Uh huh"

"We listened to some Stockhausen after that which was amazing. It's chaotic but there is a rhyme and reason to it. I really liked it. It was completely unlike anything I'd ever heard before. It was difficult and challenging. It sounded like the end of the world." She sighed. "But Marvin doesn't really know much about modern classical and avant garde music. It's not his thing."

"Marvin's quite set in his tastes," laughed Cajmere.

"He sure is an old grouch, a very compelling old grouch nevertheless," said Rachel with a giggle. "According to him all music has been creatively bankrupt after 1976"

"Why 1976?" wondered Cajmere

"I dunno, just some random year he plucked out of the air. Beginning of disco and punk rock I suppose. Beginning of the end for him. Miles's best work was behind him. Marvin Gaye's best work was behind him. Stevie Wonder's best work was behind him. Berry Gordy had done the unthinkable and relocated Motown to Los Angeles in 1972."

"Yeah but George Clinton was still going strong," interjected Cajmere.

"That's a minor point for Marvin, I don't think he'd concede it destroyed his thesis."

Cajmere was back in the studio. One of his protégées on Rings of Saturn, Carl Drake, had brought a track in of quite austere beauty – tinged with sadness it foregrounded an obscure jazz vocal sample that was a trickle of pure female pain.

"This is an amazing track," he conceded as Carl, who was a 17 year old black kid stood beside him nervously waiting for his verdict.

"How did you find the sample?"

"It was in my Dad's record collection."

"Some record collection! I'm making a Rings of Saturn compilation for the record label and I'm definitely keeping this back for it," nodded Cajmere, almost slightly crestfallen that one of his protégées had exceeded him in producing something so starkly gorgeous.

"How is your album going," Carl asked him innocently enough.

"Ah yeah, yeah, it's going good," he lied. "The record company want a rough cut in the next two months," he cringed inwardly. The pressure was mounting and Cajmere knew it.

"How was your day," Rachael asked him later that evening.

Why the fuck are you on my back now," you're as bad as the record company. Just lay off," he snapped.

"Look I'm just asking, there's no subtext, no innuendo. Just a simple question," she raised her voice. She was not going to take his bullying.

"Well if you must know it's not going well. I've got two more months to make this album and I've only got one or two tracks. The thing is, for the money they've paid me, this record has got to be pure killer."

"N one of my kids just brought in a track today that was astounding," he mumbled as an adjunct.

"There's no point being jealous or bitter," Rachael stared at him. Where's the Nietschean Superman now? Anyway I thought creativity had to come from a place of questioning and soul searching, not hubris."

"Probably." He grabbed the remote and turned on the TV.

Marvin had started paying Rachael in records. There was no real point in her accepting money from him. They didn't need the money. They didn't really need any more records either,

Cajmere already had thousands stacked up in the living room and his studio. But, she figured, you could never have enough records, it was like an art collection, vinyl would give you pleasure for the rest of your living days. Sure there was a folly and indeed an obscenity in amassing a considerable stash of objects just for the sake of it. But records were different say from say shoes or perfume. They were works of art. They soothed the soul. They were medicine for the spirit. Love them and care for them and they repaid you by lifting your life out of mundanity into the realm of metaphysical bliss.

Rachael started to stockpile her own little collection of 20th century avant-garde and modern classical music that she'd earned from working at the shop. From Stravinsky and Strauss to Messaien, Ligeti, Stockhausen and Pierre Boulez. The minimalism of Steve Reich and Phillip Glass was her special passion and she was aware that it was more melodic and tuneful, more accessible than atonal music and serialism. She took a few books out of the library about this era of music and educated herself on the theoretics behind the sounds and noises. Of an evening, Rachael would turn off the cable and play the records to Daniel.

"I'm broadening your horizons," she said one night as she hovered over the record player, cueing up some Arvo Part.

"My horizons are already broad," harrumphed Cajmere. I used to listen to the Electrifying Mojo on the radio in the 80s. He used to play Krautrock and Tangerine Dream and The Cure and all kinds of weird and wonderful shit."

She explained that she thought he needed to know what had been going on in the classical genre to give his music an extra sphere of reference.

"I mean what if you were to take very subtle elements from the avant-garde and work them, almost invisibly into your music."

She reckoned he could make a music that was like an onion, on the surface it was melodic Detroit techno, but then when you peel back the layers, there was some quiet serious allusion to the experiments of modern classical. The more astute critics would realise he was attempting something intellectually radical but doing it with the sugar coating of techno music, repetitive music that people were going to dance to mindlessly. It would be a subtle form of subversion, knitting in passages of quite radical musical endeavour.

"Yeah, yeah," he was coming round to it. "I do want to do that. Something with those orchestral undertones."

When he went to the studio, he took some of her records with him. He built a track on a sample of Steve Reich's Music for 18 Musicians and he also played around with lifting from Terry Riley. It worked. The textures melded into the oozing synths of techno and he felt like he'd added some kind of leitmotif of experiment to his work, questioning the very nature of music itself.

And so, over the next six weeks he built an album. Not, perhaps the album he'd expected to make of pure Detroit techno, but a much more sophisticated, intelligent work, one that incorporated all sorts of encoded elements of avant-garde music from the last 100 years. There were a couple of tracks he needed to get a live vocal recorded on, Carter had put him in touch with a vocalist called Etta, a heavy set black girl from the burbs who worked as a hairdresser and had discovered a talent for singing in church.

Etta arrived at the studio one morning - she was tall and full figured wearing a black leather blouson jacket (rather 1980s and dated, must be from a project thought Cajmere) – and eating corn chips. Cajmere noticed her elaborate tri-colour weave (black, bronze and gold) coiffed into a huge bun, feathery fake eyelashes and long acrylic nails – airbrushed with a Miami sunset and pierced in several places with little silver charms dangling off the piercings.

Btu she was nervous and shy, he could tell by the way her shoulders were slightly rounded and she struggled to meet his gaze. He could crush this woman like a fly he thought to himself, he could make her cry. He felt like taking out all his anger at the album's slow progression on this stupid woman. What man would want a fat girl anyway? Only freaks who wanted a mama.

"Carter tells me you're a musical prodigy!" she exclaimed, eager to please him.

"Something like that," mumbled Cajmere, although he was genuinely pleased Carter had praised him. Carter didn't praise anyone lightly.

"I've got a couple of tracks I want you to vocal on Etta," he delegated rather dismissively. "Are you familiar with the techno sound?" He knew she would not be but he wanted her to admit her lack of knowledge.

"Not really, I don't know what it is. I'm kinda like an R and B and soul girl myself."

"It's the vanguard of what's happening now," he declared. He doubted she would know what the word vanguard meant.

Oh okay, she nodded, he could see she was slightly visibly cowed.

"Let me play you something."

She sat down and he played her the Steve Reich sampling track on the album, it was, he considered, his best so far.

"Hmm pretty good," she crunched her corn chips and nodded approvingly. "Like I say not my thing but I can feel the groove."

"I want you to sing the vocals on the lead track for the album 'Celestial', I'll play you the backing track,"

"Uh huh,"

Carter played the soundbed for the vocal. It was classic Detroit, mellifluous and warm but he'd added in a sample of a harp to lift the synth chords into a more ethereal realm.

"I wrote the lyrics myself, they're quite simple. The song is the lead song on the album and its called Celestial."

"Do you really think you're capable of putting in a decent performance?" He didn't trust weak neurotic shy women. They made him angry. He wanted to test her.

He handed her the sheet then played a brief rendition of the melody he wanted her to sing on the keyboard. "Think you can do that?"

She opened her mouth to sing and the most luxuriant honeyed strain of sound was emitted. Cajmere was quite breathtaken. But he was too proud to show it, he still wanted to demean her.

"Okay not bad. But let's see if you can do better next time."

"It was pretty good when I laid down some tracks with Carter," she confirmed, a little nervous still and not quite sure about how she'd been received.

They spent the rest of the day working on the track. Etta was like a dream to work with, she had a spectacular voice and no problems with staying in tune, or getting the right emphasis on words and phrasing. Cajmere had taken an immediate dislike to the shy girl though. He made her repeat the song again and again.

"Surely one of these takes must have been okay?" she ventured nervously. In fact, Cajmere thought to himself, they had all been perfect. But her meekness had irritated him and he wanted to punish her.

He congratulated himself for discovering this unknown. The record company had offered to fly out various high-profile vocalists to record with him but he'd refused and taken a chance instead on this unknown girl because Carter had recommended her. He was delighted that his gamble had paid off. And he had avoided the potential diva histrionics and ego clashes that might have resulted from working with a big name.

By the end of the day, Celestial was finished. That night he told Rachael he'd cracked the big track on the album. He related how Etta had irritated him.

"But how was her vocal?" demanded Rachael.

"I gotta admit it, it was incredible. But I dunno what it was about her. She just rubbed me up the wrong way. She came in all eager to please and nervous and shy. Neurotic people bore me Rachael, its pathetic and boring to see a grown woman so weak."

"I hope you didn't try to crush her...." Warned Rachael looking at him dead on.

"Ahh – he emitted a mixture of a sigh and a groan. He wanted the conversation to end now.

"How do you know she was weak?" continued Rachael, relentlessly. "Shyness does not necessarily equate to weakness Daniel. Shy people can have powerful personalities and talents, they're just lacking in social skills, or the confidence to realise those skills. Perhaps she couldn't help how she was brought up, perhaps she's been abused, perhaps she's just modest. Who are you to know her backstory?"

"Don't make excuses for her. We can all make excuses for why we're not strong. Besides, she's got an amazing talent, she should be shouting it from the rooftops."

"But perhaps she's not aware of how good she is Daniel. Perhaps you should be building her up and telling her. After all, you're lucky to get someone so brilliant for your album. You've been struggling with the album for weeks and this is a real breakthrough. This shy girl, however much you dismiss her, has brought you some real good karma. Don't dismiss her for being a bit timid. Not everyone is blessed with the confidence you've been given."

"Well you're a more patient person than me Rachel and you're probably a better person than me."

"You've got to give people a chance and not crush them. That's not strength."

"Okay okay, just leave it will you."

By the next month, the album was finished. There were ten tracks in total, Celestial, the opening track that Cajmere had destined to be a first single. There was the Steve Reich sampling track and another that he had constructed by embedding a short excerpt from Stockhausen under a very sweet Rhodes piano melody. Cajmere had been closely following what was happening on the ambient scene in London. Since the arrival of The Orb in 1990 he had become very interested in beatless washes, textural experiments and the narcoleptic fantasia of producers like the Black Dog and Global Communication. He'd tried to get his hands on as much Brian Eno as possible, starting with Music For Airports and there was a track on the album, devoid of beats, that was a homage to Eno and David Byrne's landmark avant-garde album My Life In The Bush of Ghosts. Another track "Terraforming Mars' he deemed to be a potential single. It built a syncopated jazzy refrain from warm melting chords over a 140BPM four to the floor beat.

"I suppose I do want it to be like an onion," he told Rachael as they sat a the kitchen table eating tomato and mushroom pasta she had cooked one night. "On the surface it's just another Detroit techno album, but hopefully an outstanding one. But as you peel back the layers, there's an intellectual gravitas to it, it's dealing with some serious ideas and musical innovations. It's in part a meditation upon the progressions of 20th century modern classical and avant-garde music. Y'know it's like in the 80s The Cure talking about Camus and Morrissey talking about Keats and Yeats. At it's very best pop music, even if it's underground like ours, should be an entry level cultural format that inveigles you into exploring some of the serious ideas of our culture."

"I think you're right," said Rachael, "it has to have those resonances. Without exploring something more profound, you're essentially just turning out another Detroit techno album. Albeit a good one. And you know, now Detroit is established there are dozens of techno albums and it's becoming more and more formulaic. By evolving it you're keeping the genre alive and you're keeping it relevant. The record company are gonna love it you know."

"You know what. I *know* they are."

The master tapes were sent off to the record company and a few days later Cajmere got a call, to his studio from Simon Wanstall."

"Hi Daniel, how are things?" he said in his studious way.

"Yeah not so bad," replied Cajmere casually. "Did you get the master?"

"Yes. It's incredible. This album is incredible. This is exactly what we wanted. I think we've got a hit on our hands." Wanstall was effusive.

"You're not just saying that," Cajmere knew that record company people had a habit of talking things up, of indulging in hyperbole and Wanstall's studious nerdiness rather annoyed him.

"I'm not. I mean with Celestial, if it's PRed and plugged properly I think we're looking at UK top ten."

"Wow, Well I mean I did put some quite serious ideas into it. It's not just an album I banged out. It was crafted. It took time. At times the process was difficult."

He didn't like to admit that anything was hard for him. But Wanstall was so unthreatening he thought it safe to divulge a weakness to him.

"What I think we should do is get some test pressings and white labels of Celestial out to a few movers and shakers on the club scene and build up some buzz about it. I'm going to circulate it amongst the Marketing and PR teams and see what their thoughts are. I think we may well need you to come over and do some initial promotion for it – I'm thinking NME and Melody Maker, Mixmag and DJ magazine and the style titles too – i-D, The Face and Dazed and Confused....."

"I love The NME and The Face....I pick them up on import downtown. That would be so cool."

Several weeks later, Cajmere found himself travelling back to London on the red eye from Detroit to do a big press junket for the album. Now he had Rachael and they were settled in a routine in Lafayette Park he felt, for the first time in some years, that he had a home. He still did the occasional DJ date abroad, but he was loath to travel unless he absolutely had to. The glamour and novelty of travelling had dissipated some years ago and these days airports only left him with a profound sense of ennui (and often low level depression at their bad design) and a longing for Rachael at his side to share his thoughts.

He arrived back in London and took a taxi to the record company. The offices hadn't changed much, it was still full of glamorous young girls, except now a year or two on he noted their hair was in little bunches like schoolgirls rather than bobs and they wore cropped t shirts exposing firm tanned stomachs, A line mini skirts, knee high socks and metallic silver trainers. The first thing that happened was that he went into a meeting about press strategy for the album.

"This is Sarah," Simon Wanstall introduced him to a slim serious looking girl in trousers with short dark hair. "She's going to manage your interview schedule."

"Erm thanks," grunted Cajmere disinterested. "I hope they're not expecting a performing monkey."

"We've got the music papers first: NME and Melody Maker. Then the style mags Face, i-D, Dazed and Confused and then Mixmag and DJ. I doubt we'll get coverage in the broadsheets unless you do something live. Very hard to crack the broadsheets with underground dance music," she considered.

"Am I gonna have to do any stupid photo-shoots," he grumbled.

"Possibly something for Mixmag, they do like novelty. You might have to wear a space suit or something like that. Just bear that in mind. It shouldn't be too bad though. They do it to all the DJs." Continued Sarah in a business-like fashion.

"Do I have to do that shit? I mean this is a serious album. My reputation is on the line." Cajmere was disgruntled.

"You don't *have* to do anything," said Sarah, herself feeling rather annoyed that she had a stroppy DJ on her hands. "But I would advise you that the press junket is part of your record company contract and Mixmag is an influential title that we don't want to miss out on. Their circulation is soaring these days."

"Yeah, yeah. I get it," sighed Cajmere defeated.

Cajmere faced two days of interviews and photographs in the same Kensington hotel he had been staying at when he signed his deal. He noted the plastic foliage in the foyer, the brown tinted windows, the Memphis approximation carpet and felt vaguely depressed. He missed Rachael, although he barely admitted it to himself, such sentiment counted as weakness.

The record company installed him in a three-room suite with capacious sofas on the 32nd floor. At first he got quite excited by the array of food and drink they had provided. There was a large banquette table with flasks of coffee and tea, freshly squeezed orange juice, a platter of exotic fruits, croissants and Danish pastries and rows of carefully triangulated sandwiches.

Cajmere sat on the sofa sipping coffee and juice alternately and in the journalists rolled. The first one was an enthusiastic and studious black guy with thick tortoiseshell oblong spectacles and a smart fitted Crombie coat. 'Nerdy' thought Cajmere and was vaguely irritated.

'Can I just say Celestial is amazing. It's a flight into the unknown, riding on wings of fluttering harps," said the guy with a hint of poetic licence.

Creep. Thought Cajmere. Supercilious creep. How easy it would be to crush this sycophant with a caustic remark.

Although the writer kept talking about black science fiction and Afrofuturism which did pique Cajmere's interest.

"I want the album to sit in the avant-garde tradition as well as the Detroit techno tradition," he declared confidently. The conversation lapsed into one about cyberpunk, William Gibson, Phillip K Dick and Bruce Sterling.

"I wouldn't say I'm a cyberpunk per se," mused Cajmere. "When you live in Detroit – where there is this ever present urban entropy - there is a strong propensity to want to escape. You're constantly looking for vectors to ride into the unknown. And I guess space travel is one of them. There's that balance in the music between humanity and warmth and mechanisation technology. There's a constant tension, a dialectic between the two things."

The black guy seemed to hang upon his every word as though he were spilling forth gold dust and Cajmere responded with an even more inflated sense of his self importance. "This is easy" he thought. And even though the black guy was dazzlingly bright he was deferential to Cajmere. Cajmere was the artist after all.

The next journalist, a blond bobbed haired young man wearing a hooded Gap top and jeans was from Mixmag.

"So, it's all about spaceships then. Do you think you've been beamed in from another planet?"

"What?" Cajmere looked at him through narrowed eyes, quite unable to believe this spectacularly simplistic and childish reading of his music.

"C'mon Daniel – did you watch Star Trek as a kid? Did you like the aliens?"

The questions started to become puerile. He half expected to be asked "What colour socks do you wear." He spat out answers almost contemptuous. Anger surged in him like tidal wave.

"Sarah, can we just take a rain check," he asked the PR girl through gritted teeth.

"Sure," she replied and together they went outside to stand in the hotel corridor.

"I can't take this moron any longer. This guy is retarded. I swear I'm going to punch him if he continues this line of questioning," hissed Cajmere.

"Okay calm down a minute Daniel," Sarah took hold of his arm. She could see his clenched fists, fingernails digging into his palms.

" You're right he is pretty stupid and the questions are verging on the ridiculous but you've got to bear with this. Firstly it's in your contract to do the publicity for the album whether you like it or not. Secondly we can hurry this one along and get him out in 15 minutes if it's really doing your head in."

She looked at him pleadingly in an effort to placate him, using all her interactive skills.

"Look I'm really really sorry about this Daniel, yes it is an affront, but just take it easy. We don't want a fight. C'mon you're better than this. Just grit your teeth and humour him for 15 minutes and then I'll get him out."

"Okay" he grimaced

Back inside, the journalist, who was young and ebullient and eager persevered with an optimism and friendliness that made Cajmere clench up inside.

"Yeah I guess it is space music," he caught himself modifying his language to escape using any sophisticated vocabulary that might go over the young man's head. Instead he emitted the most prosaic and simplistic explanations possible for his music. He found himself gritting his teeth and speaking very slowly.

"It's alright - I do understand what you're saying," continued the young man earnestly, unaware he was being roundly patronised. "You're a space cadet just like all of us ravers."

"Yeah something like that," responded Cajmere rubbing his face wearily. "Just put that."

In streamed the interviewers, one by one and the questions merged into one. "So what was your inspiration?" "What's it like living in Detroit" "What do you think of the new breakbeat jungle sound?" One guy DJ magazine he thought - was really psyched by all the equipment he was using, kept asking about 909s and 303s. This was boring even by Cajmere's standards. There was one girl, was it i-D magazine, a young girl in her mid twenties wearing a short camel coat with a bright orange handbag who was so shy she could barely look him in the eye. She constantly shifted on the sofa nervously. He wondered how someone so introvert could have become a journalist. Surely a journalist was meant to be thrusting and interrogating – sure of themselves – cocky even. Not this forlorn young woman. Where did they get these UK journalists from? he wondered, they were like students. He imagined them contemptuously in their run down flats at home with piles of undone washing up and mould creeping up the walls. He was under no illusion about who was the glamorous one in the room.

"Well done," said Sarah who'd been sitting in on proceedings. "You did really well today Daniel."

She just wanted to tick boxes, thought Daniel 'cover all demographics'. He was exhausted.

"Wow I never knew talking could be so tiring." He shook his head. "I need to lie in a darkened room."

" Don't worry we've got a really nice suite booked for you for tonight," cajoled Sarah. She was used to getting what she wanted from the grumpiest of artists. "Then tomorrow a few more interviews and some photos too. You cool with that?"

"I guess so," he demurred reluctantly. He went back to his suite and took a very long, very deep bath. He gave a cursory thought to phoning Rachael, only she would understand, but he was too tired to talk. He had thought he liked talking about himself. But there was only so much to say about music. Although he was far too smart to trot out hoary old clichés like 'I don't like to be labelled," or "I let the music do the talking". He'd read these kinds of limited responses before in articles and found them intensely frustrating. It was the duty of the artist to expound on his creation, that was part of the deal. He didn't believe in mute intransigence, much as it appealed to his moody nature. He knew the press game and he was going to play it, even though it could be decidedly trivial and mindless at times. Cajmere gritted his teeth through another day of interviews and photographs in the hotel. There was a uniformly positive reaction to the album – which only served to inflate his already considerable ego further. Although he found himself intensely irritated by what he saw as sycophancy.

"I almost wish someone would tell me they hated it," he grumbled to Sarah at the end of the day. "All these fanboys make me feel nauseous. Don't they have any dignity, any pride." Despite Cajmere's admiration for Carter King who functioned as a kind of mentor or father figure in his life he would never have dreamed to articulate it – it would have been a shameful moment for Carter and himself had he admitted his platonic ardour for him.

The black guy had been right – Celestial did fly on wings of harps right into the top ten of the UK record chart. "Radio 1 have put it on their playlist," Sarah told him triumphantly after the second day of interviews in Kensington. "We're looking at top ten and we're expecting the album to chart high too next week."

Cajmere felt validated as he lay in the bath that night at the hotel. His work and his vision had paid off. Rock critics had said that Detroit techno wouldn't translate into an album format. He had proved them wrong. He knew instinctively that he had made one of the albums that would define the decade for generations to come. Everyone would know Daniel Cajmere now. His time had come. And he was going to capitalise on it.

Cajmere stayed on in the UK for a month. He was about to embark on a DJ tour to promote the album's release. The record label had wanted him to do a series of live PAs rather than DJ and to bring Etta over to vocal but Cajmere had argued against this. He didn't like the idea of performing the music, or even miming to pre-recorded tracks whilst Etta sang live. Besides, he didn't think Etta was robust enough for live performance, he could envisage her going to pieces if she had to stand on a stage and sing to a crowd. So instead, he put forward the idea of a compromise. He would embark on a ten-date UK DJ tour with a view to possibly working on a live PA for festivals in the future. That seemed to keep the record company satisfied.

The first date of the DJ tour was to be in Glasgow at the Halcyon club. It felt like home territory for Cajmere. He knew there was a strong Detroit following in Scotland and various DJs who had supported his tracks since the early days. He was missing Rachael so he paid for her to fly out and join him. The thought of traversing the UK staying in bland corporate hotels didn't thrill him. He needed someone to talk to, to support him, as life on the road could be lonely and thankless – even though he was currently flying high.

He met her at Glasgow airport. It was pouring with rain. But she had dressed up, she was wearing lipgloss and thick foundation and combat pants and a little pink cropped t-shirt - just as he liked. He could see her full breasts and her flat stomach and her dangerously rounded hips. Upon meeting her, he couldn't resist boasting "Did I tell you the record's gone top ten?"

"I know I know and you're brilliant. Even though I know you'll hate me for saying that."

"It's okay, you're the only one that's allowed to say it," he laughed.

"Just keep that ego in check, " she warned him.

They took a cab into Glasgow under wire wool skies. "Lets go spend some money," said Cajmere in a rush of omnipotent fervour. "Let's go to a designer store." The cab driver obliged and took them to a large clothes boutique with a Japanese name on the edge of the city centre. Inside, there were concrete floors, clothes suspended from wires dangling from the ceiling and an industrial feel. "I like this interior," noted Cajmere approvingly.

"Choose what you want," he ordered Rachael. Normally she couldn't muster much enthusiasm for clothes shopping. But she wanted to find something he would like. She picked out a figure fitting tailored shirt in a raw lapis lazuli blue silk and some bootcut hipster trousers in black. She tried them on to show Daniel, unbuttoning the blouse to her bra exposing a pleasingly rounded cleavage. Her hourglass figure swelled beneath the skintight fabrics.

She wanted, more than anything, in that moment for him to tell her she was beautiful and alluring to him. She looked at him expectantly. But Cajmere was not prone to compliments. He looked at her and grunted approval and then they went to the cash desk and paid. He was high on the knowledge that his single was soaring in the chart and he was thankful to see her – but he wasn't going to let her know that. He couldn't take another soulless trek around the UK on his own.

They were staying in a new hotel. "It's called a boutique hotel," observed Rachael as they sat in the lobby, which was all dove grey – but not the bland grey of those deadening corporate Hiltons they often had to stay in. This place was a new kind of designer hotel that Cajmere had never experienced before. The furniture was all minimal and ultra contemporary. The interior was a 'concept', with contemporary art on the walls, what looked like a Bacon and staff all clad in black Nehru jackets, possibly Armani. "I'm not sure if I like this or not,' considered Cajmere. On the one hand it's all very considered, very tasteful. It's certainly exciting. I've never been in a hotel like this before. But is it too calculated – has any trace of messy humanity been expunged."

"I have to say the designer lifestyle leaves me completely cold," retorted Rachael. " I'm not really bothered about aesthetics personally. It's all so irrelevant to the human condition, it really is. It's only set dressing. I just hope there's a nice big comfortable bed."

"Yeah but you've gotta admit this is a design revolution for hotels though, when you consider what we're used to," continued Cajmere. "I mean some of the cheap holes I've had to endure – sheez. This is a hotel for our generation, for groovy people. Hotels just got cool."

"You sound like a travel brochure," she was tired and rather irritated by his soaring yet detached mood.

The Halcyon club was a small black walled sweatbox in the environs of the city centre. You reached it by descending a narrow flight of stairs. It smelled chemical of dry ice, vinyl and just discernibly of perspiration. Rachel descended the stairs with a sinking feeling, Daniel was in an ebullient, egomaniacal mood and she was tired of trying to bring him back down to earth. His excitement at being back on the club scene, 'The King Of Detroit' was palpable.

The crowd were dressed down. There was a lot of black and navy denim, sombre colour t-shirts and trainers. Smarter than a rave, no tracksuits or catsuits or glosticks but it was not overtly fashionable, unlike some of the places they'd been to where avant-garde attire was favoured. The music was hypnotic, deep house with tribal drum patternings or strings, very few vocals. It was quite a make environment and there was not the tangible fervour of ecstacy taking apparent, although the crowd seemed locked into the groove, tranced out, feeling the rhythm but displaying no emotion.

"They're very serious about the music" noted the promoter, a laconic Glaswegian called Ronnie as he bought them a drink at the bar. It was true, there was nothing frivolous about this club, no emotional hyperbole, it was hedonistic, but dark, nocturnal, saturnine.

"Why don't you come to the back room and chat wi-us properly. You can't really have a proper conversation in here," urged Ronnie.

"Yeah sure, I'll come to hang out," smiled Daniel. "It's okay, you don't need to come." He signalled to Rachael to wait on a nearby seat. "I won't be long."

She retreated to a corner banquette with her drink. Her heart sank.

Daniel entered the back room. It appeared to be a rather dirty and dimly lit space, walls painted red with about six plastic chairs. There were six people in it that night, one was chopping out lines of white powder on a small table as Daniel entered and there were two girls, one blonde, cropped hair, wearing a metallic babydoll dress sitting on the lap of the other, a brunette. Daniel went and sat down next to them.

"Well hi there ladies," he could sense the night was going to be fun.

Daniel Cajmere – right," said the blonde one.

"I do answer to that name," said Cajmere suavely, raising an eyebrow.

"You're everywhere right now Cajmere, you're a media whore," said the blonde girl in a provocative act of flirtation.

"I can't help being naturally gifted," said Cajmere, only half in jest.

"Well I never, the new Prince of Detroit techno is sitting next to me," said the blonde, mock aghast.

"That's what they call me. And what name do you answer to lady," ventured Cajmere playfully.

"Why I'm Emma Milton," she pouted, her lipglossed lips fully ripe and lucent. "I'm in record promotions and PR at XXX" she mentioned a major label whose name Cajmere didn't quite catch.

"Oh yeah, tell me more," smiled Cajmere gazing at her lips and her tanned cleavage.

"I'm here to service the DJs," she giggled naughtily.

"I'm gonna be obvious here, but why don't you start by servicing me." Cajmere just couldn't resist asserting his masculinity.

"Oh I'm very good indeed at servicing, I think you'll find Mr Prince of Detroit," she said in her saucy, cheeky, accentuated little girl voice. ": What are your particular needs?"

Cajmere continued chatting to the girl, appreciatively noting her long slender legs entwined rather suggestively around those of her brunette friend. She had sleek cat eyes, grey blue and fashionably cropped hair somewhere between honey blonde and platinum. Her face had been made up expertly – the glowing bronzed skin, the strawberry milkshake lipgloss. She was a peach, thought Cajmere, all thoughts of Rachael sitting forlornly in the main club had vanished from his mind.

They continued to chat, teasing each other, in what was a blatant preamble to certain sexual contact. Emma Milton had all the light vivacity of a thousand expertly chatty PR girls hired for their attractiveness and extrovert personalities and personability as much as any in depth knowledge of music.

Perhaps it was inevitable they would kiss. She hadn't even asked him if he had a girlfriend. And the last thing he was going to mention was that he was married. It was an unspoken pact. At this very moment the electricity between them seemed to transcend all. He honed in on those polished and lustrous lips like an epicurean biting into a juicy red apple. Their tongues entwined lasciviously. *It's my right*, thought Cajmere, *to take what is given*. She slid off the brunettes lap and onto his.

"Blimey you move fast" commented Ronnie the promoter glimpsing Cajmere from the corner of the room.

"He knows a good thing when he sees it!" said Emma glorying in her conquest.

When he left Rachael, she was sat alone with a gin and tonic on a black vinyl banquette. After fifteen minutes had elapsed, she started to feel vaguely irritated. *Where had he gone and what was he doing*? She barely noticed that a blonde haired young woman had sat down beside her. The young woman had hair that sprouted in a little halo of natural curls from her head. She was wearing white – a white crop vest top and a white A line skirt. "I haven't seen you here before," said the girl in a broad Glaswegian accent, "I know most of the regulars you see."

"I'm with the DJ," sighed Rachael, "or at least I was, he's disappeared somewhere and left me on my own."

"Don't worry hen," the girl assured her, "I'll look after you. Is it Daniel Cajmere you're with? I've heard his sets are amazing."

"Yeah, yeah. They are," admitted Rachael grudgingly.

"Wow so I'm sitting with Daniel Cajmere's girlfriend. That's very cool."

"Wife actually."

"Crikey, married to a top DJ, somehow I imagine that's quite stressful. Like being married to a rock star. Always off playing somewhere, you never quite know what they're up to."

"Something like that."

"C'mon love, cheer up, this is the best club in Glasgow. I know it's a cliché but we're like one big family. *How about an eccy?*" She whispered the last sentence conspiratorially. "Go on, you know what these DJs are like. He's probably getting wasted somewhere with Ronnie and Dave the resident DJ. Beat him at his own game, have yourself a bit of fun."

Rachael perked up, it was like the girl was echoing thoughts running concurrently in her own mind. Yeah, whatever Daniel was up to, why shouldn't she enjoy herself too. She'd never taken drugs but she'd wondered many times what all the fuss was about. Yes she was suspicious of the effects of ecstasy in dampening the rebellious and political potential of a whole generation. But her antipathy towards it had been eroded since she'd been with Daniel. She was curious as to his secret life before he'd met her. She wanted to sample the hedonistic delights she thought he had sampled to bring them closer together. What the hell, it would certainly serve to distract her from the gloominess and loneliness of this particular nightclub on a Saturday night. And the girl seemed friendly – after all she'd told her she was going to look after her.

"What's your name?" she asked the girl.

"Susan, what's yours?"

"Rachael"

And so, without more words, the deal was done.

Susan slipped a small white pill into her hand. "What are you drinking?" "Gin and tonic" "You shouldn't really drink with it, it won't work properly. Here, have some of my water"

She swallowed the pill. "C'mon lets dance," urged Susan. "Let's go flying!"

For a while she was dancing and nothing was happening. *It's not working* she thought as she sidestepped rhythmically to the minimal hard house beats.

And then suddenly it was. It was a little bit like taking off in an aircraft. A very slow insistent surge, a lifting up, warmth, positivity. It was the sound of the music she noticed more than anything else. In fact there was nothing else apart from the sound of the music, urgent horns and klaxons coming through the speakers and speaking to her, *her alone*. All doubt and nervousness and anxiety at Daniels disappearance had dissolved in her and instead she was shining bright, gleaming from every pore. Oh and she was light and she was beautiful, sprinkling fairy dust with her smile on all around her. All was beneficent and friendly and good in the world. "Are you coming up?" asked Susan who was still there, swaying beside her. Rachael felt the urge to talk to pour out all her hearts desire to stream her consciousness into the ether, but all she managed was to turn to Susan and beam, everything about her body had morphed into one big smile, she wanted to give so much of herself and she was emanating goodness and kindness and wonder.

Soon, she was in full flight, weightless, floating in space. It felt like all the platelets and cells in her blood stream were effervescing – dancing through her body like bubbles in a champagne glass. She was brimming with love and brilliance. The music was coursing through her body along with the MDMA. Suddenly she heard synths, arpeggiating up her spine like wings of angels, and she realised, hazily that is was Daniel playing the grafts he'd sampled from Bizarre Love Triangle. *It was for her. It was for her. It was all for her.*

Hours passed or was it minutes? Hours compressed into minutes. Minutes distended into hours. Time had a whole new elasticity about it.

"You okay?" Susan passed her some water.

"He's great isn't he," she felt a snapshot of clarity at that very moment, her love for Daniel was oozing into the ether.

"Yeah, he's amazing. As good as they say," replied Susan.

She felt like she wanted to do something. She felt so burgeoning with potential at that moment, when Susan said "Do you want to sit down for a bit" it echoed her need to do something. Even though the drug had made the gates of possibility swing wide open and she felt compelled to do something great, to say something profound, to produce a great work of art or change the world in some way. And yet, all she was in actuality going to do was take several steps from the dancefloor to the banquettes.

"Are you rushing?" Susan asked her

Yes it's very powerful," said Rachael

"These are the best doves I've had for a few months, they really hit the spot."

"Do you take them every week."

"Oh Gosh yes and you?"

"Well actually this is my first time"

Susan grabbed her with both hands "You're an eccy virgin. You should have told me! Oh there's nothing as good as your first time," she said with the true fervour of an evangelist. "I think I spend half my time trying to replicate that buzz but it's never quite the same. Still good though. These ones are particularly good quality though."

Rachael nodded, absorbing what seemed like the sage incantations of a guru. At the time, this felt like a profound interaction. Everything felt profound. These utterances were felt more intensely than anything that had been said before. Rachel smiled at her beneficently. They sipped their water and danced some more.

And finally Susan said:

"I guess we better get you back to your husband."

"Oh crikey," Rachael wanted to see him but she felt a very vague flash of a thought that he wasn't going to like this.

She floated to the DJ booth. Daniel had finished his set and was getting ready to go organising his box in the booth. Rachael vaguely acknowledged a girl with short blonde hair hovering beside him.

"Hi there, how are you? Are you okay? What's going on?" conversation rushed out of her with little thought for its meaning or the reaction it would elicit. She felt such intense love for him at that moment and she just wanted to talk to him and share the feeling with him.

He was immediately aware that she was more garrulous than usual – and suspicious – he knew the signs – he'd seen them a hundred times before. "Rachael, I think we should go," he urged curtly.

"Oh but I want to stay. I want you to dance with me. The music – it's amazing here."

"I think it's best if we go back to the hotel," he was very definite now.

"Are you off darling," trilled a voice from the other side of him. It was Emma. He'd half forgotten about her. "Yeah I'm going now, let's stay in touch." She pressed her phone number scrawled on a piece of paper into his hand.

"Who was that?" said Rachael, half aware in her reverie that it was unusual for another woman to be in the DJ booth with Daniel.

"Oh just some record company promotions girl," he shrugged it off casually. "A pushy one."

She noticed he was walking very quickly now – there was aggression in his gait. She fell silent as they walked. She wanted to sober herself up and gradually the rushes were wearing off giving way to a vaguely somnambulistic detached feeling.

Finally they got back to the hotel room.

"Are you angry with me?" she heard herself saying, like an echo in her own head.

"Have you taken something?" he felt an urge to take her in both hands and shake her hard. But he resisted, violence was not going to help matters.

"I just. I just wanted to find out. What everyone was going on about. You must have done it – haven't you?" The words were suddenly slow and hard to force out. She didn't want to talk. She just felt like curling up in the bleached white of the duvet, in a beautiful soft snow drift, and lying there prone for time immemorial.

He was properly angry now.

"You know what. I haven't. You should see yourself. You're a gibbering wreck," there was sharpness in his voice. "You're no better than all those other kids at the raves I play to sucking on their dummies and waving their light sticks like grown babies. It's infantilising and pathetic. I suppose you love everyone now, I suppose you were going round that club like a child trying to hug everything in sight. Think the worlds all soft and fluffy now do you? You need to get real. The world is cruel and you're pathetic Pollyanna.

She was stunned by this onslaught. Although the visceral punch of his bile was blunted by the haze of chemical abstraction she was experiencing. A solitary tear rolled down her face. She had only wanted to tell him….. just how much …..

She wanted a hug. That was all.

"I'm going to bed," he said decisively. "I might have a bath," she murmured. She needed to get away from the bad feeling that hung in the air like thick smog.

So she closed the door and ran a bath. And Daniel Cajmere, who felt utterly justified in his rage, eventually calmed down and went to sleep.

Some days passed. They travelled back to Detroit. Nothing more was said about the episode.

Weeks passed and life continued. Rachael went to the record shop a few times a week and continued her informal research into the modern classical oeuvre. Now she was listening to and ordering in rare recordings by Messaien, Boulez and John Cage. Daniel was busy assembling tracks for a Rings Of Saturn label compilation. He was trying to mentor some of his artists – although he didn't really have a nurturing nature –it was more bullying them mercilessly into producing something good and verbally abusing them when they didn't meet the strict deadlines he set.

One day Rachael happened to join Daniel and Carter in the studio as they messed around with tracks to sample. She'd brought in some music she enjoyed listening to, vocal garage tracks on Eightball, Murk and Strictly Rhythm, loud with oestrogen fuelled diva vocals, upbeat pianos and thickset basslines.

"Hmmph, this is pussy music," observed Carter grumpily as she put another track on the turntable.

"That's a rather misogynistic assumption," countered Rachael. "Why is it that techno heads imperiously condemn vocal garage and house music with diva vocals as somehow lesser? – not as serious or worthy of revering. Surely it's actually more difficult to lay down a really brilliant vocal than it is to programme a few chords."

"The techno sound is tough, it's serious, it's a man thing,. Garage is what you play if you want girls to dance or if you want to get a girl into bed." retorted Carter, rather piqued that he had to reply to this and defend his music. Surely it went without saying.

"I'm kind of offended at your sexism frankly," said Rachael, she wasn't going to back down whilst this ignorant pig derided her taste in music. "And I think it's a very reductive binary to make techno and garage into antithetical genres."

"I dunno about you," said Carter looking at Cajmere for support, "but for me there is only techno. Its got gravitas. Whatever college language you might use, it's more intelligent. Cajmere help me out here, you know what I mean."

"He mean's there's a kind of rigour in techno production." Interjected Cajmere. "There's intelligence in its austerity and restraint, there's subtlety in the textures and in the science fiction tropes we deploy. Techno is the music of the head – its cerebral. Garage is just rumpshaking - music for the body."

"Oh so techno for the head, garage for the unthinking body. I get it," Rachael shook her head. "You can't posit one type of music as superior to another. It's crazy. It's only your opinion. Besides Celestial had a female vocal. You used that to make a commercial song. You're hardly a good one to talk Daniel."

"Well Celestial was different. You know Rachael that the label were pushing me for a single. I had no choice."

Rachael had her own theories about garage music anyway and she wasn't going to explain them for Carter to mock her. For her it was essentially a music about female power – those hormonal vocals – even though the producers were nearly all male. She wondered why the vocalists had such little acclaim in the equation, they tended to be an obscurist transitory part of the equation as far as music consumers were concerned. It was the producers who were the main stars. When she thought of the soulful vocals in garage she immediately thought of Ecriture Feminine, the theory she had learned at university which was coined by Helene Cixous in Laugh of the Medusa. She wondered if this theory could translate to the diva vocals in garage, the vocalists were 'writing the body' in their shrieking exaltations, inscribing a feminine language into the heart of the male oeuvre of electronic music. But she noted, the words of the lyrics were often about love and desire and whilst desire in itself had become a modish topic for post-structuralist and post-modernist theory, the lyrics themselves were not the 'writing'. It was the texture of the voice and the timbre, the tone: the twists and turns of each exhaled note, these formed the script of this particular 'ecriture'. And the feeling she, and she reckoned many others must derive from these records was, in the words of Cixous again, jouissance – an explosion, a diffusion, an effervescence, an abundance...the taking of pleasure in being limitless. Jouissance was a font of female creative expression – and so were these records – they spoke of the very essence of femininity itself – of the encoded language of the soul set free by the sheer muscle and unstoppable force, of the black female voice.

Rachael was curious, not to mention suspicious, about how Daniel was treating his protégées on Rings of Saturn. She and Daniel discussed inviting them round for dinner to talk about the progression of the label. Rachael cooked stir fry chicken and vegetables for the three guys that came and they all sat down afterwards to discuss the work they'd done for the album and how to progress it.

"I'm only accepting excellence for this album," decreed Daniel belligerently.

"I'm sure these guys are striving for it," said Rachael defending the youngsters. "I'm sure they want to give you their best. It's your job to guide them and mentor them to do that. Not put the fear of God into them."

"Hmmp" grunted Daniel.

He had to concede that Rachael was good with the youngsters. He watched on that evening as she played them her favourite modern classical tracks and encouraged them to talk about their tastes in music.

"Personally, I think what's going to keep this genre fresh is miscegenation," she mused. "You kids need to be listening to other stuff, in the same way Daniel was listening to 20th century classical for the Celestial album."

She talked about how the originators of the genre - Juan Atkins, Derrick May and Kevin Saunderson were listening to the radio show of The Electrifying Mojo. And how he'd play everything from The Cure to Kraftwerk, Can, Neu and Tangerine Dream. "What you have to remember is that Detroit techno was fused from some very disparate influences. If you only listen to Detroit techno yourselves, your music might become flat, whereas if you open yourselves up to lots of other genres you'll keep that freshness, that evolution."

Daniel sighed, Rachael was providing the mentoring, the teaching that he seldom had the patience to do. He'd never thought of spending much time with these kids, they were too reverent towards him and that was boring. They tended to roll by the studio, drop their tracks off and leave. But now it was occurring to him that if he hung out with them, he might be able to coax better material from them and guide them in the right direction.

"Have you thought of letting them have some time in your studio?" Rachael asked Daniel.

"Uggh no. But that's a good idea." She'd put him on the spot now. He felt slightly exposed. He hadn't been giving these youngsters the support they needed and that was obvious now.

"I think you should schedule in time with everyone here. Just spend a day each in Daniel's studio. He can afford a lot more equipment than any of you have got in your bedrooms and it might be an opportunity to evolve your sound."

Some weeks later a fax came through. "I've been booked to play in Berlin," announced Daniel, pulling the paper out of the machine. Will you come with me?"

"After last time?" She really didn't like the idea of another night in an strange city with Daniel disappearing on her again. Much as the thought of visiting Berlin, especially the Eastern side, in the wake of the wall being pulled down, did interest her, she thought of a night spent alone, waiting for Daniel in what was likely to be some kind of subterranean cave, with hundreds of sweaty bodies she didn't know and who didn't speak the same language, would be alienating and dispiriting, not to mention boring. She'd heard him play so many times before now and clubs held little allure for her any more.

"Not keen?" he grunted.

"Not really, I've got to be honest." She was not afraid of him and she was not going to comply with his wishes.

"Look it's a fascinating city, I'm really keen to see the Eastern Block architecture. Why don't we make a couple of days break of it? Go there and hang out, walk round what was the old East side of the city, hit some cafes and some restaurants. I think it would be a great little holiday for us. C'mon, don't be so resistant to my ideas. Give me a break!"

"You're not going to disappear on me in the club again?" her voice was slightly cracked.

"Look you know I've got to hang out with the promoters a bit in the club. I'm sure it'll be fine. Anyway you'll be okay, you can handle yourself. Just don't go and do anything stupid like you did the last time."

"I wouldn't have done anything stupid if it wasn't for you deserting me."

"Look, for goodness sake let's go. It'll be a blast. Anyway I need you to help me with my set. We'll stay in the best hotel. I'll get my agent in London to book the flights."

There was no point arguing any more.

Two weeks later they departed for Berlin. Daniel was playing the most famous and legendary club there and he and Rachael had spent hours preparing his set. Sampling modern classical albums in the studio and creating test pressings to play them off. Daniel's set was going to be a symphonia of groundbreaking sonic textures and early electronica, all grafted onto some classic Detroit tracks. He'd also created test pressings of some rough cuts of the forthcoming Rings of Saturn compilation to play the same night and he was very pleased with some of what his protégées had produced, especially in the wake of the night Rachel had mentored them.

It was a rainy Friday morning when they got to Berlin, the weather was especially inclement and they were tired from flying. "Let's go and rest in the hotel and then lets go for a walk round the city," suggested Daniel. "I want to see what remains of the Eastern Block."

The hotel, as promised was a monolith of luxury, a newly refurbished gleaming tower block on the West side of Berlin. It reminded Rachael of the hotel they'd stayed at in Vegas – the polished floors in the lobby, the low key but comfortable greige furnishings, everything lambent and optimistic in its wealthy veneer. And so they lay down on the ocean liner of a bed and slept off the flight.

Berlin Alexanderplatz, with it's mid century futurism, captivated Daniel. For some reason the pale expanse of concrete reminded him of an ice rink, which in turn made him think of watching Eastern Block ice skaters and gymnasts in the Olympics as a child. An oblique train of thought. They walked along Rosa Luxembourg Strasse "I always wanted to walk along a road called Rosa Luxembourg Strasse," remarked Rachael. "You're such an idealist," teased Daniel. "You said that to me on our first date, do you remember?" she said. "I do"

It was soon enough after the destruction of the wall for the east still to have a vaguely backward feel. "It's hard to pinpoint why this still feels dated." observed Daniel. "But I love the architecture, it's so bleak and uniform, all traces of individuality have been relentlessly expunged." He pointed at the spherical TV transmitter that seemed to be suspended above the city, a satellite floating in the sky. "Remember when we still had faith in the space age." He mused. "We were children then," she said, vaguely reminiscent of the seventies.

The club was located in a subterranean bank vault. Daniel and Rachael descended a flight of stairs with the promoter. He pointed out the iron grills that still remained where the vault had been sectioned off. His English was incredibly good thought Daniel. And these Germans were more enthusiastic and knowledgeable about techno than even the British and the Americans. "I've got all your records Daniel," he told him, "I can trace a trajectory from the early and naïve tracks where it sounds like your equipment was fairly limited to the more recent material and the album where what you are trying to do is a lot more sophisticated." "Yeah," I tried to embed a lot of different ideas into the album," said Daniel in a rare moment where he actually wanted to explain what he had done." We had some more digital equipment in the studio, although I still prefer the analogue synth sounds." "Much warmer, more human," added the promoter. "Exactly" agreed Daniel.

The club started filling up. Rachael observed that the German clubber's clothes were more sober. There were a lot of combat trousers and grey sweat tops, girls with plaits and boys with close-cropped hair. She and Daniel had a drink as the music started to accelerate. This was very hard chiseled unromantic techno. Techno with flinty edges, nails being hammered into wood relentlessly – one after another after one. This music was projecting out towards the jackhammering violence of gabba she thought – hard, Teutonic, impactful and rhythmic. Dancing to this the body became a mere automaton, it was like the machines had taken over. It was very very masculine and linear, there was no more room for humanity in the music. This wasn't the kind of techno that she liked. She wondered how Daniel's set, with its textures and flights of fancy would fit in with this crowd. They seemed to merely want reductive beats, a decisive, pared-down four to the floor with little embellishment. Melody and seeping atmospherics would almost be too soft, too evocative, too subliminal for these hedonists. Down in the crepuscular blackness of this bank vault extremity reigned supreme.

Daniel and Rachael stood at the side of the bar having a drink. "Look I am going to have to go and hang out with the other DJs, you'll be alright staying here won't you?" Daniel was feeling the lure of the back room.

"I suppose so." Sighed Rachael. Another evening alone with this stark, sharp, needling machine music for company. She stared into her drink. She was bored of nightclubs. What was a peak experience for other people, an entry into a magical transformational space where they dressed up and could become something other than the everyday, had become mundane and tedious for her and she struggled to stay up all night, by midnight she was yawning and longing for a soft pillow. Suddenly Wolfgang the promoter was at her side.

"You okay?" he asked.

"Yeah, I think Daniel's gone to hang out with the other DJs."

Yeah he's in the back room," confirmed Wolfgang. "Look this is my girlfriend Hannelore, you two should hang out. "Hi" said Rachael rather gloomily. "Hey there," said Hannelore in heavily accented English, a statuesque peroxide blonde, two plaits hung down the sides of her face playfully. "I think you got DJ girlfriend syndrome! Too much hanging around. Don't worry I've got club promoter girlfriend syndrome. So – let's hang out and forget about them."

Hannelore bought her a drink, gin and tonic. The music was giving her a slight headache by now; she noticed it seemed to be louder than in other clubs. 'Why is the music so loud here?" "I dunno, Germans like their techno hard and fast no!?" laughed Hannelore. Rachel smiled, but she felt weary. "Need a little something to pick you up?" asked Hannelore, as though she had sensed Rachael's ennui.

"I don't know," the night in Glasgow flashed through her mind. Daniel would be angry. It was an unfamiliar club in an unfamiliar city, he might even desert her, she worried. Oh damn him, ran her internal narrative. He could be remarkably callous, yet again he'd gone off with little thought for whom she would spend the evening with. Besides by the time he'd DJed, he was on late, it would have all worn off, she reasoned.

"Makes the evening go quicker. Makes the music nicer," shrugged Hannelore. *She was only trying to be helpful*, thought Rachel.

"Okay go on then, what the hell." Hannelore pressed a small white tablet into her hand

And so they started to dance, and Rachel could feel the familiar feeling swelling up in her, not as powerful as the last time, but a surge nevertheless and she danced, biding her time to be swept away with the arrested orgasmic shimmer of blissfulness that was ecstasy.

She waited, predicated herself on those staccato beats, but all of a sudden she was standing in the middle of the dancefloor and the music had become even darker, more oppressive than before.

"I need to sit down," she stuttered.

"Are you okay? Want some water? I'll come with you. Let's go sit on the stairs," said Hannelore guiding her from the dancefloor to the entrance stairs where Wolfgang had initially led them in."

"I feel sick," said Rachael, she could feel nausea overtaking her body.

"Here please drink this quickly," said Hannelore urgently handing her water. I think you are dehydrated.

Gradually, gradually, dark thoughts were taking over Rachael's' mind. She was finding it hard to breathe. Each inhalation was labored. She could feel herself lurching irrevocably towards something. Was it death that was looming towards her with inevitability? She was certainly under a storm cloud, if not being enveloped by it. It was becoming harder and harder just to stay alive.

"Please – help – me" she managed to utter desperately to Hannelore.

"I think you must have had a toxic one. Sometimes I think they are cut with heroin. Don't worry, I had a heavy one a few weeks ago. It's just a panic attack. Stay there whilst I get you more water. I can talk you through it. Stay with me."

"Don't leave me, I'm scared," Rachael was overcome with panic.

She sipped urgently on the water, glugging to down in the hope it would save her.. Surely the water would wash it through, make it better. She gasped for air.

Each expiration seemed to get shallower. It was harder and harder to breathe. She was in a long dark tunnel. Teenagers ….. she'd heard about in the news ….. that had died taking E. She was terrified. She was going, too. Away. Away. Far. Away.

As her breath became shorter and blackness enveloped her she was vaguely aware of Hannelore shouting out in the distance.

"Somebody fucking help her she's had a bad pill and she's passed out…." And then something vaguely audible in German.

Daniel, who was sat in the back room deep in conversation with a Dutch label owner called Joachim, suddenly felt a tugging at his arm. It was Wolfgang and he looked desperate.

"Daniel, Daniel, come quickly, it's your girlfriend. She's had a panic attack and she's passed out."

She's actually my wife, thought Daniel, irritated that he'd been interrupted. His first thought was – she's taken something again. Stupid cow. But then he could see Wolfgang racing towards the exit and his pulse quickened and he followed him.

Daniel arrived at the scene of Rachel's collapse on the stairs.
"What the fuck is going on?" he demanded of Wolfgang and Hannelore.

"Calm down Daniel," Wolfgang urged him. "She's taken a bad pill and passed out. Don't worry the ambulance is on it's way."

Daniel put his head in his hands. He was furious. How could she make this mistake again. He'd only left her alone for half an hour. He clenched his fists. When they got back to the hotel he would really let her know what gives. And then suddenly he felt anxious. A UK promoter had told him there'd been a number of well-publicized deaths from ecstasy recently that had rocked the club world. He blanched, a shiver of froideur went through his body, his stomach turned over. *What if she was to die.*

He turned to Wolfgang.

"Do you think she's going to be okay?" At that moment the paramedic team arrived and put her on a stretcher. From that moment on Daniel felt himself disembodied. It was like he was standing outside himself looking in on the situation. He was frozen.

"C'mon Daniel, Hannelore's going to go in the ambulance because she speaks German and we'll go in the car and follow them to the hospital" urged Wolfgang.

It seemed like they were travelling in slow motion in that car. They seemed to be stuck in traffic for hours. The blur of city lights out of the window. He felt paralyzed. Numb.

"For God's sake how long is this journey going to take?" he asked Wolfgang at one point through gritted teeth.

"Don't panic, we're nearly there."

And then the hospital. They were ushered to some chairs in a corridor in what must have been the accident and emergency department, Daniel guessed. Hannelore came and sat with them.

"Her heart stopped in the ambulance and they're trying to revive her now."

"Oh Christ," said Daniel. He put his head in his hands. This wasn't happening. He was cold and blank and anaesthetized. Extreme panic had propagated a kind of stasis in him. He could not move. All around him was movement, lights, action. But he was frozen.

"Come on let me get you guys a coffee, there's a machine in the waiting room." Hannelore was trying her best.

An hour elapsed. It was a strange, sterile period of time. Daniel lurched from one minute to the next, suddenly very aware of his stomach, aware of his breath.

OhmyGodIloveheromuch. He was desperate

She's so vulnerable. So innocent. Please let her be okay.

Finally a doctor appeared. He ushered Daniel into an empty room. Daniel felt the air of gravitas in the man's voice.

Are you her next of kin?

"Yes I am Rachel Hurst's husband, Daniel Cajmere."

The rest was a blur, something about how they had tried to save her but toxins in the bloodstream and failure of major organs.

"I'm so sorry" said the doctor. "Do you want to see her?"

He felt tears swell up in him. But he could not cry. Just keep breathing. In and out. In and out.

OhGodpleaseletthisnotbetrue. Come back to me my love.

A month later and he was back in Detroit in his empty house. There had been a funeral, in Rachel's home town about an hour out of London. He met her family, her mother and father. They were just an ordinary middle class suburban couple in their mid fifties. They had all been so nice, hadn't blamed him. "I suppose it's the lifestyle, it goes with the territory," her mother had said, touching his arm, yet looking impossibly sad. He couldn't help wondering what they were thinking. *I killed their daughter.*

He hadn't been able to do much since the funeral. Initially, there had been this compelling urge to join her in the grave. For the first time in his life, in his invincible consciousness, his thoughts had turned to something he'd once deemed as an option for the weak and cowardly: suicide. He wanted to leave this world. There was nothing left in this world for him. It was a void without her. He could travel to the ends of the earth and there would be nothing, anywhere. He wanted, seriously, to join her in the grave. He considered how he might do it. Hanging – he didn't have a clue how to rig up a noose. Slashing his wrists – too messy – he didn't like blood. Pills and booze. Yes, that was how he would end it. To drift into oblivion slowly and blissfully and then he would join her – wherever she had gone. He would follow her there.

The first week back in Detroit he had been shell-shocked. It was like learning to talk, learning to walk, learning how to put one foot in front of the other all over again. The record company had been understanding, Simon Wanstall had called a number of times, and they'd given him more time to sort out the Rings of Saturn compilation which was pending. There was no one he could really share what he was going through. His mother had been so shocked by the revelation of drug taking she'd just mouthed 'Oh' and then quickly added 'You didn't take anything did you?" Carter King had expressed gruff condolences one day at the studio, there was no way Daniel could elucidate to him what the process of grieving was like. And his young protégées on Rings of Saturn had been too awkward to mention it. He was left alone in his grief.

The aching void was a constant. He had taken her for granted. It was only without her there, without her colour, her life, her intelligent conversation, that he could conceive of how much she had given to him. It was true now, he told himself, she had indeed been his soul mate and it was the cruellest blow of all that she had been taken away.

Sadness and loss became habitual in his life, those first few raw months after Rachael had died. But sadness was also mutative – like gradations of the grey and black of the concrete metropolis there were incremental fluctuations in his consistent low mood. Sometimes it was characterized by emptiness – what wasn't there - the hollow echo of the cubed white house they once inhabited. Other times there was a kind of tenderness – he would hug her pillow – trying to discern the last traces of odour of her and he would cry because there was no one there to see his pain.

The constant sense of his culpability for the death plagued him. *I did it. I did it.* Eventually this emotion solidified into a lump in his stomach. His digestive system started to breakdown. All food tasted of sawdust anyway since she had gone. But he could feel each piece of food travelling down the tract, slowly progressing through his body in great wooden clods that distended and scraped through his alimentary canal, one by one. Eating became a source of discomfort, however diligently he chewed his food. A few trips to the doctor followed and he was directed to try Pepto Bismol. He gulped it down desperately, however it wouldn't alleviate the problem, just left a strange aniseed aftertaste in his mouth and throat for hours afterwards.

Everyday a train of thoughts would enter his mind. If only he hadn't deserted her in Glasgow. If only he hadn't kissed Emma Milton. If only he hadn't left her with Hannelore in Berlin.

And then the big philosophical questions would come. Where had she gone? What had happened to her? What happens to any of us?

He didn't know whether there was a God or not. Surely no God would take away this beautiful intelligent wife of his, with so much potential, so much ahead of her, so much they were going to do together. He was cognisant that he lived in a faithless world – the West of the late

20th century. There was no comfort to be had in Jesus or churches for Daniel Cajmere.

Then the worst-case scenario would occur to him, the unthinkable. What if, after death, *there was nothing.* What if the light had been switched out and there was Rachael, alone in the dark, a void. This was when it became unbearable. He would walk in slow motion to the fridge and get a beer. Anything to expunge that thought, anything to blank out the pain, anything to slide into oblivion.

One day he decided to take his camera to Highland Park again. To visit the factory where they'd wandered around together. A solitary pilgrimage. To remember her.

As he walked around the dilapidated factory with his camera, he wondered what she might be saying to him. The ruins had had a profound effect on her and she'd wanted to help rebuild this decaying city. They were both happy back then and they had seen an otherworldly beauty in the corrosion of these industrial buildings, a poetry in the rotting wood and crumbling plaster. But it had been safe, he reflected, to indulge in a sort of tourism of melancholy when you felt secure and well adjusted. Now, on the other hand, looking at the smashed in windows now he could hardly bear it, they were like the mirror of his broken soul. The jagged remnants of glass in those windows frames pierced his trembling and vulnerable heart. It started to rain and the sky was compressing the cityscape with dark clouds. He let himself get wet as the water poured through the leaking roof. The desolation resonated in him. In the end it was unbearable, he wandered around and took a few desultory picture of rusting metal structures that, he imaged, had once comprised a production line, and then he had to leave. He ruminated on the building. He was haunted by it. Once there had been voices and life and productivity. That was all left behind. Now all there was was loss and he only realized then that it was loss that truly defined and underscored *what had been.*

As the months progressed and he slipped un-noticed back into the routine of his own normal life, he found himself conversant with her in his head. "What do you think of this track?" he'd ask her when one of the kids submitted something for the compilation. But nothing no reply. So he'd imagine what her answer might be. "I think they should listen to some Messaien or Sun Ra or John Taverner's The Whale" she would say. But all the while he was aware that he was concocting what she would say and he yearned for her answer, across the seemingly impenetrable divides of time and space and heaven and earth. If, indeed, there was a heaven. He now found himself clinging on to the idea there was.

Finally the Rings of Saturn compilation was completed. He realized that since Rachael had mentored the young producers their output had improved considerably. Instead of just aping existing Detroit tracks and producing a weak, watered down version of the original landmarks of the genre, they were trying to evolve the sound and move it into new sound worlds. There was one track that Cajmere was particularly fond of, that even used breakbeats. This was controversial for Detroit, breakbeats had gained traction in the UK with the recent explosion of the jungle and drum and bass sound, but many Detroit producers had stayed stubbornly with the four to the floor formula. However using breakbeats creatively, deconstructing them, making sure they were the same timbre as the original Detroit drum programmes and then laying over classic contemplative synths could make a very convincing evolution of techno, noted Cajmere.

His protégées had been adventurous in their productions and he was pleased. There was one very tuneful jazzy track, it could almost make a breakout single, thought Cajmere, if the album was to have such a thing, although it probably wouldn't. There was another ambient track with dulcet melodies woven around the metronomic spine of a ticking clock. And there was an anthem in the 'Strings of Life' mould, a real rousing orchestral clarion call – perhaps they could send out a number of test pressings to the most influential DJs in the US and UK thought Cajmere.

He sent the master tape off to the record label, a week or so elapsed and then the call came. They were happy with the album. Would he come to London to do some press and a DJ tour to promote it? Cajmere couldn't say he was enthused about the thought of returning to the UK. For him it was so embedded with memories of his time with Rachael. He couldn't envisage touring without her at his side. Travel generally, and the UK specifically held very little allure for him any more. It was bad enough being in Detroit, with all the memories of the life they'd had there. But to return to the UK – the prospect served to depress him further. A leaden lump formed in his stomach.

However, he couldn't say no. He didn't need money from the new album but he was locked into a cycle of producing releases for the label – it was part of the contract he'd signed and he couldn't escape.

A day or two before he was scheduled to leave, he found Emma Milton's crumpled phone number in a pair of his old jeans. He contemplated phoning her. He couldn't muster much enthusiasm for it. And yet he had to admit that a night out with a glamorous woman would at least serve to alleviate the gloom of the treadmill of record promotion.

He found himself picking up the phone.

"Hey there is that Emma Milton,"

"Yeah sure, who's that?"

"It's Daniel Cajmere the DJ, remember, we met a few months back in Glasgow."

"Oh darling, how could I forget you! How come it took you so long," her voice growled with pleasure. She had one of those voices that sounded as though nicotine was coursing through her veins and indeed she did smoke, albeit rather casually.

Daniel found himself getting back into his old stride of handling a woman.

"It's a long story. I had this and that to deal with." He didn't think now was the time to explain he'd just lost his wife.

"Hey I'm back in London next week though,"

"Are you darling?"

"I was thinking, we should hook up for dinner,"

"Wow I'm being asked to dinner by *the* Daniel Cajmere," she exclaimed. "How could I refuse?"

"I generally find women don't" he laughed. Cajmere was getting back into his cocky bachelor stride now. Ah the old days were coming back.

They chatted casually for a few minutes. She was travelling to a few clubs at the weekend to promote some new twelves. She was easy to talk to and convivial, flirtatious, engaging. She made him feel like a man again, rather than the shell of a human being he'd become, longing for what had been. He wondered if he was in some way being unfaithful to the memory of Rachael. What the hell – he needed company – no one could object to him just wanting to hang out with a girl – he reasoned. Emma Milton was a means to alleviate the pain and pass the time. Female company was just what he needed to salve the wound.

It was springtime when he touched down in London. As his taxi sped through the different boroughs he noted the acid bright yellow green of trees in new leaf as luminous as glow sticks against the crisp blue sky.

His stomach lurched as he passed through the streets near the record shop where Rachael had worked. It was almost too much to bear. He daren't go in there. He knew they would blame him – Mark and Tom – her innocent friends. He didn't need them to reprimand him. He blamed himself. Anyone else telling him he'd killed her would merely be reinforcing what he already felt.

"Hey there," said Simon Wanstall as he entered the record company offices. "Firstly, I'm incredibly sorry about your loss," Cajmere was glad to see Wanstall. He felt vulnerable and there was something intangibly warm and comforting about him.

"It must be hard for you coming back here," Wanstall had read his mind. "Is it your first time back since the funeral?" Cajmere nodded. "Look I just want you to know Daniel, in the industry, no one blames you. People see it as an unfortunate accident. These things happen in our world. Let's face it, it's unusual if someone doesn't take drugs, isn't it?"

"I don't take drugs,"

"Yeah I know, but you Detroit guys are different. I don't know one DJ or producer from Detroit that's ever had an e. Which is remarkable since you seem to make music that sounds otherworldly when you're on one!"

Cajmere cheered up a bit at his humour. "I guess we're just naturally psyched." He was relieved. It was as though Wanstall had alleviated some of his pain. He felt bad he had dismissed this guy as an over-intellectualizing geek. He was earnest and sensitive to others, and those were decent qualities. He needed to see someone like Wanstall in the industry right now, not some brash, swaggering jerk who would damn her for 'being a lightweight'. Rachael would have liked Simon Wanstall, he thought. It was a shame they'd never met.

"You know my wife had a huge influence on my tracks," he'd never admitted this before but he knew he could confide in Wanstall.

" She worked in a record store and she had an encyclopedic knowledge of music."

"It must be great when you have that synergy," nodded Wanstall sympathetically. "It's not often when someone comes along with that."

Cajmere mused on that idea. Could it be that Rachael was his one chance and his one chance was now gone. Would it be back to endless sexually gratifying yet meaningless encounters for him now? His stomach clenched and his throat went dry.

"Do you think there are many other women out there like that," he asked, voice noticeably half-cracked.

"I honestly don't know," replied Wanstall. "I met my wife at University and it so happened we had the same interests – avant garde music and film and books. Look, you know how it is as well as I do out there. Yes there are a few women who've got a specialist knowledge and are interested in the mechanics of the music, but lets admit it I guess there's a contingent who just want to go out with a DJ because he's rich and famous."

"I know. I think I know both sides of that equation," pondered Cajmere quietly, almost half to himself. There was a self doubt and a sorrow about him now, her death had given him a jolt and he was no longer the infallible 'superman' he'd read about in Nietsche.

"Look Daniel, I'm sure you'll find someone nice. Just give it time. And if I think of any eligible female trainspotters to introduce you to I will! Unfortunately, all my wife's friends are happily married. Now come on, let's talk about the compilation – it's bloody great."

They talked about the album. Wanstall told him it was interesting that he'd got his protégées to push the boundaries of the genre, rather than simply produce weak homages to it 'in the style of'. "I'm impressed," he said. "That was kinda down to my wife too," recalled Cajmere. "She's really got to take credit for encouraging our stable of producers to indulge in some stylistic miscegenation. She was really against out and out purism. Although I'd argue that the constraints of a genre can sometimes be a good thing, sometimes discipline and rigour can heighten emotion I think." "Well there's arguments for both," surveyed Wanstall. "Personally I'm glad there's a breakbeat track on there – we can get some hot producers to remix it, speed it up a bit and get it out to the drum and bass DJs – you must have heard how that music has exploded here in the UK in the last year or so." "Yeah I read about it," replied Cajmere "and I do like the bits that I've heard." "I'll take you down to Speed one night, that's the club all the junglists go to. I think you'd love it," said Wanstall. The following week Wanstall fulfilled his promise and took Cajmere to Speed. It was somewhere in central London, Cajmere wasn't sure where, down a side street. The queue snaked for a few hundred yards along the wet pavement but Wanstall confidently circumlocuted it and guided Cajmere to the door. Inside it was a large milky pod of an interior, lots of boys in combat trousers, t-shirts and trainers on the dancefloor and industry types shuffling around near the bar. The music, as you'd expect from the name, was what was now called drum and bass and it was a maximum velocity hurtle through the stratosphere. Wanstall explained that the producers everyone was name checking included LTJ Bukem, Photek, Peshay and Goldie. Cajmere noted how the lumped hardcore techno of the early nineties had now evolved into this spangled rush of percussive multiplicity. The breakbeats were now diffuse and highly wrought, rather than lumpen and grinding. The producers had cleverly deconstructed them so that they took on an almost improvised form, stuttering, spluttering cycles of drums circulated over a syncopated two step. He could almost see these beats, pyrotechnics in the sky, dazzling and twinkling like filigree patternings before him, see sawing and circling, dotting the air with magic.

"What you thinking?" asked Wanstall as they had a beer at the bar. "I'm thinking this is the most incredible music I've heard since Detroit techno came about," commented Cajmere, genuinely impressed. "I never really liked breakbeats before, I thought you know, there was something clunky about them speeded up. But these guys are amazing. I don't know how to describe it. It's like a new kind of jazz. The beats are very light and fragmentary. It's like they broke them down and built them up again in new formations. Very clever." He felt invigorated by this new music. His immediate thought *was what would Rachael have thought*? The thought that followed was, perhaps inevitably, *it is my fault she's not here to hear it*. Suddenly, he felt saddened. "Of course all the other major label A and R's are all over this scene like a rash now," mused Wanstall cynically. "In some ways it's a shame. They're going to use it up and wear it out I reckon. Like Detroit techno I don't know if it's going to translate into that many hit albums. Everyone's talking about Goldie's album which is out next month. If anyone can make a decent long player out of this scene, it's him. But it's touch and go."

"I guess we were pretty lucky in that our scene got a chance to develop before the major labels moved in," replied Cajmere. "I think if something like this is pounced on in its infancy there's a tendency it's going to be exploited and become a flash in the pan. Youth culture is such a product now – and like all products it's got an expendable nature. Once it's been consumed people are hungry for the next new thing."

"Yeah, you're absolutely right," said Wanstall, "and I hate to think that I'm part of the mechanics of under ground music's exploitation. But I like to think, on my better days, that I'm nurturing and evolving these scenes, rather than stamping a sell-by date on them."

"I wonder if what we're seeing is the start of the end of the underground," added Cajmere. "These days the uptake is so fast from subculture to pop culture. It seems like there's only a very small window where these movements have the potential to be insurrectionary and shock before they are absorbed into the mainstream. It makes me sad. Sometimes a scene can't survive the amount of mythologisation heaped on it so quickly."

Cajmere was staying in the same Kensington hotel that he'd been in originally – again, at the expense of the record label. He was earning enough in royalties now from his chart hits for them to indulge him. He would go back to his room at night and feel a profound loneliness – the night stretched out before him without promise. Inevitably perhaps, thoughts of Rachel would come in the dark. He yearned for her presence, for her wisdom and thoughtfulness. Every minute spent in the black was full of loss and longing. And then, there were the recriminations. *It was my fault. It was my fault. I shouldn't have kissed another woman. If only she hadn't come to Berlin. I shouldn't have left her alone.*

To ease his anguish he would scribble notes to her on the hotel stationery. He would write down all the things he should have told her when she was alive. Part of him, the part of him that hoped there was a God and an afterlife, wondered if she, or at least someone up there could see what he was writing. *You make me*, he wrote in his angular scrawl. *You were my guardian angel. You saved me.* He would cringe at the clichéd nature of his output. And yet these written exhalations were such a heartfelt exhortation of his feelings. Feelings he could never share with anyone else.

Wanstall, who was secretly worried about Cajmere since his bereavement, was making subtle gestures to look after him. He phoned him daily, on the pretext of minor issues to do with the compilation, but really he wanted to check on him. To make sure he was coping in the aftermath of his loss. Cajmere was too wrapped up in himself, at this point, to realise the support he was getting. But he was thankful of the opportunity for human contact, during these empty, aching days and nights of hotel ennui.

He had a week left in London and he decided to call Emma Milton. He was desperate for company, anything, anything to alleviate the gaping chasm in his life. He couldn't even face going to the record shop where Rachael had worked, for fear that Mark and Tom blamed him somehow. Everything in London reminded him of her, where they had met, where they had gone shopping, where they had gone clubbing. It was now a city of ghosts, a city bereft of life for him. He thought some female company – in the form of Emma - would at least provide distraction in his empty and unrelentingly bleak world.

"Darling, how wonderful to hear from you," she greeted him.

" I didn't forget you," he ventured suavely.

"Well I'm impossible to forget," she retorted, a half-joke. He recognised her hubris, the mirror image of himself.

They arranged to do dinner. A big new architect-designed restaurant in West London that Cajmere had never heard of.

"We can see and be seen," said Emma Milton excitedly; she was an inveterate networker – even when dating. But Cajmere hardly noticed. In his current state, he was just glad of the company, the distraction from the current emotional entropy of his life.

He turned up at the restaurant early that night. He was nothing if not punctual – and it was not like he had anything else to do. The exterior was a sheer wall of glass with a skeleton of industrial structural supports beyond it; large stainless steel pipes ran horizontally suspended from the ceiling. It reminded him somewhat of the Pompidou centre in Paris, of which he was a fan. The chairs at the tables were rainbow coloured Robin Day chairs and the tables were white moulded polymer. Cajmere was seduced, he had thought he was the only one interested in forms and structures, design and architecture - he had never seen visited such a design-aware restaurant before. Like the hotel he'd stayed at with Rachael in Glasgow it seemed to signal, the dawn of a new evolved era.

All along one wall ran a bar. Cajmere went and sat here, staring into a beer or watching the people go by. The staff were outfitted in designer clothes an approximation of Thai fishermen's smocks and Thai fishermen's pants in a hemp-like fabric and the diners were a mixture of business men and creative types in ultra baggy indigo denim selvedge jeans, imported Japanese trainers and t shirts in off –key shades like petrol blue and khaki.

20 minutes late, in swung Emma Milton. She was wearing baggy combat pants slung low on the hip with a large Chinese dragon embroidered in red and yellow down one leg. A vast swathe of tanned midriff was visible, she had a belly button piercing and above that there was a sports luxe red crop top through which her erect nipples were protruding. Her lips were lambent and polished with clear lipgloss over a nude lipstick. Cajmere felt his groin harden.

"You awright darhling?" she greeted in a saucy faux cockney lilt.

"Yeah fine thanks," Cajmere sounded depressed by comparison. "You chose a cool place to eat. Well done. I've never been anywhere like this before."

"It's brilliant isn't it," she was self-congratulatory. "Last time I came here Leonardo Di Caprio was at the next table."

"We just don't have restaurants like this in Detroit. It's either dated places in large hotels of neighbourhood diners. I guess quite a few Indian and Chinese too in the burbs."

"London's getting a lot better, quite a few hip new places," she said scanning the room avidly for people she knew then taking a cigarette out of her cross body bag and lighting it.

They sat down at a table and read the menu. The food was fusion, Emma informed him, a melange of South East Asian and European, apparently it was very fashionable at the moment. She was chatty, light, breezy company, observed Cajmere,, almost the opposite of Rachael with her studied sincerity. She would look into his eyes and touch his hand briefly as though it were the easiest most natural thing in the world, like a butterfly alighting upon him before fluttering off elsewhere.

There was certainly something about her......
He tried to talk about music, her knowledge seemed to be mainly confined to a cursory grasp of very commercial house and European trance, of which Cajmere was not fond.

"So you're a top DJ, tell me your vices? Pills? Charlie? C'mon, everyone's a little bit naughty these days, aren't they? Everyone I know at least."

Cajmere didn't really know how to respond to this. No one had ever challenged him about his morals before. Besides he was pretty boring these days in the wake of losing Rachael.

He smiled. "As if I'd tell you that,"

"I love it, an elusive one. Hard nut to crack. Don't worry I'll get it out of you sooner or later." She smiled back, but there was steely intent beneath the saccharine grin.

"Did I tell you about Paul Reeves?"

"No, go on, what?"

"Everyone in the industry's talking about him. Apparently he picked up a 17-year-old girl at Cream one night and he's flying her to all his gigs with him. His wife, who's famous fashion editor on Chic magazine, knows nothing about it. But everyone else is in on it. Can you believe it?! Ha ha ha. She proceeded to laugh in outrage.

"I didn't know that. I don't know Paul. I know his name, of course."

"Gosh and what about Andy Silver! Did you hear about him?" she was revelling in disseminating this information. She delivered her anecdotes with relish.

"No can't say I did, I know he is very big in Ibiza, though." Cajmere could hardly wonder what she was going to say next.

"He's such a caner! The last time he got wasted he absconded from the club he was meant to be playing in. I mean completely disappeared. They had to put out a search for him. They found him a few hours later staggering about in some bushes on some waste ground near the club with his trousers around his ankles! Crazy huh."

"Wow, some guy," Cajmere managed a little chuckle.

"Eddie Wright has ended up in rehab – what a lightweight," she crowed with a cackle. "Someone can't take their drugs!"

She proceeded to regale him as to the exploits of various famous house and techno DJs as their fusion plates of food arrived – Cajmere had ordered a chicken and mango Laksa. Drugs, sex, money – she was a font of scurrilous information about the main players on the scene. Who loved groupies, who was a coke head, who had got a gargantuan £10,000 out of the record label for one remix.

Cajmere had always felt slightly out on a limb there in Detroit. Half invested in the UK scene and half detached and concentrated on the small coterie of Detroit DJs and producers in his hometown. It was interesting to hear what really went on with the DJs over here. Sure, he'd had his own peccadilloes as an eligible bachelor DJ on the scene. Not that he was going to tell her that. Although he wondered if she already knew.

"So what did you hear about me?" he enquired casually.

"Oh not much, I don't know much about Detroit in all honesty. I heard your girlfriend died. Yeah, I'm sorry about that." Her voice withered and she became awkward, she'd been hoping not to talk this subject all night long, but now it was unavoidable.

"Yeah," tears welled up and his eyes glassed over, although thankfully she was too busy evading the topic to notice. "A few months ago, in Berlin. I'm kinda still recovering."

"Don't worry, you'll be okay," she touched his arm affectionately, whilst having absolutely no knowledge of the depths his pain was plumbing that day.

Suddenly she picked up, she was, to her relief, distracted. A thirty something man with brown spiky hair, indigo denim jeans and a Junior Boys Own record bag sat down at the table next to them. Emma got up out of her seat to greet him, air kissing him on both cheeks. "Jo, oh my gosh, Jo you corker. I didn't know you were going to be here? You naughty boy! I heard all about you in Brighton the other night. Bad boy! Daniel, come and meet Jo – Daniel Cajmere this is Jo Barber. I'm sure you know each other's names. Jo's just about to do his first remix for a major. Aren't you babe? And Jo, you must know Daniel Cajmere – he's a legend!" She went and sat at Jo's table and chatted for a while to Jo and Daniel finished his food, feeling somewhat abandoned.

She came back shortly "Oh my gosh, you'll never believe what Jo's just told me. Steve Tarporley's in hospital. Snowboarding accident. But I bet that wasn't the only snow going on if you know what I mean. Har har." She clapped her hands together in glee.

Cajmere looked at her. She was attractive; she was light, easy company, fun to be around. Yeah, he would see her again. It was a nice distraction from the pain of everyday life, the emptiness that wouldn't go away.

After they meal had finished they were stood outside the restaurant. He kissed her tentatively. He wasn't as confident as he used to be, there was shakiness in his stomach. But no one else could sense it. He was a tough act.

"I'm not going to fall into bed with you tonight Daniel Cajmere. I hope you're not expecting that. I'll bet all the girls want to hop into bed with you with your melted chocolate eyes. But not me, I'm a femme fatale me."

He laughed. "It's not mandatory, you know, sleeping with me. But I'm going back to Detroit the day after tomorrow. So I guess I'll see you the next time I'm in town."

"Call me, won't you," she still sounded casual and noncommittal. Because she knew he would call.

Cajmere travelled back to Detroit soon after. He wasn't looking forward to going home. That lonely house, however pleasing the design was, was not the same without her. Emptiness. It was all-pervasive. He had assumed she would always be there you see. These houses had been built with couples and families in mind. It was inconceivable without her bustling around, cooking something or rearranging the records. He had assumed she would be there to infinity. Assuming, he thought, it was almost taking for granted. Almost. How arrogant he had been, he thought, not once had he considered losing her. He had it all, the prince of Detroit, a hollow laugh followed. How completely it had slipped through his fingers. Nothing was left. Except his money. And he would have given all his millions to have her back. He knew that now. Life was so fluid, the feelings it would go continue forever and ever. Then here was death to sever that infinity. Death was an absolute. There was nothing malleable about death, it was not mutable and flowing like time and emotions and very breath. It was a hard severance and *humans are not built to cope with hard severance* he thought. We can't conceptualise finality, endgame, brick wall where the soft pulsing body or the expansive mind is concerned. Or at least its fixity is so problematic for us to conceive of a life ending, so unlike stories and books where we crave the end, we race towards it blithely.

He still couldn't think of death without some outburst of anger. He was angry at himself mostly, the recriminations, leaving her alone, kissing another woman (although his anger didn't make him want to give up Emma Milton – he needed someone right now he figured), not caring, not knowing that someone was offering her dirty pills. A couple of times he had even thought of phoning Wolfgang and Hannelore and telling them what he thought of them. How dare they, he would reach a pitch of fury. *They killed her. I killed her. They killed her. I killed her.* There was even one rare time where he wondered if someone was out to get him. Someone jealous of his success had spiked his wife's ecstasy to attack him in the worst possible way. But he batted this thought away immediately. This way lay madness. But still, he looked back on his life, he was the one that should have died not her. His former arrogance, his abuse of women, Cajmere was well aware he had been a toxic character, but so sure of himself he didn't care. She was innocent, she had only ever been kind. I was cruel. I should have died. There were still these moments. He wished himself dead. But suicide no. He would not go down that road. She would have wanted him to continue. There was more music to be made. But love would never be the same again. There would be women in the future, he reckoned, but there would never be a love as pure as that.

He was listening more and more to ambient and avant-garde music – Laraaji, Brian Eno, Harold Budd and alternative rock like Japan, David Sylvian and Talk Talk. He took his Talk Talk albums into the studio one day to play to Carter King.

"Interesting production on this shit," noted King. "Yeah, it's more contemplative than a lot of other Eighties rock," mused Cajmere. "The Colour of Spring is such a good title for an album, it's like, you know exactly what that looks like and you can imagine exactly what it sounds like."

Everything he played he played for her. The whole soundtrack to his life like a Requiem mass. Things she would have liked.

"I'm going to make a track for Rachael, should have made it whilst she was alive really," he told King.

"Uh huh," King grunted. He didn't really know what to say. "You still miss her?"

"Hell yeah."

"I guess it will take time," he tried to console him in a sort of gruff male way. It wasn't something they could really talk about.

"I don't think the pain will ever go away," murmured Cajmere softly, his brow furrowed, a lump of lead in his stomach. The days of acute grief, where he could barely put one foot in front of another, had passed now, but there was still a persistent ache. Where love had once been.

"What sort of sound are you thinking of?" safer to focus on the music, thought King. Talking about emotions felt uncomfortable.

"Something like Carl Craig's 'Neurotic Behaviour' or Eddie Flashing Fowlkes' 'Check One Boy'. I think the Detroit sound lends itself really well to that kind of melancholy excursion….. Yeah …. Reflections…… Sense of loss."

"I got some library music samples that might be helpful," offered King

"Yeah, they might be King, but I think I might play it on synth myself,"

"What you gonna call it?"

"For Rachael."

And so Cajmere set to work on his opus, sat alone in the studio, with only his records for company, the sorrow seemed to flow out of his fingers onto the keyboard. Almost a howl of anguish, but muted by time, distance and the cavalcade of events that had elapsed since then, the scenery of a half-life lived. For yes, he thought, it was only half a life without her, a dwindling sense of hope, optimism, future. He tried to think of Emma Milton, her lips on his, her chirpiness, her breasts, but it was a fleeting distraction, a mirage that couldn't take away the sour taste of lost love like a bitter pill in his mouth.

Later that day, one of his kids came into the studio –a tall, skinny, dark-skinned youth with bug eyes. He was dressed in a marl grey tracksuit and scuffed white shell toe trainers and seemed to shuffle agitated from one foot to another. Usually Cajmere would have dismissed him with a wave of his hand, but this time he wanted to coach him. He wanted to do what Rachael would have done. "Hey Tony, come and play me what you've done," he urged and the kid stepped forward shyly with a tape in his hands. Cajmere listened to it attentively, it was a straight up four to the floor anthem, in the mould of Underground Resistance's Jupiter Jazz, but a little rudimentary perhaps. "Come here, let me show you some stuff," Cajmere went to the keyboard and showed the kid how he could improvise and riff on what he'd done and make the syncopated shuffle of the melody a little more lithe and elastic.

"Wow, I can see that's much better," said the kid hopefully, delighted that he'd managed to get some time with the great Daniel Cajmere. Daniel thought of how good Rachael had been with the youngsters, *she would have been a great mother,* now he was cracking inside like a brittle shell. He gulped back emotion and tried to focus on the keyboard. "Where are you getting your samples from? Have you tried listening to some early 70s jazz fusion? That might fit well with your sound? Herbie Hancock, that kinda stuff?"

Yeah, I never thought of that," said the kid, whose knowledge of music was still in its infancy.

"Why don't we go record shopping one afternoon," suggested Cajmere in a fit of benevolence. He thought of going to visit the shop where Rachel used to work, a kind of pilgrimage. He hadn't been in since she died.

"Wow that would be so cool," said the kid, astounded that Cajmere was taking such an interest in him.

"I reckon if we shape this track up a bit we could put it out on the label," nodded Cajmere. "I need a single for next year and this could be it. How about that then? Your vinyl debut?"

Tony was overcome with elation, his admiration for Cajmere was palpable and to have this seal of his approbation was too much to bear. Besides he'd heard that Cajmere didn't really have time for many people in Detroit apart from Carter King.

Cajmere went home that night, to his white box of a house, and he felt some sense of achievement at having coached Tony. It was satisfying to impress his thoughts and skills onto a young mind. He felt invigorated. *It was what she would have wanted.* He cooked himself a meal slowly, fried chicken with greens. He had hardly been bothered to cook or eat in the few months since she had died. Food all tasted bland, with the texture of sawdust. He'd had to force it down; even chewing, once pleasurable, had become a kind of perfunctory grinding and he was aware of every mechanical gulp his throat made.

The studio was his only refuge at the moment. There, immersed in records and surrounded by his computers, keyboards and drum machines he could lose himself in sonic possibility. It was lonely, sure, but in the six months since she had died there had been not one person that had understood, really understood what he was going through. He felt set apart from humanity, singular, alienated. Sure there had been brief distractions, momentary diversions – his meeting with Emma Milton, hanging out with the record company guys or the kids in the studio. But they were finite associations. At the end of each day there was emptiness, and that could not be escaped from.

Cajmere had been fiddling around with some samples of Talk Talk. The early nineties albums had some interesting drum patterns on them – deconstructed and he was wondering how they could dovetail with some classic Detroit chords. Later that day, around 4pm, the phone rang. It was Simon Wanstall, he sounded a bit strange, over friendly, thought Cajmere. He must want something, he immediately thought.

"Yeah look Daniel, I know it's sensitive but I just don't think we can release for Rachael as a single,"

"Uh huh,"

"It's beautiful, for sure, but it's quintessential Detroit and it's probably too melancholy for most people's tastes,"

"Sure,"

"I think it should go out as a single on your Rings Of Saturn subsidiary imprint,"

"Yeah I had wondered that," replied Cajmere wearily. Too weary to argue or contest this, besides he knew in his heart of hearts that it wasn't commercial enough.

"What we need," continued Wanstall (and Cajmere had an inkling what was coming) "is another Celestial. We need a massive single that's gonna crash the charts and put you back in the spotlight."

"Ohhhh."

"Can't you get that girl back in the studio? Her voice is amazing"

"Sure, I can try, but I'm telling you now it's very hard to replicate something you've already done,"

"No I don't mean replicate. Do something different, something original but keep it upbeat, you know diva vocal, punchy chords, you know the formula,"

Cajmere was vaguely agitated now. Wanstall had assured him at Speed that night that he wasn't one of the bad guys trying to urge everyone to be commercial. He remembered his sincerity describing how he wanted to gently 'evolve' the music rather than force producers to go poppy.

"Formula," spat Cajmere, some of his old bile coming back, "I'm not having no formula. This is exactly what they did to Kevin S----, they wanted a big smash second album and you can't force it."

"I have to remind you Daniel that you are under contract for two albums with us and it's my duty to guide you forward."

Wanstall sounded like a robot now. A record company robot. And he, Daniel Cajmere had thought he had integrity, he was a nerd, he wasn't a sharp suited manipulator like the other record company schmucks. Wanstall continued, he wanted Cajmere to do a remix. It was a novelty record by a cartoon character called Chirpy Chick.

"Chirpy wuhat!" exclaimed Cajmere incredulous.

"Yeah huh, Chirpy Chick," Wanstall laughed nervously and lamely, not convinced by himself. "Sure, it's cheesy but do it right and it'll put you back on the map. You'll be in all the right record boxes."

"Sheez, Chirpy Chick, what is the world coming to," Cajmere sighed. " You told me you were all about evolving the music. This isn't evolution. This is a joke. How can you claim to be a guardian of the underground when you're urging us to do this rubbish? Don't you care about my reputation? My integrity? Look I don't know, it might be the most awful sell out going. I need to discuss this with Carter King."

"Sure," replied Wanstall, "I'm just doing my job and that includes offering you any opportunities that come up. There is no agenda. If you want my honest opinion, yeah I mean, between you and I Chirpy Chick sucks, big time, and the record company would gain kudos from having your name on it. I mean you're not under contract to do this but it's a nice chunk of cash for you, £5000, and you know, like I say, back on the map."

"Back on the map huh," Cajmere repeated, only half engaging. He bid Wanstall goodbye and tried to comprehend the conversation they'd just had. When they'd signed him, they couldn't get enough of the Detroit sound they said. It was going to be, their words, 'massive'. But now it seemed they didn't want a classic piece of Detroit like For Rachael. He pondered, had it fallen out of favour in London? Now that this drum and bass had come along. The half-life of a dance music subculture appeared to be only months now, rather than years. The music industry was a factory, a production line, for a small window of time your product was hot, to be sold to the highest bidder. And now, in a matter of 2-3 short years Detroit techno, just another electronic subgenre, was old stock, to be sold off at a cut price, the producers reduced to reviving children's novelty tunes like Chirpy Chick. He covered his face with his hands. It wasn't the money. He didn't need any more money, he was set up for life after his initial deal and his top ten single and album. But he'd envisaged his career having more longevity than this. His stomach lurched as he hit the realisation. *Am I over?*

The next night he repaired to a bar with Carter King. It was a neighbourhood drinking place, near his studio, yellowed pine cladding and sports memorabilia on the walls. Not his favourite bar but it would do as a venue for a serious discussion. The music was Country and Western ballads but the volume was low.

"Lord I hate Country music," announced Cajmere as they sat down in a booth with their beers. Carter, who was wearing a burgundy baseball cap and a blouson leather jacket agreed. "Redneck music, pure and simple."

"Who listens to this crap?"

"Hillbillies," sniggered Carter.

"You know most music I can find something to like, some kind of hook that I can get into. But not this. This can never be redeemed. It's like, beyond…" he was always on a roll when he could find some piece of music that was execrable to spit his dislike on.

"You're the one that brought us here," observed Carter ribbing him gently.

"Oh sheez it's always my fault," laughed Cajmere loosening up.

"But seriously man, he continued "Chirpy Chick. CHIR – PEE CHICK. What the hell are the record company doing to me. It's gotta be some kind of joke."

Carter stared into his beer philosophically. "Well you know they wanted me to remix Aerosmith. I was pretty psyched by that. And then I thought, well they did that collaboration with Run DMC. Perhaps its not so bad after all."

"Yeah but we're not talking about metal here. This is some goddamn kiddie record, I mean under fives. Cheep cheep robot chickies. I'm not sure if any of these sounds are redeemable in a remix. At least with an Aerosmith ballad you've got some nice strings to play around with."

"Yeah, I guess so. I kinda lost all the Steven Tyler vocal outta there. That had to go," laughed Carter. "So….. don't do it. Seriously, tell them where to get off. You can't sell out like this, it's crazy. Who do they think you are, some cheesy rave producer? You're a credible artist."

"You know what's even worse. They want a follow up to Celestial. They want a formula. I made this track 'For Rachael' kind of elegiac, a requiem and they just canned it, said it can go out as a minor release on Rings of Saturn. Not mainstream enough to be a follow up single. I'm so over being signed to a major. If it wasn't for the money I'd do it all myself."

Yeah boy but you took the golden dollar, don't forget. " You danced with the devil and now you smell of sulphur you don't like it," said Carter, maintaining his higher moral ground as a DJ and producer that hadn't succumbed to major label offers."

"Yeah yeah, I know," said Cajmere putting his head in his hands, "they made me and they can break me. They know my sell by date. I've got this feeling in the pit of my stomach that Detroit's gone off the boil for them. They're all talking about drum and bass now in London. We're old news."

"Well they're gonna have a hard time cracking the drum and bass nut, I'm telling you now," mused Carter. "If they thought we were resistant to commercialisation, well those guys, those guys are hardcore. I've gotta friend in London, D--, he's a drum and bass producer, also makes techno in the Detroit style. He's more militant than Mad Mike and Underground Resistance. Won't do press, hates the media says they dissed his music in its infancy. Says they're all racists. They hate the majors. Gonna take a hell of a lot for the music industry to turn that attitude around. Drum and bass ain't to be messed with. They can't pick that one up and then spit it out like they done with so many others"

"Yeah pick it up and the spit it out. That's how I'm feeling right now," sighed Cajmere, "they just spat me out."

"Well you need to thank God that you don't need their money any more, some of us gotta work for a living."

"I'm not sure if DJing is work Carter,:" smiled Cajmere.

"I tell you if I've got to get on a plane to Europe one more time I'm going to explode. The travel is exhausting and it's killing me." opined Carter.

"Well I guess neither of us is sweeping the streets. We have to give thanks for that."

It was late at night now and the stars – or was it space hardware – something, anyway hung in the sky fizzing brightly as Cajmere walked back round the block to the studio. Cajmere brooded on Chirpy Chick. *What would Rachael have done?* She would have said no, he was absolutely certain of that. She wasn't avaricious, yeah she loved the luxury of Vegas, but she wasn't motivated by money, if she'd had a lot she would have given all away. Money was not her thing, her thing was musical knowledge. He could learn from that. There was a time, when he was young and impressionable, when he felt high on the money, invincible. But he could see now it was a pay off. A dance with the devil as Carter had observed. The arrogance and obstinacy in him that still remained after the bereavement wanted to really piss the record company off. He was thinking about starting on his second album and suddenly the idea occurred to him of a vast concept album. The sort of album that would have had a gatefold sleeve had it been released in the 70s. It could be complete folly of course, all the overblown pomp of progressive rock transposed to dance music. But he loved the idea of something so abstracted and conceptual that it couldn't be pinned down and marketed by the record label. A big two fingers up to commercialisation, a record with 20 minute long tracks that just ran and ran into the ether. He went back to the studio and listened to some old George Clinton and Kraftwerk. Yes, that was it, a concept album and the whole thing would be a veiled tribute to Rachael, he would create a narrative about an alien girl with Medusa-like green locks who lands on earth and teaches humans how to behave with more compassion. Her name would be Rayli – an amalgamation of 'ray' and 'light'. He would write ten fabular short stories, or extended essays anyway, one to accompany each track, he might even write them first and create narratives for the music before it was composed, to expand his creative lexicon. He didn't know if he could write, but he figured Wanstall could get some serious writer to help him.

Yes! He'd cracked it. He would rail in the face of Detroit being commodified and sold off cheaply because it wasn't as cool any more. He would produce an album that was beyond categorisation, off the chart and he might even use breakbeats too, just to unnerve the purists. An opus that ranged through techno, drum and bass, avant-garde music and jazz funk to the very limits of the imagination. He was perhaps less enamoured of his onion idiom now for accessibility. He wanted to produce something tuneful but also experimental, that people would have to listen hard to to understand properly. He stayed in the studio till 2 am that night, playing tracks and doodling refrains on the keyboard. At last, he had had an idea on how to move forward, despite the mire of his grief, his mind was still fertile at least, he thought.

Some days later, a Saturday to be specific, when he was home alone and the house seemed particularly empty, Emma Milton drifted into his mind. In truth, it was perhaps not so much her in particular, it was the thought of a woman, of a body to keep him warm, of full breasts and warm breath exhaled from lip glossed lips. He needed someone, anyone. He could just go to a bar and pick up some random chick. But those days seemed distasteful to him now. He hated to admit it but he wanted something meaningful: he wanted love. He waited until 6pm that day, it would be around midday in the UK and he called her at her house.

She answered the phone seeming a little enervated. "Hi darling, I am shattered." She admitted rather dramatically, "I was out with some industry people last night promoting our new single."

She explained the single was a 'big tune' a trance anthem. "I can send it to you but you wouldn't like it, I can tell you now," she laughed. They talked about what had been happening in their lives. "Are you coming to London soon," she asked him casually, hoping the reply would be yes.

"Yeah I am. I've got a date in Rotterdam first but I'll be in London after that."

"Hmm Rotterdam, don't know anything about the scene over there,"

"Me neither, there's a lot of trance and techno coming out of Holland and Belgium but I don't know about the club scene. I've never been booked for Melkweg in Amsterdam. " he admitted.

 "Oh boy, I gotta say, I need to see you." He was almost shocked at the way he came out with this. It was completely out of character. Nearly desperate.

"Okay okay, that's a bit heavy!" she joked, she was shocked too, but pleased she had lured him. It was a cliché, a cliché that Emma Milton was unable to discern in her world where romance and fairy-tale were childishly entwined but Cajmere was a catch – wealthy, famous, still young, handsome. Any girl on the scene would have been delighted to have landed a date with him.

A week before the Rotterdam date Cajmere's DJ booking agent phoned him from London. "Er hi Alice, wassup," he said casually. "Well it's this Rotterdam date," responded Alice, his agent, a slight hardheaded woman of 30 who spent her days organising DJs schedules. "They don't want your usual set. They want you to play Jeff Mills style, you know very staccato, jackhammer, banging stuff. It's going to be one of those nights I think – hard, fast, loud."

"Yeah sure, I can do that, it's not really my personal taste but I've got a limited selection of those records in my bag for emergencies. They're still paying the same aren't they?"

"Great, yeah still paying the same. Don't sweat it. Just a one off. I'm only asking you to compromise this one time. I appreciate it," she said in her clipped way.

Cajmere came off the phone. He thought it was a little strange. Why hadn't they asked Jeff Mills if that was what they wanted? He supposed he was still a fairly fashionable name and they were just after names. It was depressing. But sometimes you had to do this sort of thing.

And so Cajmere packed his record box for another round of dates. Making sure there were records for Rotterdam in there, what he called headbanger – crashing, acute, apocalyptic music that made you feel that the world was ending. *Oh well, if that was what they liked.* But it wasn't his usual style. He liked melody and texture. He liked to take a crowd on an emotional journey, where nuanced melancholy would surge unmistakably into optimism at the end – what he called the arc of life – he figured *there was always hope.* Although it had been hard to translate this mantra into his own life, in the period following Rachael's death. There had been times when he'd played his set and been dismayed as he retrod the path to happiness and major key tunefulness in his own sets. He found it meaningless now, saccharine, twee, Pollyannaish. He wasn't sure that things always ended up that way – happy. There were no certainties any more.

But he was glad to be going away this time. During this last year without her his house had become a sort of refrigeration unit, cold and empty and devoid of life. The echoes of conversations they'd once had resounded around the walls. All was haunted, all was ghost. As his taxi sped through the outskirts to the airport, he dreamed of sometime when the pain would be just a memory. Although even now it was subsiding. Time healed, they said that didn't they? It was certainly true.

When he touched down at Rotterdam The Hague airport he was tired. Red wine, more antidepressants and some melatonin tables had made for an uneasy cocktail. He felt woozy and slightly queasy. The taxi sped to his hotel. He just wanted it to be over and to be back in London with his friends.

The rave was in a stadium, a football pitch of bobbing heads and outstretched arms. Everything was blackish. "Our clubbers are quite enthusiastic", the promoter Joachim told him, a tall guy with a mousy pony tail bobbing at the back of his head, as they walked down a back tunnel to the stage. "They like it hard." Cajmere saw this for himself as he checked out the DJ booth, already busy, on the side of the stage. It was certainly harder, harder and faster than he'd ever heard techno before. It must have been about 160 BPM, an insistent heavy thud of a beat. "What is this music?" Asked Cajmere. "It's too hard and fast to call it techno" "We call it gabba," said Joachim, "the kids are crazy for it – ha ha."

Cajmere suddenly felt uneasy, the music was far louder than he'd ever experienced before and he was worried it would damage his hearing. And it was a very dark music, darker even than what they'd been playing that night in Berlin when he lost Rachael, a pounding, a banging, a thousand goose-stepping stormtroopers stamping in unison. It was undoubtedly a violent sound, he thought of punching, kicking, bullets peppering metal. "You might need to pitch up your tracks a bit," advised Joachim, indicating the records needed to be played at a faster tempo. Cajmere had no idea how he could tame this crowd. Kids who liked this sort of music – and he could just about witness rows and rows of skinheaded males as the lights swept over the crowd – they weren't the usual loved up Ecstasy heads. They seemed to be on the verge of a riot. A fizzing of electricity hung above this crowd. A force field. It was as though black clouds of foreboding were hanging in the sky. He entered the DJ booth and took a deep breath, he had never felt trepidation like this before. He cued up some Jeff Mills as the DJ before him finished up. But even Jeff Mills wouldn't keep these kids happy, he reckoned, why they had booked him he had no idea. He cued up some Robert Hood. It was what people called 'nosebleed' on the techno scene, very aggressive, tenacious, dark music. For the first time ever in a DJ booth he felt uneasy, "pitch it up" didn't bode well. Suddenly waves of cheering and shouting were emanating from the crowd. He couldn't decide whether this was good or bad. His stomach was turning over. "Juden, Juden Juden" he pulled off one side of his headphone and asked Joachim what they were shouting. "Oh just jews jews jews, it doesn't mean anything, just kids, youthful energy." The realisation shot through his mind. *Were .. they ...Nazis?*

It deadened him to be playing this sort of music – with no melody, no mood apart from an insidious gloomy pall. Beats like steel, chiselled into poison darts that could wound and rupture human flesh. It was inhuman. How people could dance to this and enjoy it. The machines had taken over and they were on the march. He decided there and then to never accept a booking like this in future. It was hard to modulate a set based on this punishing hard, fast tempo and texture. His natural inclination was to build emotion, a kind of chiascuro, to move from dark to light. But there would be no subtlety or nuance in this set, if anything it must become stonier, more unyielding and that was just to stop a riot taking place. This rave felt like it was on the verge. It could erupt at any given moment.

He looked up from his decks. There was a young man, can't have been more than 17 or 18, moving towards him. His face was contorted into a torsion of anger, his chest was bare, white, lucent with sweat and knotted with muscles from working out, baggy khaki camo pants sat around his hips. "Play some f---ing gabba you bleck b---ard" he shouted and he shook his fist as though about to punch Cajmere. Cajmere blanched and stepped back from the decks. Others were following the first young man, there was a small stream of kids approaching the DJ box in seeming protest. Cajmere's immediate instinct was to flee. He picked up his record box leaving a record revolving on the decks. "I think we need to get you out," urged Joachim, ushering him out of the DJ booth and into a back tunnel. Cajmere raced down the tunnel with Joachim at his side. The tunnel seemed to go on forever. His heart was pulsating furiously in his chest. He looked back and further back they were shouting down the tunnel at him 'bleck b---ard, bleck b—ard' It was survival instinct. Fight or flight. There was no way he was taking on a legion of angry young gabba ravers. His neck was throbbing –a pulse of urgency. He was gasping for breath as he ran. Finally he was outside, out of breath after the running, Joachim handed him his fee in cash and bundled him into a waiting cab saying something like 'get him to his hotel fast' in Dutch to the driver. Cajmere could see a few random ravers hanging around outside the rave. He was in no mood to loiter. At last he sat in the cab which swerved onto a dual carriageway, his chest was heaving and he was gulping back breath.

He slept fitfully that night. Even though the hotel was an anonymous, corporate beigey squat tower block of a place, he wondered if they were all around, these fascists. He couldn't wait to leave Holland. Never again.

He touched down in Heathrow and swallowed an anti-depressant and an anti-anxiety drug alongwith the dregs of a glass of rather acidic airplane red wine. He always vowed never to drink the wine on planes, but he always succumbed for the pure mellowing, woozy, warmth of the afterglow. Back in Detroit, in the early days after his bereavement, the doctor had prescribed some anti-anxiety tablets. He now had a supply of pills to alleviate depression, pills to quell anxiety and pills to help him sleep. He wasn't dependent on any of them, he took them sporadically, when the pain and distress became too much to bear, or when insomnia hit.

After dropping his luggage at the hotel in Kensington he decided to walk to the record company where he had a meeting. It was one of those bright, late winter days where the sky seemed very high above and was a hue of the clearest crystalline blue. Cajmere inhaled the bright air: it was good to be in London after the shock of the gabber rave in Holland. London had its ghosts but perhaps he could start anew here.

It was funny, he would walk through the record company offices now and he didn't notice the glamorous PR girls at their desks, lipgloss glinting at him with promise. After `Rachael's death, life had become more than a series of libidinous opportunities, he was focussed on the record he was going to make, more than ever now. Everything hung on the album to come.

"Hey Daniel Cajmere," Wanstall greeted him with a smile. "I hope you've forgiven me for Chirpy Chick."

"Please don't mention Chirpy Chick," grimaced Cajmere sardonically. "The chick can chirp right off as far as I'm concerned."

"How was Rotterdam? You've just been in Holland right?" asked Wanstall as they repaired to a meeting room with low black leather sofas.

"Oh boy. You have no idea. For some unknown reason my agent booked me for a gabba rave. You heard of gabba? It was like the ninth gate of hell."

"That bad huh? Yeah I read a feature about gabba in i-D recently," nodded Wanstall, "it all sounded rather nasty. The dark side."

"Nasty doesn't even cover it, they were punching the air and chanting Juden Juden, which means jews, all these angry skinhead Dutch kids. Really horrible. I got racially abused and had to escape down a back tunnel."

" Probably on amphetamines rather than ecstasy I imagine. Strange that they wanted to book you in the first place, no?"

"Yeah I mean I think they thought they were going to get something like Jeff Mills, or nosebleed, harder still which I can do, I mean I've got those records, but it's not my style. It really kills me to play like that. I'm never going there again literally and metaphorically."

" The horror, the horror," mused Wanstall bleakly. "You really saw the dark heart of rave culture. I always used to think, standing there in a field, you could be right next to a football hooligan with a knife, it's just that he would be wearing a blissful chemical mask – psychologically speaking - and handing you water. Sobering stuff though, I'm really sorry to hear that Dan," Wanstall looked rather disturbed, as though racial abuse and fascism didn't really often impinge on his comfortable, rather intellectual middle class world.

They discussed the issue of racism in music further. Wanstall wondered whether, with the rise of very white dance subgenres like trance and big beat, dance music had been hijacked from its predominantly black origins of disco techno and house.

"Yeah but then I guess you had Kraftwerk, they were white and European and they inspired us," said Cajmere. "It's a complicated relationship."

" I dunno, I think Kraftwerk were an anomaly. The general drift is for black music to be appropriated by white people, watered down and made palatable and commercial. The white guys cash in on black innovation. Look at rhythm and blues and the Rolling Stones. Twas ever thus." sighed Wanstall, "In confidence, because we've just signed a big beat act, it's a very white student scene that seems to be in denial that dance music ever had black origins, even though it uses hip hop beats."

"I don't really know about big beat being in the states," offered Cajmere.

"Well its quite a rudimentary pop music based on hip hop breakbeats with lots of quirky samples and hooks," explained Wanstall. "The producers are mostly white and pretty middle class. It's definitely predominantly a student demographic. Dance music for people who don't like dance music. Now tell me about your album."

"Ahh Rayli," Cajmere sighed exhilarated. The moment he had been waiting for. "Well it's going to be very different to Celestial…."

"Okay, riiiight," Wanstall sounded somewhat guarded.

Cajmere went on to explain about his concept, a ten track album based on the narrative of an alien girl, Rayli, fallen to earth and exploring the geography and anthropology of the human race. Wanstall seemed particularly enthused about the idea of a book of short stories to accompany it. "You know Reload, Tom and Mark from Global Communication did an album called 'A Collection of Short Stories,' don't you?" "Yeah, I love that album," enthused Cajmere "I guess that must have been a subliminal inspiration for me". They discussed writers for the short stories. Wanstall was a prodigious reader. He suggested Neil Rushworth "He's a brilliant neo sci fi dystopian writer who's kind of followed in the wake of William Gibson. Based in the UK. Very dense and quite florid descriptive prose style. Very immersive. I think you need someone who can really bring alive these landscapes, the idea of tropical lush rainforest vegetation and high arid mountains and saline oceans. There's quite a travelogue element to his work and that's what you need, a reimagining of earth through fresh eyes, someone who can make it vivid but also slightly strange. And his stories are skewed, they're not traditional tropes and motifs, he thinks up odd little twists that confound you."

"Yeah that sounds like what I need," agreed Cajmere.

"I think it's a great idea in essence, but you know all the things people are going to say about a concept album, that it's pretentious and bloated and symptomatic of all the excesses of prog rock in the seventies when there was too much money floating around the record industry and artists were indulged. Then I guess punk came like a new broom and swept all that concept stuff away. People might say you've gone too far, been too ambitious if you don't come up with something truly dazzling. You've had a lot of glowing press so far. I'm warning you right now, there could be a backlash."

"I know what people might say. But I don't care, this is the future," railed Cajmere. "Ideas and concepts, that's one of the things I'm good at. I'm sick of dance records that are just churned out to please E'd up clubbers. I want to make something for posterity's sake that lasts, something that you can put on at home in ten years time that still stands up as an experimental piece of music. I want Rayli as my epitaph." What he didn't tell Wanstall was that Rayli was based on his bereaved wife Rachael. He didn't feel like talking about it any more. It was something locked inside him that he would carry forever.

"So, I hate to say it, but how about another single, a follow up to Celestial." Ventured Wanstall tentatively

"How did I know you were gonna say that," sighed Cajmere "To be honest I don't want to make a conventional single on this album. You are gonna hate me for saying that but I'm afraid this is going to be one artwork that you will have to accept in it's entirety and I envisage some of the tracks being very long. As I said it's going to be about ideas, not commercial compromise. I checked my contract and it says two album deal – no stipulation about singles. Now if you want me to produce a single separate to the album that's another matter, but you'll have to pay for it. I'm sorry, no more major label bullshit. You guys packaged me up and put me on a conveyor belt like a commodity and I'm saying – 'no more'." At this juncture he held his hand up to signify a halting. "You say you're one of the good guys but Chirpy Chick nearly pushed me to the brink. I don't care whether Detroit ain't the hot property it used to be. I'm just not going there."

"Well I think I learnt my lesson with Chirpy Chick, no more novelty record remixes for Daniel Cajmere," laughed Wanstall a little uneasily.

"You got that right" said Cajmere flatly and with finality. He felt he had made this case.

After two hours sat in intense discussion with Wanstall and the early morning flight from Rotterdam, Cajmere was tired. He went back to his hotel and slept for a couple of hours. He was woken by the sound of his new acquisition, a mobile phone, bleeping.

"Hullo"

"Darling" it was Emma Milton, sounding rather husky and come hither.

"Hey Emma, what's up with you?"

"I just thought I'd call you and say 'welcome to London.'

"I gotta be honest, I'm pretty glad to be here."

"Why's that darling?" she sounded faux concerned, although Cajmere didn't notice

"Oh the gig from hell in Rotterdam. My stupid agent booked me for a gabba rave. I got threatened by some psyched racist and had to run out the place with my record box."

"Lordy, you should have taken him on. I bet you could have beaten the hell out of him. I don't know gabba, I thought they were all into that brilliant Euro trance stuff out there?"

"It would have been unwise to have got into a fight Emma, there was a whole football stadium of these racists and a group of them were coming at me in the DJ box. I wouldn't have come out alive."

"Right. Oh. I still don't know what gabba is?"

Gabba's that 160bpm four to the floor stuff, faster harder and louder than you've ever heard techno before."

"Wow scary, but don't you think it was an isolated incident, I mean it's never happened before, right? Aren't you making a bit of a fuss about nothing."?

Cajmere sighed, there was no use explaining the visceral punch of racial abuse to the soul to a complacent white person who was never likely to experience it, and it would have been unmanly to have admitted how terribly scared he had been in that rave, surrounded by angry young white men punching their fists to the toughest music he had ever heard.

"Yeah just forget it, it was nothing."

"I'd still like to see you giving some guy what for in a fight, I bet you could smash his brains out."

"I'm a lover not a fighter," joked Cajmere

"I think I need to feel some of that love," it was a cheesy opportunity to flirt but Emma Milton was not above cliché, in fact she was unable to see the cringe worthy irony in it. "You want love, come see me play tomorrow night at this new venue in East London then."

"How could I refuse," she had clinched it. A night out with Daniel Cajmere. She felt elated.

It was early spring now as Cajmere arrived in the area of central East London where the new warehouse club was situated, round the corner from the old meat market. Red brick Victorian mansion blocks jammed up against grey office block monoliths in this rapidly gentrifying area. Several media corporations had their offices here and there were photographic studios up high in these buildings, skylights facing upwards and printworks and graphic design agencies down below. Cajmere jumped out of his cab, he had dressed down, as usual, in selvedge indigo jeans (a Japanese import), shell toe trainers and a khaki record label t-shirt. Emma Milton was waiting for him at the bar inside, which had a high black ceiling and was painted a pleasing grey green colour, noted Cajmere. She was wearing a mushroom hued shell top with a thin fluorescent orange stripe horizontally bisecting the middle. It was tight and her nipples were visible – back in her flat she had rubbed them with an ice cube to make them stand up. Tight dark denim clam diggers embraced the arcs of her hips and on her feet were a pair of soaring wedge sandals with pink fluorescent straps. Cajmere's eyes alighted upon her nipples and he felt his penis become tumescent in his baggy jeans.

"I'm expecting nothing less than magic, you know," teased Emma Milton licking the top row of her white teeth visibly and tantalisingly with her tongue, "I've heard you've still got it."

Cajmere's heart sank a little 'still' suggested he was on the cusp of being a has been, or at least Detroit techno was. That was the implication. He swallowed hard and tried to overcome the slight.

"Well you know, we try to please," he retorted meaning nothing of the sort. The only person Cajmere ultimately aimed to please when he DJed was himself – although of course part of this was demonstrating he could seduce a crowd. It was an exercise in creativity but also a skilful balancing act for him: how much could he innovate and how much could he cajole the crowd into a paroxysm of ecstasy.

They were drinking now, Cajmere a whisky sour and Emma Milton a sea breeze, everyone drank sea breezes now, cranberry juice was a recent vogue.

"Why don't you come and stand up in the DJ booth with me? I'm going to start preparing now. I'm on soon."

The club was filling up. It was a typical mid to late 90s London crowd, lots of combat pants slung low on the hips – boys and girls, lots of obscure trainer brands, and, if you looked closely enough girls with bindi spots on their foreheads, scrolling henna tattoos on their wrists and toxic blue and algae green nail polish on their fingertips.

The remit of this new club was eclectic, there was an element of hegemonic middle class good taste about it all, from the grey green interior and grapefruit yellow Helvetica font of the logo to the roster of DJs: techno, drum'n'bass, trip hop, hip hop, ambient. No trashy brash big tunes or superannuated superstar DJs with their retinues of spangly clad groupies, no ersatz rave and hardcore, which was now relegated to the working class suburbs and post industrial wastes of East London proper.

Cajmere started to play, he figured this crowd, with it's cosmopolitan air of specialist music appreciation, could take some experimentalism and he built his set gradually, at first blending very classic Detroit jazzy melancholy from Kenny Larkin and Blake Baxter and then building, building, building with excerpts of film scores like Apocalypse now that he played over simple beatscapes. The crowd were appreciating his nuances and details he could tell, a steady stream of head nodders approached the DJ booth to speak to him after the set. He could just spot a girl and a boy in the crowd and something about them flicked a switch in his mind and reminded him of things past. They were swaying together in time to the music, her a petite Bjork-like creature hair in two knobbly buns like horns atop her head, garbed in a Suzie Wong type cheongsam dress of embroidered cobalt blue satin, him in baggy indigo jeans and a shell top tousled peroxided hair with the long roots plainly visible, like a techno head Kurt Cobain. They didn't look e-d up, just intensely locked into to music, arms wound round each other, eyes closed as they stepped to the beat - occasionally they would smile at each other in recognition of a track. Cajmere watched them in between mixes, they seemed somehow to epitomise young London at that precise, beats per minute regulated moment in time. Cajmere's set was climaxing now and the kids in the crowd were raising their hands aloft, although this was less uniform a gesture than it had been in those high early 90s days of rave and techno. His set was peaking now, he was playing a ten minute long mix that a talented piano virtuoso called Nils who lived in Berlin had made for him specially. It started with flickering modulating ripples of synth, as clear as the water of a calcified blue lake and the built and built like a tsunami of insistent arpeggios, culminating in a lucid, major key tidal wave, a swelling ocean of loveliness that he saw himself sprinkling on the crowd like a benediction of drops of holy water. He sensed there was a gasp of appreciation as this track worked its spell on the crowd, who were, by now, rapt and in the palm of his hand. Whilst the room now seemed to be at an ecstatic pitch of fervour, he kept the mood euphoric by dropping Underground Resistance's Jupiter Jazz. It proved to be a masterstroke, the couple were smiling and the girl had her hands raised aloft, kids were cheering and clapping in time with the music, the place had erupted, at least as much as a cool metropolitan knowing London crowd could do. Cajmere's greatness was undisputed by everyone who heard him.

All except Emma Milton. She stood by the DJ box sipping her drink and occasionally moving to the beat.

"So how was I?" Cajmere joined her with his record box,"

"You were great babe, I mean, not my taste in music really but I can see you know how to work a crowd."

He didn't quite know how to take this backhanded compliment, on the one hand she could acknowledge he was a proficient DJ, on the other she didn't like his music. "So what sort of music do you like?" he asked. She explained in return that she liked the music she promoted – commercial house and trance with Euro leanings, a very synthetic strain of music devoid of funk and black influence in his opinion, as he had discussed with Wanstall previously. "Detroit a bit boring for you perhaps?" He ventured. She smiled evasively "Detroit's great for the real techno heads." She replied ambivalently. Cajmere found himself wanting to please her. He had to admit, that by this point he was infatuated with her, although it was more the persistent image of those lipglossed lips and those breasts that had aesthetically imprinted themselves on his waking imagination. He longed to possess her, her body was a mantra that he was mentally chanting with increasing frequency. No, she was not Rachael, she would never replace Rachael and he knew that in his heart of hearts. But she filled a void, she was a distraction from the aching pain, she was fun, or at least she appeared to be. He needed that right now.

They moved to leave the club. "So are you coming for a drink at the bar of my hotel?" he ventured smoothly. "How could I refuse," This was going to be easy. He hadn't lost his touch. A few drinks. The lights low. Then, inevitably, if it all went according to plan, bodies locked together on clean white sheets.

The cab sped through London and he tried to explain the construction of his sets to her. How he was sometimes sent tracks that had been tailor made for him. His use of film scores and modern classical to create interesting test pressings to intersperse with more classic Detroit. She appeared to be vaguely interested.

"Have you ever thought of playing more big tunes in your set?" she wondered resting her head on his shoulder on the back seat of the black cab.

"Yeah I mean it's not really me. I've got a style and I'm known for it. I don't want to sell out."

"But the big name house DJs haven't sold out really," she cajoled, " they're just a knowledgeable as you. James Pearce (a famous big name house DJ who played at all the big 'superclubs') has got a massive old disco collection, I mean worth thousands and thousands of pounds. Surely you like old disco?"

"Yeah, yeah I do. I think it's probably the area where I'd cross over with the more commercial names. Although it's rare that I play disco in my sets, it doesn't really fit with my aesthetic. Obviously there were some more experimental disco producers like Giorgio Moroder and they are interesting to me."

"Oh you think you're so intellectual you Detroit DJs don't you, well I'm telling you, you're not the only ones who are clever, a lot of those commercial DJs you pour scorn on are just as meticulous in building their sets, they're just more savvy in the style of music they play. Not so worried about stupid 'principles and 'integrity', whatever they mean." Her tone was still friendly but there was an undertone of quite overt criticism to what she was saying. Cajmere was taken aback. How could she say that? *She was resting her head upon him amorously and yet telling him, in no uncertain terms that he was some kind of intellectual and musical snob.* His impulse was to please her, to show her how great he was. What she was saying was partly true, he did put himself above the commercial house DJs playing all the big tunes. He felt piqued that she had identified this.

"Okay so let me ask you, how much do you get paid to do a set?" she continued

He was taken aback that she would ask him such a direct question about his finances so soon into their friendship. Caught off his guard, he told her.

"Well I can tell you now that DJs like James Pearce get four or five times that playing Ibiza."

Cajmere liked money, but it was not his only motivation and integrity was far more important to him. In truth he wanted both, to stay true to the style of music he was pioneering and also to remain wealthy. He had become used to a certain lifestyle.

"You've got to admit I have got a point," he felt her slightly pressurising him now. He tried to be polite, he did want to end up in bed with her after all.

"Yeah kind of," he tried to compromise. "I can see where you're coming from."

"*It's just that I'm boring and set in my ways,*" she mocked, pretending to be his interior monologue. She was teasing him now.

"You got me," he gave in and laughed.

They arrived at the hotel, the bar was still open – it was all-night at weekends and it had that strange anonymous low key ambience that international hotel bars in big cities tended to have at 2am. She ordered a cocktail and made a big deal of sliding her fingers up and down the straw provocatively. "You often end up with strange women in bars after your sets." It was meant to be a flirtatious gambit but it suddenly made him feel serious. He wasn't about to give away his insalubrious past pre-Rachel with her now. "Not since my marriage and not since losing my wife, no," he felt a little sad at the thought. "Cheer up babe, you're with me now." She proffered.

He was feeling a little woozy and mellow now, cradling his whisky sour in his hands as he perched on the bar stool.

"I am fixated on your lipgloss." He intoned, a little drunk, staring at those cherry ripe lips, beckoning him like ruby hued glace fruits. *Just one bite....*

"Well it's a very obscure Australian brand called P---, and very expensive too. You buy it from a little beauty boutique in Covent Garden. The colour is maraschino, in case you are interested.

"MmmmmMaraschino" he mouthed drunkenly as though it were some mystical incantation to unlock a treasure chest of gleaming jewels. He was close enough to smell the lipgloss odour now, a kind of ersatz watermelon. He leaned forward and closed in to her dazzlingly pretty visage and stole a kiss. She reciprocated by licking her lips slowly and inserting her tongue into his mouth. Their heads surged into one entity and their mouths danced as he sucked on her succulent embouchement.

"Shall we go to my room?" She slipped off her bar stool and picked up her handbag in assent. In what seemed like minutes they were in his double room with its pristine bed and floor to ceiling windows. She stood by the window. Cajmere stood behind her and started French kissing her neck. Soon they were on the bed, Cajmere sitting on the end of it, Emma Milton straddling him, arms wrapped round his back, acrylic pointed nails lightly scratching the skin. It was the first time he had been with someone since Rachael and he felt a little tentative under the surface, although it didn't show. Daniel Cajmere was an expert lover, perhaps it was a cliché, he thought, to have this gift for seduction, to be so measured in caressing female flesh, to mould it sensually between the fingers, to knead it, to know when to stroke lightly and when to press into it meaningfully. In his bachelor days, there was no meaning behind the touch, except pure libidinous greed. But these days, he needed to be at least infatuated, to crush on someone before he could parlay that passion into skin on skin. He examined her body with his hands, she was like a perfect Barbie doll he thought with full pert breasts, the tiniest waist imaginable, his two hands could circle it easily, and plump buttocks, but firm, not so big they were cushiony. Her skin was lightly tanned and golden from a recent holiday to Thailand, he noticed as he surveyed her body with relish. He slid his hand up her top and tweaked her nipples, the nipples he had gazed upon expectantly, she arched her back in pleasure and pressed her groin into his. She began gyrating on his lap, but it was jerky he noticed and a little aggressive rather than the sensual circling he had envisaged. Minutes later she had her hand down his jeans and suddenly her tongue was flicking over the head of his penis. And then aargh, he went cold, she had clamped his penis with her teeth – it hurt and it was sore. "Take it easy baby" he tried to urge tactfully. "Don't worry this is one thing I'm expert at," she boasted with characteristic hubris but she continued to sink her teeth into his member like a child gnawing on a stick of rock. "Let's move back onto the bed," he urged, the pain was palpable and she was now clamped onto him like a barnacle. He lay back prostrate and she sat atop him, grabbing his penis and stuffing it into her vagina in a hurried, slapdash fashion. She then started rocking on him, somewhat mechanically, as though her hips were fixed and rather rusty, as opposed to swivelling sinuously. Cajmere tried to concentrate on her lips and her nipples rather than her spiritless and perfunctory bobbing on his penis. Her vagina was dry so he decided to stimulate her clitoris, manipulating it with his fingers. Suddenly she was screeching and screaming in a completely over-the-top fashion and jogging her hips upon

his sore penis in a frenzy of ecstasy. "F--k me, f--k me baby"
By this point his penis was so raw from the attempted
blowjob he had given up all hope of an orgasm and as she
spluttered out a melodramatic orgasm he felt his penis going
limp. She flopped down next to him, spent. "*That. Was.
Amazing.*" She gasped. "You're so masterful" "Now you
sound like a heroine in some cheap romance." He sighed.
She coughed. "There ain't nothing cheap about me darling,
I'm only going to the highest bidder, ha ha ha"

Cajmere wondered how many women had lain in his position
in years gone by, chafed and unsatiated, lying next to a
partner who neither knew nor cared about their enjoyment of
the sex act. Crikey, he thought, I'm almost becoming a
feminist. It must be Rachael's influence. And lying there next
to Emma Milton, who almost immediately started dozing
after her orgasm, a solitary tear rolled down his cheek as he
though of his dead wife with whom the sexual chemistry had
been so electric, so right.

The next morning he found himself wanting to talk to her, to
take her for breakfast and linger over coffee. Surely there
was nothing worse than a fruitless sexual encounter than the
morning after when one party awkwardly tries to abscond all
to quickly. In this case it was her. "Babe I've gotta get into
work, we've got a new single to plug," she remarked off hand
as she pulled her clothes on hurriedly. "You won't stay and
have coffee with me?" "Sorry mate, this is a big new Euro
trance single, banging actually. Love it. Gotta go."

And so Cajmere was left alone, alone with the rumpled
sheets and half full glasses of the night before. It was just an
off night, he thought, trying to excuse her. It would get better.
She seemed so sexy, so delicious, so ripe for plucking when
they were sitting in that bar. And yet. He felt a twinge of
discomfort in his still slightly inflamed penis.

He couldn't bear to stay in the room after what had
happened the previous night so he grabbed his army surplus

jacket and headed for the rather bland looking interior of the dining room. He felt the need to indulge himself and ate what was called on the plastic menu a Full English Breakfast – eggs bacon, sausages, mushrooms and tomatoes with toast and hash browns. And ever so gradually the depressive hangover from the night before began to fade.

He was getting the tube today, out to the burbs of North London to the studio of D—and his production partner Michael. Carter King had arranged for him to spend some time with them. They were jungle or drum and bass producers with a strong interest in Detroit techno and they had put out a compilation of Detroit tracks on their record label recently. Cajmere found their address with some difficulty, a three storey terracotta brick Victorian villa, slightly dilapidated, tucked away in the corner of a street. Michael, who was a tall black guy dressed in a burgundy sweatshirt, jeans and trainers wearing a round black Rastafarian hat, came to meet him as he buzzed at the front door. They ascended three flights of stairs with threadbare black carpets to get to their studio, which was in the loft or attic.

"You just in from Detroit?" asked Michael gruffly. "Actually Rotterdam, I had a DJing gig there," replied Cajmere. "What d'you wanna go there for, they only make gabba and Euro trance in Holland from what I heard. Isn't Belgium a better place for hanging out with techno heads?" "I wish someone had told me that before I went!" said Cajmere with a hollow half laugh. "I got booked for a gabba rave which wasn't a walk in the park." "Too right, I heard they're racists," Michael sounded concerned in his gruff way. "Yeah, something like that," said Cajmere too weary to explain it all over again.

The attic was a small cramped space stacked floor to ceiling with black recording equipment, computers, drum programming machines, samplers, amplifiers, speakers and keyboards. Wooden beams criss crossing overhead meant they had to crouch in places. There was the warm smell of vinyl, rubber electric cables and dust. Michael pulled up a chair for Cajmere and D— (a short stocky black guy) and he sat jammed up against the keyboard.

'Carter told us you were thinking of doing a breakbeat track for your new album," said D---

'That's right," responded Cajmere, "I went to Speed and I loved the sound of the tracks they played."

"Yeah we don't go to Speed, we're not scenesters, we're hermits!" proclaimed D--- "Besides from what I heard that place is full of record company parasites and PRs now, all trying to get in on drum and bass because its trendy. Makes me sick. To think of three or four years ago, we were like the lepers of the industry, no one would touch breakbeats with a bargepole. We were thought of as too ruffneck. And now look at this stupid frenzy about the music. Pah" he virtually spat out the 'pah'

"Yeah I've seen it all. I'm sick of the media and the majors too," sighed Cajmere rubbing his eyes. 'Recently, they've been making subtle digs that Detroit ain't so fashionable any more. Offering me cheesy mixes of novelty records and telling me it'll revive my career. Like my career needs reviving."

"You should have seen the attitude we gave them when they started to come knocking on our door!" D—and Michael both started laughing at this point.

"Oh boy they were probably wishing they'd never been born! One journalist ran out of here virtually in tears after we ranted at him for half an hour. Then, when we had three majors chasing us for a deal we didn't half give them the run-around. Not returning their calls, making them sweat, ha ha ha, we had some fun, didn't we D—"

"Did you sign a deal in the end then?"

Michael heaved a big sigh "In the end yeah, because you just can't say no to the money. It's life changing. It means a new flat, new studio equipment, financial security doesn't it? Can't say no to that. Even though the whole thing sucks. As soon as you sign on the dotted line, that's it, you've done it, you're over, you've sold out. Although it's that thing isn't it, can you still make good music when you're signed to a major or do you lose the plot. We ended up signing to XL because at least the MD Richard Russell had some form on the rave scene. He'd been in it from the beginning and he was actually quite a nice bloke. It helps if you like the guy."

"Yeah I like my A and R," continued Cajmere, "he's really sound. At first I thought he was quite geeky and intellectual, not very streetwise. But he's been pretty decent. Apart from offering me the cheesy remixes. But I've forgiven him for that."

D—made Cajmere a cup of tea. Like Cajmere they did not take drugs and they rarely drank. They all sat down and played Cajmere their first album, Quantum Physics, which had not been released a major but their own label, Vortex. As they sat in that cramped dim room, with it's tiny windows and airless fug, the sound of deftly deconstructed breakbeats, like fireworks spluttering into the ether and Catherine wheels whirring around, filled the space, like magic. Michael and D--- were fans of the Detroit sound and their synth chord harmonies were quintessential Detroit. Cajmere found himself thinking *they do it better than we do*. But he didn't articulate this thought.

"I hadn't heard this album before, it's pretty good, " he offered. "I'm thinking of doing a breakbeat track myself, on the new album I'm working on, Rayli,"

"Shall we mess around together programming some beats?" said D--. 'yeah that would be really helpful for me guys," Cajmere was grateful.

They spent the day doodling on the keyboards and showing Cajmere what they did with beats, sampling the Amen brothers break that was so famously used by junglists to base their tracks on, taking the beats apart and then reconfiguring them. It was detailed and painstaking Cajmere noted. They used a bassline from The Reese Project's Just Another Chance, now known as the Reese bassline, it underscored many of the most famous drum and bass tracks. Cajmere finally felt that after all this talking, he was starting to envisage what Rayli would sound like. If he could get anything as close to the optimistic futurism of Quantum Physics he would be happy, he thought. "You must come and visit me in Detroit," he promised them. "Yeah we're probably coming to see Carter and some other producers at some point," said D---. They discussed the bitter irony that dance music, and house and techno in particular, had never broken big in the US as they had in the UK and Europe. "There's just not the culture of raves and clubbing back at home," Cajmere told them. He continued that he imagined that in 10 – 15 years time the music might break and that there would be a massive DJ star dominating it all. "Probably white knowing the way things go," "That's how it generally rolls," shrugged Michael fatalistically.

That night Cajmere phoned Emma to reassure her after their relationship had developed in this new physical way. She sounded slightly offhand. Once more Cajmere felt the need to please her. A thought entered his mind. He asked her if she wanted to take a day off work so he could take her shopping and buy her some new clothes. Suddenly her interest was piqued "Of course babe, I would love that!" she exclaimed with a little helium giggle.

The next day Cajmere met Emma Milton in the champagne bar of a large department store at lunchtime. "You *are* my prince," she declared as they sipped champagne cocktails at the bar. "How did you know that shopping was my favourite leisure pursuit?" A man that wanted to go shopping was a very rare prize indeed, she thought to herself, but she wasn't going to tell him that. Feeling that slight sense of hazy, warm giddiness you do after a lunchtime drink, Cajmere and Emma proceeded down the escalator to the womenswear floor. To Cajmere, the pale grey shopfittings and rails of clothes were a colourful blur. He was just happy if she was happy. "Oh gosh, this is the one I saw Victoria of the Spice Girls wearing!" Emma seized upon a dress, a copper lurex bandeau piece - as shimmering and iridescent as burnished metal - which she proceeded to try on. As she strutted out of the changing room Cajmere was transfixed. It was virtually spray on, pulling in the tiniest hint of stomach she had so that that her lissom waist was foregrounded and bulging breasts and buttocks, curvy yet simultaneously firm and neat. It was dangerously sexy. "What do you think? She asked triumphantly, revelling in her own delectability. "Yeah I like it – a lot, let's take it" laughed Cajmere. He knew he was no expert on women's fashion but without doubt he could see her body was booming in this skintight sheath. He thought she might be finished after this one purchase (which was not cheap at £360) – after all shopping with Rachael had been so quick and easy. But she seemed to assume that the offer of a shopping trip would proceed until she had exhausted her desire to purchase. So off they went to another mini boutique in the store, a jewel box full of lingerie-like silk-satin pieces in coruscating fuschia and turquoise hues. Emma tried on a slip dress, a languorous lick of frippery edged in lace that flowed over her hourglass body in a waterfall of suggestion. "Yeah I like it too," said Cajmere. After paying £500 for it at the cash desk he hoped she would be finished soon. "Ooh shoes," she squealed and pulled him by the arm to a gallery area at the back of the store where there was shelf upon sculpted shelf of leather accoutrements of every permutation imaginable: from sensible patent loafers to sparkly showgirl strappy stilettoes encrusted in glittering rhinestones and crystals. "These, oh my gosh, these are so me," gasped Emma Milton seizing on the showgirl stilettos. "For when I'm doing cabaret in Vegas of course!" he felt sad at the mention of Vegas, but was silent. In the blink of an eye she'd stacked up 5 boxes of shoes, the showgirl ones, some high chunky heeled brown patent loafers, satin kitten heels in the palest baby blue, lilac Mary Jane flats with ergonomic moulded trainer soles and a rather shiny dominatrix pair of knee boots. Cajmere was about to say something, this was more than enough. The shoes and boots came to more than £1000. She looked at Cajmere with imploring eyes "You're ever so generous, I mean I can hardly believe it, I feel this is like a dream come true" And he couldn't resist her. He handed over his credit card at the cash register and flashed her a smile. "Honestly it's my pleasure honey, all mine." This new happiness, like a saccharine sweetener on sour fruit, had taken away some of the hollowness of bereavement and loneliness. He figured she was worth it.

Cajmere was still thinking about developing Rayli. The album was at the back of his mind and he couldn't wait to get back to Detroit and work on it. Wanstall had arranged a meeting for him with Neil, the prospective writer at the record label offices. Cajmere had read one of Neil's books and enjoyed the writing, it was futuristic but highly evocative and dense with ideas. His taste in literature tended towards sci-fi, the beats, some theory and the avant-garde, he liked high concept writing, writers prepared to take risks and play around with literary convention. He was well read, despite not having a degree, a fearsome autodidact. He scorned DJs who were so immersed in the music they had not taken the time to read and educate themselves. He felt there was no excuse for ignorance.

Cajmere sat waiting with Wanstall in the record company meeting room, lounging on a black leather sofa and sipping a coffee Wanstall had made for him – milk – no sugar. He related how he had spent a day in the studio with Michael and D--- working on breakbeats for the new album. "I heard they signed to XL," said Wanstall. "Yeah," laughed Cajmere thinking of how they had told him they'd given the record company a hard time. "I don't think they are crazy about majors but they couldn't refuse." "Comes to us all," said

Wanstall soberly, "We all sell our souls sooner or later in one way or another. It's called making a living." Cajmere wasn't in the mood to discuss the pros and cons of major label backing right at this moment. He felt he'd made his point about Chirpy Chick, now he was focussed on making an album to really impact the scene – and also the cultural landscape at large. He had his sights set on highbrow arts coverage for this album, it would be a multimedia event rather than a mere record release.

Shortly, Neil arrived. He was a lean figure with mousy hair in a very short bob, parted in the middle. He was dressed similarly to a DJ – navy puffa gilet, long sleeved red t-shirt, jeans and trainers. Must be early thirties Cajmere assessed.

Cajmere waited for him to settle and get a coffee then began to explain his concept. Rayli, the name of the album and the heroine, was to comprise ten tracks and ten accompanying short stories. Or indeed ten short stories and ten accompanying soundtracks.

"Do you envisage them being long short stories of 8-10 thousand words, if that's not an oxymoron," interjected Neil, "or a short collection – ten stories 5,000 words each, like a novella."

"I would say short," Cajmere was decisive in what he wanted. "We want the words and the music to approximate each other as much as possible so that people can consume each medium as easily as possible."

Cajmere went on to describe Rayli herself. She was to be a beautiful alien, but not the conventional Amazonian beauty of a supermodel, a luminous otherworldly beauty "I'm thinking of Bjork," said Cajmere. Bjork was his current obsession although she was not a woman he would have wanted to date. "But with rainbow coloured hair." She was to have superhuman attributes – gills to breathe underwater and wings on her back so she could fly. And her personality would also extrapolate human traits like bravery, purity and compassion.

He had already conceptualised one of the stories, it was to be about Rayli in Oceania, diving to the lost city of Atlantis and finding a rare black pearl which was indestructible. Rayli was subsequently going to be chased around the world for her black pearl by various shadowy global corporations who wanted to get hold of it. But she would refuse to relinquish it and instead, use it herself for the power of good. "So I guess that story and track would be called Oceania, all about her journey to the bottom of the sea, what she sees, the texture of the water, her discovery of the lost city of Atlantis." Neil was making notes in a large A4 pad, carefully transcribing all of Cajmere's directions. Of the other nine tracks and stories Cajmere wanted one to be located in the jungle or rainforest "with all kinds of wonderful and weird vegetation and you don't have to stick to what actually exists on earth, you can use artistic licence." And another to be mountainous, set on the dry, arid, snow capped peaks of either Kilimanjaro or the Himalayas. "Remember what I want you to convey, more than anything is the strangeness of earth, the earth viewed through alien eyes." He continued. Another track and story, he elaborated was to be about war. This was to be the breakbeat track, with beats spluttering and stuttering like rounds of ammunition being fired through the air. He explained that the music would be saturnine and unsettling, especially when compared to the aqueous lullaby of Oceania. So the short story would need to channel this atmosphere too. Cajmere continued to elucidate the theme or setting for each track which included oceans, rainforest, mountains, desert, glacier, war and love.

Neil said that he would sketch out plots for the nine remaining tracks and either fax them or email (email was the very latest communication method) them in around a months time when Cajmere was back in Detroit. Then, once Cajmere had some of the music down, he would send a master tape back to Wanstall so that Wanstall could play it to Neil.

"You can make the writing as abstruse and highbrow and conceptual as you want Neil, but keep the stories quite simple and quite focussed on their environmental backdrops."

I think I'll wait to hear the master tapes before I start writing proper," said Neil "I'm a great believer in what Walter Pater said," added Neil "that all art constantly aspires towards the condition of music."

"That's good," contemplated Cajmere. "I like that a lot."

That night he phoned Emma Milton. She was in an ebullient mood, one of her tracks had just made No1 in the Mixmag Update DJ chart. He asked her to go for lunch the next day. She told him she couldn't get out of the office for long, but they arranged to go to a noodle bar near her office. He phoned his mother in Detroit straight after. He rarely talked about emotional stuff with her but he felt he needed a second opinion. She was one of the only people he could talk to. "I'm gonna ask her to come back to Detroit with me," his Mum did not sound enthusiastic. "Remember what happened the last time," Cajmere countered that what had happened with Rachael had nothing to do with her moving to Detroit, it had been an unfortunate accident with a dodgy ecstasy tablet. She kept asking. "Are you sure" she reminded Cajmere that he hadn't known Emma that long. "Do you love her?" asked his Mum. "I honestly don't know, I mean infatuation, yes, crush yes, love, I'm not sure. I do know that I need her," 'I don't think its her you need, it's anyone," assessed his Mother insightfully "you need someone to fill the void left by Rachael and you're grasping at anything or anyone. I think you need to wait and see how the relationship pans out. It's still early days." She paused. "Remember you're a very good catch, you're handsome, you've got a lot of money in your bank account, so much that you never need work again. What woman is going to say no to that. You need to be careful. But then these are the sorts

of things I'm going to say. I'm your Mum, I'm protecting you."
Cajmere knew she was right but he was resolute. He
couldn't bear to think of being alone once more in that white
box of a house in Lafayette Park. The emptiness was
unbearable. Emma was light and fun and easy company.
She would distract him from what was no longer. Sure, the
sex hadn't been great, but that was probably a one off and
she was irresistible to him. Her face, her body were
imprinted on his consciousness.

And so Cajmere and Emma Milton met over soba noodles in
an ascetic wooden table-and-bench populated Japanese
canteen. It was full of twentysomethings in the latest trainers
slurping from wooden bowls. They got a quiet table by the
window.

"Darling I am so psyched by Helios, our big tune, it's
amazing." Cajmere felt uneasy with the way she swooned
over other producers records, especially when they were as
cheesy as the track Helios, which to Cajmere was the
epitome of aural bad taste, all insistent synthetic trance
crescendos and hands-in-the-air breakdowns. It was as
obvious as it got. Why couldn't she enthuse about his
records in the same way. His ego was slightly dented by it.

"Yeah I'm not so into Helios personally, I can't get excited
about it," grimaced Cajmere.

"That's because you're boring and you think you've got
integrity," said Emma Milton, half teasing, half serious.

"Yeah yeah," said Cajmere trying to laugh it off lightly. But
something about her comment stung.
"Look Emma, I didn't bring you here to talk about your trashy
tune," he decided teasing her back with an undertone of
serious critique was the best approach.

"How dare you call it trashy! But go on."

"Seriously though, I want you to come to Detroit with me."

"Phew, that's a heavy one to lay on a girl on a Thursday lunchtime. When did you come up with that brainwave?"

"I've been thinking about it for a while. What do you reckon?"

She looked into her bowl of noodles for a second. Of course she was flattered. He was asking her to live with him. A rich, handsome millionaire DJ and producer wanted her to live with him. Had all her dreams come true at once? But she would have to give up her whole life in London, her bachelorette flat, her job that she loved, frequent trips to clubs around the country, hanging out with DJs, being free. What would it be like in Detroit? It could be a dump with no shops. What would she do all day? Just be a rich DJ's wife, spend his money. Although, she could cope with that, she thought.

"That's a big question, Daniel Cajmere, You're not shy about coming forward are you?"

She wondered if it was the house that he had shared with his dead wife.

"Did she live there with you?"

"Who, you mean Rachael, my bereaved wife? Yes, she did live there with me. Does that matter?" He had been very careful not to mention Rachael to her, even though she was constantly at the back of his mind.

"No no, I mean it doesn't bother me." In her incorrigible egotism Emma Milton was completely convinced that she was far more impressive than any previous wife would have been anyway. She was just curious. She decided to leave him dangling a little bit. She would agree to a holiday in Detroit, to test the water so to speak. But not concede to living with him. Not yet anyway. *Always leave them wanting more* she smiled to herself.

"Yeah, come for a holiday, you'll love it, I'll show you all the sights," Cajmere was elated. Someone to share his life with. A future without pain, or at least, without so much pain and loss. He asked her if she could come the very next week, go back when he was going back. "Yeah, why not," smiled Emma. "I can get some leave from work. Is it cold there? Are there shopping malls?" She had heard the shopping was good in the US, although she had never been before.

And so, some days later they met at Heathrow to make the long flight back to Detroit. Emma Milton was on a high pitch of excitement, Cajmere was more sober, but nevertheless happy to have a companion to travel back to Detroit with him. Emma had dressed up, even for the flight, a v-neck embroidered lace top and a knee length A line skirt and kitten heels. "You shoulda worn trainers you know, your feet won't be comfortable," said Cajmere looking down at her heels. "Darling, glamour is just my middle name." she replied, nothing was going to depose her from her cloud. She had a huge suitcase – she'd heard the shopping was good in the US and intended to bring clothes back with her. "Shall we go for a drink and a snack before we head to boarding," asked Cajmere unthinking. "ooh darling come and look at the duty free perfumes with me, it's not often I get to see perfume with such a great discount." Cajmere sighed to himself, he was not really in the mood for shopping, he would rather have been at the bar cradling a whisky and gently sedating himself for the journey ahead. She led him by the hand to a boutique area with searing bright fluorescent strip lighting, a sweet smell of flowers and fruits hung in the air. "I love this one, she said spraying from a conical green bottle. It smelled of cucumber and seaside air and ozonic freshness. "What do you think?" "Yeah that's nice," said Cajmere hoping this would be over with as soon as possible. She seized upon another bottle with a blue container. This one smelled of caramel and vaguely of patchouli, it was sweet and toffee-like. "Yeah that's nice too, I prefer that one." Cajmere tried to muster the semblance of interest. Next a bottle that looked like a woman's torso with a corset on it and peachy-pink liquid within. Smelled like women's face powder and all those things women kept on their dressing tables, generically floral and vanillic. "Yeah not bad," said Cajmere less enthusiastic. Then finally a bottle with what looked like the American flag on it, the perfume smelled of apple and cinnamon, it was a hyper realistic rendition of American apple pie. "That's my favourite," said Cajmere decisively trying to muster enthusiasm by thinking of her bare ripe breasts emanating this 'gourmand' odour. "Ooh I don't know which to choose? I can't decide." "C'mon" said Cajmere, desperate to get out of this perfume concession "I'll get all of them for you, I don't want you to go without." "You are just the best," she murmured thoughtlessly into his neck as they stood at the cash register and the shop assistant rang up £200 on his credit card.

Within the hour they were sitting in business class, on the plane, bound for Detroit. Cajmere was trying to read a book, Neil Rushworth's latest collection of short stories. Emma Milton wouldn't stop chattering; something about some girl she worked with, not doing her job properly and some DJ who she was marrying. Finally Cajmere lost his patience. "Do you mind watching a film or something, surely there's a romantic comedy on the film menu? I mean or don't you have a book with you?" He burst out exasperated. "Okay Mr Serious, reading his book," she pursed her lips sulkily, crossed her arms and put on her headphones. Cajmere knocked back some of the rather disappointing red wine and hoped she would be quiet for the rest of the journey.

Cajmere was drifting in and out of slumber when the overhead speaker announced they were descending into Detroit. Emma Milton was reading – Bridget Jones's Diary – some light women's book - noted Cajmere. It was a blue-skied afternoon in Detroit. Cajmere though it boded well. Once landed they cruised through immigration and customs and went to the car park where Cajmere had his car, a sports car. "Ooh sexy car," cooed Emma Milton. "Yeah I guess so," Cajmere was tired, "I got it with the initial record company advance." "That must have been some advance," said Emma Milton hoping he might divulge the exact sum. "Yeah it sorted me out for a while," replied Cajmere tight lipped, suddenly mindful of what his mother had said about his multi-millionaire status.

They sped back to Lafayette Park and as they arrived Cajmere explained how it had been designed by Mies Van Der Rohe, a famous architect. "Oh how interesting," commented Emma Milton, plainly bored. "Can I got for a lie down when we get in, I'm tired."

She wondered round the house taking it all in. She liked it, yes, for sure. It was a dream home for any fashionable twentysomething either in Detroit or London. Cajmere thought of the song title 'in every dream home a heartache' it was Roxy Music, wasn't it? Why did he think of that, he wondered?

Emma Milton perused her minimal surroundings - a blank white box with a gleaming metal kitchen and a modern bathroom containing a huge shower room. "You like it?" asked Cajmere, hoping she might be seduced into staying. "Yeah, I really like it, you're certainly set up here." "Go lie down in the bedroom if you're feeling tired, I'll cook you something to eat later," urged Cajmere, doing his best to be a welcoming host. After all, he thought, this might one day be her home. When Emma Milton woke up, after a few hours rest, it was dark. The smell of fried chicken was wafting upstairs from the kitchen. "So, you cook too?" she wandered into the kitchen barefoot and wrapped her arms around Cajmere. "You really are the perfect bachelor aren't you?" "I try" grinned Cajmere, it was good to finally have company in this once empty home. Laughter and chatter and warmth would once again fill its well-proportioned spaces. It would be bearable at last. The ghosts would be gone.

And so, happier, more content with a fellow human sharing his space, Cajmere began to work on Rayli. Emma Milton said she would be all right for a few days just investigating her surroundings whilst Cajmere went to the studio. He was glad to be back in the studio. After all the talk of the short stories and making breakbeats in the studio with D--- and Michael he was full of burgeoning ideas for his new album. He decided that the opening track, called Rayli's symphony, would be a long one, perhaps even up to 20 minutes with an orchestral feeling to it. That would give the record company something to think about! He laughed to himself. He wanted vocals, even though it wasn't to be a single. Not Rayli's voice but descriptions of her first landing on earth and all her impressions of her basic surroundings – the sky the grass, the buildings, humans, animals and plants. He decided to call up Etta, this time he would take Rachael's advice and treat her kindly, rather than bullying her. He found that he had to talk her into it. He thought it would be easy to just call her up and get her into the studio – after all what better did she have to do? But he found she was reluctant to work with him again. "Was it because I was tough on you?" "Well yeah, I gotta be honest with you, you made it hard for me and I need to be in the right mood to sing." Cajmere told her how sorry he was and how he had changed. He had to cajole her for 10 minutes before she relented and agreed to come and sing.

In the meantime Cajmere decided to work on the Oceania track. He thought of all the music that evoked water for him such as Brian Eno's Deep Blue Day and also LTJ Bukem's Return to Atlantis, he wanted to recreate that feeling of rippling aquatic translucence, marine colours of azure and cerulean, shafts of light penetrating coral reefs, the quivering gelatinous feeling of being suspended in water. He played some refrains on his keyboard, part of him wanted to make this a beatless ambient track with washes, but then he thought about the actual motion of swimming and the questing nature of the narrative he'd contrived about a search for a location of a magical black pearl. He decided it needed beats as a result, but perhaps a low level breakbeat rather than a slamming four to the floor. With studied cool he experimented with different refrains on the keyboard and then decided to go for a rifle through some of his extensive record collection to search for samples.

 The next day Etta came in, she seemed more confident this time, after Cajmere had placated her and he decided to ask her to provide some spoken word excerpts for Rayli's Symphony as well as sung phrases. This time, with Rachael in mind, he was careful to be kind to her rather than impatient. When she became flustered that she had made a mistake he calmed her down and reassured her. His natural impulse at times was to get irritated but he didn't let this surface. By the end of the day, a fruitful day when much of the vocal was completed, Etta proclaimed "Daniel Cajmere, you really are a different person," " Ah" he sighed, slightly guilty at how he had behaved previously "my wife had a word with me" "I love your wife!" said Etta. "Yeah, sadly she's no longer around." He looked a little sad.

Having Emma Milton in the house had lifted his mood. But she was starting to get bored, rattling around the place with nothing to do. She'd made a long trip to the supermarket to buy food one afternoon, marvelling at the sheer size of it and range and sophistication of food available. She was enthused by all the unfamiliar brands. "There's nothing to do here," she complained to him one evening when he came home from the studio. "Sure there is, there's plenty to do. You can take a walk. Go to downtown Detroit, go to the cinema or the theatre, go to the bookstore and get another book. Hey" then he had a brainwave. "Why don't you go to the mall? There's a huge mall out in the burbs," he named a place. "Why don't you get a taxi and spend the day there, it's on me." Cajmere almost regretted saying this as soon as the words were out of his mouth. This woman was costing him serious money. At this rate his substantial fortune would be spent in a year – well – perhaps not – but her profligate spending was certainly cause for concern. However the idea she might be bad for him was just a vague suspicion at the moment. His over riding desire was to please her. He craved her angelic blonde looks and her curvaceous body. He sometimes felt he would do anything for her.

So as Cajmere walked off to the studio the day after, Emma Milton called a cab and set about embarking on a trip to indulge in her self-proclaimed favourite pastime. She enjoyed riding in the back of cars and as the taxi sped through various districts and suburbs of Detroit she gazed out of the window aimlessly at buildings and houses, feeling slightly dejected that no one knew who she was here, and no one cared that she was a prominent promotions girl with all the right connections. The thought of shopping cheered her up however and as they arrived at the mall she could smell doughnuts and popcorn - the leitmotif carbohydrate odours of American capitalism in the air.

As she entered the first shop, a unisex store, she was greeted by rails of denim and combat pants. She was quick to feel for the price tag and was delighted to find that prices were a fraction of what they were in London. The pound must be strong, she thought, she'd heard as much when colleagues in her office had gasped in approval when she'd announced she would be shopping in the States. She quickly picked up several pairs of combat pants to try on and headed to the changing rooms in a froth of enthusiasm. The adrenalin rush was palpable. After she'd picked up combat pants for $20, or about £10 each she headed for a beige hued department store. Here she found v-neck cashmere sweaters in a rainbow of colours piled high. She'd got into cashmere since having a pashmina, an upmarket version of a scarf that you flung insouciantly or knotted loosely around your neck. She grabbed some sweaters in a fervour of desire and then took them into the changing room to try them on. Thirty minutes later she had bought four sweaters, a chocolate brown one, an orange one, a cerise one and a lilac one. She decided it was time for a break. There was a doughnut and coffee bar next to the store. She bought a big milky mug of coffee, two sugars – she was not one for dieting, her figure came naturally - and sat down in a booth for a moment of calm. She was thinking, quite carefully, about whether she would come and live in Detroit. She would be, in effect, a rich man's housewife. An idea that she wasn't averse to in principle. It would be easy enough to make friends and make a life out here, but she would miss being centre of the scene that was in London and the UK. And all the things that made her Emma Milton, wouldn't be in place, who would she be out here? Just an adjunct to Cajmere? Of course he had status, he was a well-known producer in his own city. But she liked being respected in her own right for what she did. Her ego didn't really allow the thought of being a nobody in a foreign city. It was easy to be negative but she was erring towards staying in London. Besides, did she even like Cajmere enough to commit to him? Sure he was handsome and rich and famous, everything she could possibly want in a man. But she wasn't one of these women to give herself away completely. *Always keep them wanting more.* It was a cliché but it happened to be true.

The rest of Emma Milton's day passed in an intoxicated blur. She found plenty of shops she had never seen in London before – shops that were minimally fitted out in black and white – the height of 90s interior chic, faux-rustic shops with pretty clothes and piles of books and home décor, underwear boutiques that sold the raciest and kinkiest little negligees and g strings and pile-it-high, sell-it-cheap teen emporia where the latest throwaway young styles flew off the rails, with a never ending production line of new stock to replace them. She went wild with Cajmere's cash, buying lingerie - *he'll like that*, she thought with a touch of cynicism – and dresses and coats and trainers. You got a lot for your money, she thought triumphantly as she assessed her purchases.

"You. Bought. All. That!" exclaimed Cajmere in mock outrage when she got in that night. He didn't mind. Well, he half-minded. If it kept her happy for a while it was worth it.

"Look the deal is, you had a day doing what you want, tomorrow you're coming out with me, I'm going to show you the Detroit that means something to me."

"Wow exciting," said Emma Milton, still in a good mood after her shopping trip. She couldn't imagine what he would show her, maybe some fast cars or a plush hotel or his favourite restaurant or bar.

So there they were, the next day, outside Michigan central station. The building was a grand expansive old building, but nearly every window in its façade was smashed, the jagged glass masking black holes, windows onto nothingness, the void. Cajmere had his camera out and was happily snapping away.

"Er you brought me here to see this?" said Emma Milton puzzled. "It's a smashed up old building."

"Yeah but look at the intrinsic pain of that building, look at the violence of the smashed windows. How did it get like that? What was its story? What was it like in its heyday? It's a building that asks me a lot of questions. It provokes emotions. It's more than a building it's a metaphor for what Detroit has become."

"Are there a lot of buildings like this then?" asked Emma Milton.

"Sure," said Cajmere, "I'll show you my photographs. I generally stake them out, break into them and photograph the decay. Detroit is a bankrupt city and these buildings are its epitaph."

"Right," said Emma Milton. But she didn't get it. She felt depressed looking at it. And bored. There was something in this man's soul that she really couldn't fathom. She didn't get it. She didn't want to get it.

They jumped back in the car and headed a few blocks away. Another derelict old building, this time a bank, probably dating from the first half of the 20th century. Cajmere led her round the back where they found an old rotting door that he pushed open with a hard action. They climbed a flight of stairs, the planks on the stair treads were splitting and broken.

"Are you sure this is safe?" asked Emma Milton, she imagined the roof collapsing and she wondered if she would get out alive.

"Yeah, sure, I've been here before. Here – this is the room I wanted to show you." Suddenly they were in what must have been an old counting room or vault. At one end of the room there was a vast metal panel, a door to a vault and then along the right hand wall there was a floor to ceiling wooden cabinet with hundreds of small drawers slotted into cubby holes. Many of the drawers were missing. There was plaster from the ceiling all over the floor and some of the drawers from the cabinet had been removed and discarded randomly all over the floor.

"They must have counted the money in here, or kept the ledgers in those drawers." said Cajmere snapping away immersed in the chaos of his surroundings.

Cajmere looked at Emma Milton briefly. Her arms were crossed as though she expected him to impress her in some way. Her body language said 'This is a dump. Get me out. Now'

But Cajmere was swept up by the poetry of the debris around him. Trying to imagine the room, busy with people, filing things and counting things. What life was once there. It could have been a poignant moment, he thought, the two of them exploring this wreck with its detailed history, its decrescendo narrative of neglect and decay. But instead she couldn't wait to get out. He sighed as he put his camera in its case. "I guess we'd better go," "I really want to go and see the new Tarantino, Jackie Brown, can't we find a cinema somewhere?" there was a hint of a moan developing in her voice, like a petulant child threatening a tantrum. "Yeeeaaah," said Cajmere masticating the word ambivalently. "I'm not so keen on Tarantino myself. It's the worst kind of cynical postmodernism in my opinion, stylised pastiche, glib, ironic, no substance. No soul." "Oh get with the program, it's the zeitgeist, don't be such a contrarian" she was irritated now, "well this new one's meant to be more 'sincere' if that's what you like," "Okay," he said just tired of and defeated by her highly strung demands. "Let's go for it. I know a movie theatre quite near here."

He spent the day after in the studio, working on Rayli. But when he arrived home that night Emma Milton was in a rather dejected mood. "I'm bored,
 she opined "There's nothing for me to do here. I've been for a few walks but I don't want to go far from the neighbourhood in case it's dangerous. There's not much you can do in this city without a car. I'm going to see if I can change my flight and go back tomorrow." "Look, stay another day," urged Cajmere. "Come to the studio tomorrow and listen to what I've done on Rayli. I'd love your opinion and you won't be bored. Carter King will be there, you'll love Carter he's a Detroit legend. And I'll take you for a nice lunch in a proper American diner. How about that?" "Oh all right then," she sighed heavily. "One more day if that's what you want."

Back in the studio, Cajmere gave Emma Milton a brief tour of his equipment. "Very impressive I'm sure," she said with a hint of ennui. Cajmere played her some riffs on the keyboard and let her hear some of his favourite records by the Blue Nile and Talk Talk. "Us Detroit guys don't only like techno you know," he mused, "back in the day, in the eighties, we all used to listen to this radio show by the Electrifying Mojo. He'd play all sorts from The Cure to Tangerine Dream, Kraftwerk to George Clinton and that's where it comes from, our music." After they'd been in there an hour or two Carter King arrived. "Hello darling," said Emma Milton air kissing him on both cheeks, "I've heard a lot about you – all good of course," "I should hope so," smiled Carter, "enchanted to meet you Emma, I'm sure."

Shortly they were all sitting down on the beaten up old office chairs that peopled Cajmere's studio. He began the playback of the album tracks he'd been working on. First, the 20 minute opus that was Rayli's Symphony, this was the track that would open the album. "You get Etta to sing this for you?" questioned Carter, "she's got a great voice that girl."

Cajmere turned to Emma "So what do you think?" "I've gotta be honest Dan, I think a 20 minute track is pretentious. I mean who's gonna bother with that. I think you should ditch the idea of a concept album. It's too difficult. It sucks. I mean who's gonna wanna bother with that? Do you think people are actually going to read the book of short stories? Give me a break."

Cajmere felt a pang of pain in his stomach, how dare she criticise something so dear to him. *Criticise anything about me*, he thought, *but criticise my music and you impugn my honour.*

" So you're saying everything should be easy right, accessible, no one should bother trying or having any ideas in art in case they get ridiculed for it. Carter, back me up here,"

"I'm not saying anything," shrugged Carter embarrassed.

"Okay perhaps I'm being the devils advocate here, but I just think what you're doing is elitist and self-indulgent and yeah, pretentious," Emma Milton continued.

"Look, perhaps I'm an idealist, but I don't think people always want run of the mill big tunes. I think sometimes they do want to contemplate life and hear a 20-minute track that ignites their imagination. What I'm trying to do is to create a work of art that stretches the mind that stimulates people, where people think about the spaces between the notes as well as the notes themselves. If we all did things your way the world would be full of cynical moneymaking chart tunes like Helios. There would be no aspiration to do anything more innovative, anything that lasted, anything that strove towards important ideas. I'm not a producer I'm a concept engineer."

"For crying out loud, you seem to think you're the only intelligent one on this scene. You're an intellectual snob that's what you are. There's dozens of commercial house DJs smarter than you, and one of the main ways they're smarter is they know how to make a hell of a lot of money – and fast. The way you're going no major label is going to touch you with a barge pole after this."

Cajmere was smarting inside after this assault. Attacking his intellect, for him, was like attacking his penis size. Below the belt. All he had ever strived to do was to create interesting and different and inspiring music. Yes, he was working towards making something of worth, something lasting that challenged convention and preconception. And yes, he hoped the intellectual nature of it was elevated and although he didn't want to alienate anyone, probably not everyone would understand it. But the point was to aim for greatness, to aim for the stars, to aim to change music and maybe the world - not to go for the path of least resistance, the lowest common denominator, the easiest, the most commercial, the big money. It was integrity that counted.

After Emma Milton left to fly back from Detroit to London Cajmere decided to meet with Carter King and find out what he really thought of the album, in the light of Emma Milton's scabrous critique. They convened in the neighbourhood sports bar where they'd discussed Chirpy Chick.

"So – I gotta know – did you like it?" asked Cajmere hoping that not everyone hated the record. He was desperate for positive feedback after Emma Milton had demolished some of his idealism.

"Hmm," Carter was thoughtful, he went on to say that he had to be honest – it was not an album he would make. "But that doesn't mean its not good. And you've gotta remember that I'm a Detroit purist; I keep strictly to the sound of the genre, whereas you're deliberately stretching the parameters. You know, I think any musical style needs both sorts of people, those who replicate the sound faithfully and those who experiment and take it to different places."

It was the sort of measured response Cajmere would have expected from his mentor and he understood King's reasoning instinctively. Praise from King was high praise indeed and although Emma Milton's assessment of his music still stung him, it was fading into the background.

"Your girl didn't like it huh," said King gruffly.

"No she didn't" said Cajmere "I'm afraid when it comes to music that's one river that doesn't run very deep."

"You know what I think, for what it's worth, I think you're hooked on a bad woman. I've seen the type before, they dangle you on a string, make you feel you ain't good enough, make you run rings to keep up with them. But I doubt you'll see sense. Like I say you're addicted. She ain't no Rachael and that's for sure."

"No, you're right, she's not Rachael. But she's fun and I can't help myself."

"I didn't see you having much fun when we were in the studio the other day and she was dissing your tracks,' observed King.

"Yeah well, let me sort that one out," underlined Cajmere. By now he had an idea that Emma Milton was going to be trouble. But the craving for her face and body and general sexy demeanour was underscoring any logical thought that she was bad for him. He was still, also in denial that the sex wasn't right. The way she moved on him, it was jerky and mechanical rather than sinuous. Could it be that despite all the promise of her suggestive and glamorous mien, that *she just wasn't that good in bed*?

And so Cajmere was finishing Rayli. He was pleased with it. He thought it was the best, most profound, most worthwhile thing he had ever done. He didn't know if it was great or not, if it would be anointed in the canon of era-defining albums, but it certainly had soaring ambition. Taking the melancholy synth motifs of Detroit and meshing them with all kinds of innovative soundscapes. The seascape track, Oceania, sounded aquatic and immersive, as he pictured Rayli diving to the depths to find the rare black pearl. There was a mountain track, with wings beating and harps fluttering as Rayli soared amongst the thermal air pockets of Kilimanjaro and the Himalayas. There was the warzone track, a barrage of stuttering breakbeats, peppering the air like machine gun bullets. He just hoped that Neil Rushworth's book would extend his imaginarium into print and fulfil his vision for Rayli.

He sent the finished Master tapes to Wanstall – there was beginning to be a way of emailing music files on the computer, but he' didn't trust it, as yet. He waited, somewhat nervously, for a response. A few days later Wanstall phoned and told him he liked the album. Cajmere was relieved.

Wanstall was on his side. Apparently there had been questions at the record label – where was a follow up to Celestial? Why this concept stuff, wasn't this a reminder of the bad old highly indulgent days of prog rock. Wanstall had warned of this. He thought there would be people who didn't get it. "But when it comes down to it, you only have to listen to the record to realise these are really beautiful tracks, with amazing textures and timbres and sweet melodies too. It's just not in any sense a dance pop record or a chart record. Yet it's none the worse for it. It stands up as an album."

Wanstall arranged for a playback so that Neil Rushworth could come in, listen to the album and make notes. The idea was he would go away and work more on his short stories so they provided a very true literary extrapolation of the tracks. Neil emailed Cajmere some rough cuts of the stories he'd written and Cajmere was impressed. The poetic nature of the prose meant there were some beautiful sentences and descriptions. He imagined some of the sentences carved in stone, like immortal verse. He felt something had been achieved. Between Neil and himself they had created a new 'multimedia' experience. Cajmere was happy, he believed he had produced an album that was very true to himself and also an incredible flight of fantasy. Celestial had been the onion paradigm, a record with difficult concepts couched in a pop lexicon. You consumed it as a melody and then could peel away layers to get the more avant-garde modern classical structures and samples that underlay it. This album and the short stories were the concept, in this case, and it was not as commercially accessible as Celestial, but there was sweetness and tunefulness and stimulation of the imagination locked within this more abstruse idea.

The album was finished, and shortly the accompanying book of short stories was finished too. Spring became summer and Cajmere was booked to play in Ibiza. He rang Emma Milton "You want to come to Ibiza, I've been booked to play. We could make it into a little holiday together." He thought it might be a prelude to them living together – if not in Detroit in London. So Cajmere flew to London, met Emma Milton and the two of them flew to Ibiza. Emma Milton was effervescing with excitement as they sat on the plane. "I know so many DJs and producers that are going to be out there, it's going to be one massive party!" she exclaimed breathlessly. Cajmere was slightly apprehensive, half imagining the kind of cocaine and ecstasy addled laddish types she might be referring to. "We're going to large it big time," proclaimed Emma Milton. This was dance music parlance for hedonistic abandon, it had made it into the lexicon of Mixmag journalese. The very thought of this did strike a note of unease in Cajmere's heart. He had imagined quiet dinners a deux sampling vintage Rioja's and hanging out with a select coterie of deep house and techno producers – the serious musos that were out there – not spending time talking nonsense with brain-dead party animals 'necking' 5 Es at a stroke.

Their villa was a one storey traditional whitewashed building on a road overlooking the sea. Bougainvillea was creeping like magenta-hued lace over the frontage and there was a small swimming pool to the side surrounded by a number of padded sun loungers. "Looks like the promoter sorted us out Dan," said Emma Milton as they surveyed the gleaming white and cream interior with its commodious bleached linen sofas and artless driftwood furniture. Cajmere lay back on a settee and read whilst Emma Milton swam in the pool and sunbathed outside, slathering her silky limbs in oleaginous oils and creams until they were glossy and lustrous. She was reading a well-thumbed pink paperback with a picture of high heels and a cocktail glass on the cover. He was booked to play at an open-air club on a terrace near the beach, at sundown the next day. Until then, they lounged around the villa, grazing on over-ripe peaches, cherries, bread, manchego cheese and chorizo from the nearby supermarket.

A couple of hours prior to his set, Cajmere and Emma Milton headed over to the club in a taxi. She had grown her hair and it hang behind her ears into two champagne blonde plaits. She was wearing a tiny pink bikini top – two triangles on a string that barely covered her nipples. For the sake of decency she had put on a very brief wraparound mini skirt. Cajmere was appreciative, although he was not sure he wanted every man in the club hitting on her. He felt a pang of possessiveness about her body. His record box was full of a special Balearic selection of tunes. All his favourites – New Order, Talk Talk, the Blue Nile, Brian Eno some drum and bass as well as some Detroit techno white labels he'd acquired specially for the trip. The club, which was essentially a large veranda overlooking the sea, with a DJ booth/decks at one end and a bar at the other, was open all day as a bar. So they sat on stools round the bar sipping on cocktails with the promoter and a producer friend, Matt, who Emma Milton knew from London. Cajmere was careful not to drink too much alcohol in the heat, he wanted to be on form for his set. But Emma Milton seemed to be on a mission to drink very quickly. She downed her cocktails with relish, toasting Ibiza with her Matt – who was a loud cockney boy, tall and gangling with spiky deliberately badly bleached hair – roots showing and those wraparound shades that were so fashionable in the mid to late nineties. Once or twice Cajmere noticed them whispering together. They drank quickly and enthusiastically and gradually became louder and louder, almost shouting above the background music and laughing at full volume. At one point Emma Milton nearly fell off her stool. Cajmere refrained from commenting. Let her enjoy herself, he reasoned, getting heavy with a wilful girl like Emma Milton just wasn't going to work.

Seven o clock came around and Cajmere got behind the decks. The Ibizan sunset was beginning, he noticed and the sky was so breath taking – like Sunset at Sea by Renoir – all blue and striated pink and orange and the sun a ball of coruscating bright. It wasn't often he was booked to play records from his own personal collection, the sort of thing he listened to when he was not in Detroit techno work mode, so he played with an invigoration and enthusiasm he hadn't had for a long time. He segued into E2-E4 by Manuel Gottsching, perhaps the quintessential Ibiza track with it's hypnotic twinkling refrain – made famous by Sueno Latino and glanced up from the decks for a moment. There, right in front of him, brazen, was Emma Milton, in the middle of the dancefloor with her arms around her friend Matt's neck. Unaware he was watching, she proceeded to turn around, clasp Matt's hands around her waist from behind, bend over and grind her buttocks into his groin suggestively. Cajmere could hardly believe his eyes. This was his woman, getting intimate on the dancefloor with another man. He was furious he was in half a mind to jump out from behind the decks and punch Matt full in the face, take Emma Milton by the hand and drag her back to the villa. But he realised this would be a mistake. He continued to DJ, burning with humiliation now. What had been a supremely enjoyable rifle through his off duty record collection was now a nightmare scenario. How could she do this to him? She was out of control.

In the cab on the way home he finally exploded. "What the hell did you think you were doing on the dancefloor? Getting it on with that guy Matt right in front of my eyes." "Oh for crying out loud lighten up D, we were just having some fun. It wasn't like we were having sex or anything." Cajmere was more incensed by her casual attitude. "You may as well have been having sex – you're barely wearing any clothes." "Well we are in Ibiza, everyone dresses like this, besides, I'm a liberated woman, the times are past when women had to cove r there bodies to appear decent to men, don't be such a prude." "I'm not a prude, I'm just not a fan of my girlfriend making a spectacle of herself with another man on the dancefloor in front of me and people who know me." She crossed her arms and turned her body away from his to stare out of the taxi window pointedly. "Well I'm a free spirit, you will never own me or possess me," she retorted. Cajmere sighed, there was no point in even replying, she had no conscience, he couldn't reach her now.

Things were strained and quiet between them as they spent the next day together at the villa, sun bathing and by the pool. Cajmere went for a walk to clear his head, just along the shoreline. At least her garrulous chatter had ceased, he was thankful for that. He hoped he had given her something to think about. But he doubted she'd even given it a second thought.

When he arrived back at the villa, Emma Milton was on her mobile making plans to go out. "Yeah so we'll meet at the bar darling, around 8pm, then we can get a few cocktails in before we go to the club." She enquired as to the whereabouts of various famous DJs and producers, ascertained they would be at the same place and, charged up with excitement, began to ready herself, by showering and blow drying her hair, for the night ahead.

"I had thought we might go out for a meal tonight, just the two of us," Cajmere said to her flatly as she gazed at herself in the mirror using the hair straighteners to sleek out her thick wavy mass of blonde hair. "Do you know how boring you are sometimes?" she glanced at him coldly in the mirror. "Look Ibiza only happens once a year. I'm making the most of it. I'm going out," she mentioned the islands most famous club, a vast fortress of a place about half an hour's drive away. " Look, you can come with me if you want but it's not your kind of music, it'll be all the superclub DJs, my gang," she added although he knew there and then, it was not an invitation, it was an afterthought, tossed away, said as a token gesture.

And so Cajmere stayed in that night. He decided to cook himself a paella with some fresh seafood and rice and he accompanied it with a fairly expensive bottle of Rioja he'd found in the supermarket. He mused upon the rift with Emma Milton. The problem was, he just didn't want to go to clubs any more unless he was booked to DJ. He was over clubbing, had been for a long time. He'd never really been a dancer, apart from those teenage years trying awkwardly to bust a few moves at house parties. And clubs were now places he associated with work, not fun. Restaurants were much more his scene these days, especially now the ones in London had such interesting architecture and design. He was still only in his late twenties, perhaps he'd got old before his time, he thought. Perhaps being in clubs, rather than preserving your youth in aspic, accelerated ageing – especially if you took drugs, drank and smoked, so that you staggered out into the daylight a wizened, pallid, partied out version of the youthful you the night before. Clubs were strange places, he brooded, people sometimes came out changed, or they didn't come out at all, as in the case of Rachael. He wondered what she'd have made of Ibiza, she'd have had no time at all for this superclub nonsense. The superannuated big name DJs, the excesses. She might have liked his Balearic set though, he reckoned, the sort of music they used to listen to when they were relaxing at home.

He wondered what Emma Milton was doing and there was no denying it, he felt paranoid and jealous. Who was she with? Was she taking drugs? His trust in her was ebbing away and the thought of her caressing another man was unbearable. Rachael would have never done that. But perhaps Carter was right, he was addicted to Emma Milton and he didn't know how to detox.

She didn't get in until the next morning. Cajmere was having his breakfast: fresh fruit, coffee and some sweet bread he'd found in the supermarket. "Wow what a night" she exclaimed. "after the club we drove to the beach and watched the sun come up," "uh huh" Cajmere could not get excited by her account. She named various famous highly commercial DJs she'd been hanging out with. "You should hear what they're getting paid out here, no wonder they're caning it!" " I honestly don't want to know," said Cajmere not wanting to be made more jealous or humiliated and demeaned further. She saved him from that declaring herself exhausted and heading straight for the bedroom to sleep the night off.

Cajmere had to head back to London after Ibiza, to play some dates around the launch of his album. He was staying in his usual Kensington hotel and Emma Milton was, intermittently, staying with him. He was feeling apprehensive about the launch of the album: he was taking a risk putting it out there. He knew that. And he knew it would polarise people. A concept album wasn't something that the media were going to assimilate easily and laud universally. In some ways he was setting himself up for ridicule. He knew that too. He tried to voice his concerns to Emma Milton but she was not supportive, although she tried to be less caustic than she had been in the studio. "Darling you know what I think of your album idea. However nice the music is it's going to be over a lot of people's heads."

It was not like Cajmere to be shaky. Before losing Rachael he would have been full of hubris about the prospect of releasing an album. But since that life event that had shaken him to his foundations and since dating Emma Milton, who only served to unnerve him at times, he had found himself doubtful emotionally, where once he had been very sure of himself.

He phoned Carter King about the album's imminent release. "Look kid, I told you, it's not an album I would have made myself. But it's a good record. It stands up. It's not bad music. Once people have got over the idea of it, they're gonna love it, you'll see." This was uncharacteristic exuberance from Carter, so it must be good, thought Cajmere.

He spoke to Wanstall. "Look you knew it was risky when you started making it. But I firmly believe artists should go where the muse takes them, otherwise nothing worthwhile would ever get done. Believe me I would tell you if you were disappearing up your own proverbial. We're here to safeguard you from doing that. I think once people get over the grand idea, they will be seduced. How could they not be! It's a Daniel Cajmere record."

He had become increasingly concerned about what Emma Milton was thinking and saying about him. Ever since Ibiza she'd been going out with her commercial house DJ and producer friends to bars and to clubs without him. He figured he had to let her go, but he'd also become uneasy about her wilfulness. One morning, after she'd stayed the night he was having a shave in the bathroom. He could vaguely hear Emma Milton on the phone in the bedroom part of the hotel room.

"Darling he's just so boring, this is one boring man, he doesn't even like going to bars and clubs any more apart from when he's playing. In my opinion he's old before his time. He may as well hang up his headphones. As far as I'm concerned *he's over.*"

In a split second Cajmere realised Emma Milton was talking about him. He knew that she thought he was boring. She'd told him as much herself. But to rubbish his career. His heart sank. *She thinks I'm over.*

He wondered who she was talking to. With her loquacious nature, gossip like that about him would be all over London in a matter of days.

He stopped shaving and turned the tap off so he could hear more clearly.

" Don't talk to me about sex, she said in a low barely discernable voice. You know what, I think he's gay. I really do. There's just no enthusiasm – do you know what I mean? No chemistry any more. He can barely be bothered to turn me on."

Cajmere knew this was an exaggeration. Sure the sex wasn't right and it hadn't been right from the beginning. But he knew it wasn't his fault. He'd never had a problem before. Had he?

He quickly turned the tap back on so she wouldn't realise he had heard all of this. His stomach was lurching and he was cold. *So this is what she thinks of me.* It was a shocking and unwelcome revelation. I mean, he'd had some idea she thought he was a bit boring. But the level of contempt and slander was so extreme. It cut him to the quick. How could someone so apparently light of nature and fun, exhibit such bitchyness. He had read her completely wrong.

He found himself in the following few days, becoming rather paranoid. Emma Milton had flicked a switch in him. He felt the need to prove his masculinity. He found himself mentioning his love of women in any random conversations he might have, even casually in record shops. Who knew who she was talking to and what they were all saying about him?

He tried to compensate by taking her out for an expensive meal to the first architect designed restaurant they'd met at and buying her some new very obscure imported Japanese trainers – that she didn't really appreciate. He was even more compelled to please her now and to prove to her he was a real man. He complimented her and was more attentive. But all she responded with was "Why are you being so romantic all of a sudden? Worried I will go off with someone else?"

There was no one he could speak to about it. Carter had already told him his opinion and he had chosen to ignore him. he could hardly go complaining about her to Carter after he'd already warned him against her. His mother didn't really know the full story and he rarely spoke to her about women anyway. And besides them, there was no one else he was close to. Wanstall would have just thought he was weird if he started talking about his love life and he couldn't go around

London with a loudhailer shouting out "*I am straight*" even though that was what he felt like doing to clear his name.

As it was, he had another chance to prove his red-blooded masculinity when Wanstall invited him into the office to have a look at all the press for Rayli.

He arrived promptly and sat down once more on the record companies leather sofas. "I'm afraid, as I predicted it's a bit of a mixed bag," said Wanstall with an armful of magazines and newspapers, almost apologetic. "First week sales are looking good though, it's likely you'll chart somewhere in the lower regions of the top 20. Repeat buyers I would imagine – fans that liked Celestial."

Wanstall explained that very few broadsheet or tabloid newspapers were likely to do more than a 200 word review, but there were the style mags, the music papers, music magazines like Q, Select and Mojo the dance music press and then, because this album came with a book in tandem, the literary press.

Cajmere leafed through Mixmag. He saw a headline 'What Planet Is Daniel Cajmere On?' and read a piece that was jokey and ambivalent – and yes it did refer to the worst excesses of prog. "They're having a laugh at my expense," sighed Cajmere. "Well, it is Mixmag, it does have intelligent moments but in general it's very tabloid, pictures of girls in fluffy bras," "I know I know," said Cajmere resigned to some of the less highbrow regions of the British press.

To cheer him up Wanstall handed him The Wire, "look they've done a cover feature." Cajmere glanced at the cover 'Expanding the lexicon of Detroit techno.' "Wow, that's amazing," he was excited now "I love that magazine, although its difficult to get hold of. This more than makes up for Mixmag." The Wire had done an accompanying piece about the history of the concept album, which was incredibly well researched and well informed. Rachael would have loved it he thought to himself. This was the one you wanted to be in.

"Yeah I mean it hasn't got a massive readership but it's an influential readership for sure. People who are really invested in avant-garde music."

The Face, i-D and Dazed and Confused had all done positive pieces, the headline of the article in i-D was The Immaculate Conception with a highly intellectual deconstruction of the project. Cajmere was more than pleased about this. "The style mags tend not to cover things unless they really like them," explained Wanstall. "Again their readership isn't huge but their influence can be felt across the media. They tend to break things first and incubate trends. They're a good litmus test."

Wanstall passed him NME and Melody Maker "Music papers not so good I'm afraid. Melody Maker is more dance music friendly than NME. They sort of liked it – seven out of ten. Still a bit ambivalent though. Didn't want to entirely back it in case other people were having a laugh at it. That's the feeling I got anyway." He paused and leafed through the papers. "NME is rather studenty, also tends to stand against anything that's avant-garde. Of course it wasn't like that in the old days, they were famous for their coverage of punk and post-punk. But now it's a lot more conservative. They'll cover the scrappiest, most talentless Britpop acts and then rubbish a dance album that's going to be huge. They don't seem to realise that most of the young people of this country have been out clubbing and raving since the late eighties and that a sizeable proportion of record buyers and music fans are now into dance. Some kids who like Britpop are even going to go clubbing at night. I even heard that Noel Gallagher of Oasis like dance music and clubbing. The music world isn't as polarised as you might think."

Cajmere glanced at the review in the NME, the headline asked 'Conceptual Smart???' in a pun on Conceptual Art.

The review had given him six out of ten. They thought that the concept was overblown and that with this album Detroit techno was over reaching itself and overly ambitious. Rayli's Symphony, the 20 minute long track was 'rambling' and 'lacking in structural discipline'. But Oceania was 'a dive into bliss' and they thought the breakbeat track was impressive, for a producer who wasn't practised in drum and bass. "You know their criticisms are fair enough," said Cajmere, trying to be adult about the fact he did feel a bit piqued. "Like you said, this album was always going to polarise people."

"What I think you need to see is that the right people got it, the smart people who know their avant garde music." said Wanstall "Yeah, it's a shame about the music papers and the dance press but they're both much more mainstream, and I've told you what I think of the music papers anyway."

Cajmere still felt a bit hurt. For some reason, despite his elation at the Wire cover, he was in the sort of mindset where he could only focus on the negative press. Why couldn't they all get it? He pondered as they sat there. *He wanted the world to love his music.* But of course, that just wasn't realistic.

Wanstall sensed he was dejected and was doing everything in his power to cheer him up. "Look, look at what the LRB did about Neil's book and the project as a whole – it's amazing," he urged, showing Cajmere a long article in the London Review of Books about the book of Rayli short stories and the accompanying album and how they were created and synergistically worked together. It was not only positive, it explored in detail the writing of a book and the making of an album in tandem and how multimedia, cross genre projects like this could signal a future for the arts. "Is the LRB prestigious?" asked Cajmere. "Crikey, yes, terribly so," said Wanstall enthusiastically. "I mean who needs the NME when you've got the LRB on your side. That's the intelligentsia."

Cajmere went back to his hotel room that night and thought about the reviews. He did feel crestfallen that the NME, Melody Maker and Mixmag had half-damned Rayli and he knew how important they were in the UK and to a lesser extent globally in terms of their influence on record buyers. He phoned Emma Milton for some solace. "Do you want me to come over darling?" she asked innocently enough. "Yeah, it would be good to see you," he said somewhat melancholy.

She arrived bearing a bottle of wine and wearing a slip of a top that barely covered the full curve of her breasts. Cajmere was distracted for a moment. " Cm here gorgeous," she grabbed him and kissed him full on the lips, "I thought we could celebrate the release of the album." She said cheerfully. "Yeah well, not so much to celebrate there," sighed Cajmere. "What do you mean? Are sales down?" "No sales are pretty good for a follow up, we're going to make the top 20 at least," replied Cajmere. "Well what's not to like?" said Emma Milton, subtly questioning his vaguely gloomy demeanour. "Oh just some bad reviews?" Well what do you mean by bad? slagging you off big time? three out of ten? Hatchet job?" "No not completely trashing me, just ambivalent." "Honestly I don't know what you're grouching about?" she chided him. "So some magazines and newspapers weren't all over you. So what? It's usually the way with a dance record. There's so many factions now there's rarely consensus." "Yeah but it was the NME and Mixmag," he was somewhat inconsolable. "Get over it Dan" urged Emma Milton. 'They're not going to like everything. That's the whole point of criticism. Besides I gave you my opinion when you were making it. I told you a concept album wasn't going to be everyone's cup of tea, too overtly intellectual too elitist. You know what I think. But you're stubborn. You won't listen to anyone else will you? Always think you're right. Well perhaps its time to take some advice." There was a distinct 'I told you so' attitude to her response, not the support and empathy he had hoped for. Another telling off. He wasn't good enough. That was the crux of it. 'I don't mean to be mean but Detroit's had its day for a lot of people," she continued, its all about trance now and big commercial house tunes in the superclubs and big beat. Have you thought about changing what you do?"

His stomach lurched. Changing what he did, not being true to himself, that was anathema to him. Besides, he hated trance, it was too white, too Euro, no funk in it, no soul. Why should he conform to someone's trashy notion of what dance music now. No, he would be true to his genre – whilst evolving it of course. No one could knock him off course. Detroit techno may not be the height of fashion any more, but, like that other Detroit music Motown, there was something classic and enduring about it. Detroit – or its techno at least – would never die.

He had hoped she might give him some constructive criticism, as Rachael would have done. Could that track have been shorter? or more tuneful? were the harps in the Arial track too saccharine in their timbre? Were the beats too slow and lugubrious? He wanted someone he could discuss the album and the responses to it in depth. And not just a record company person who would give him stock responses, cheerleading it on when his work needed objectively assessing.

But Emma Milton wanted to talk about some girl in her office that wasn't doing her job properly "She had this killer tune and she failed to get it into the right boxes, it was a travesty, she's just rubbish, if I was the boss I would sack her." Then she tried to work him for gossip about the other Detroit DJs. "c'mon what do those guys get up to? You can tell me! The women, the drugs." The last thing he was going to do was to confide in Emma Milton about his bachelor life before he met Rachael. Unless she already knew of course. What he wanted to talk about more than anything was his music, he craved a really serious in depth talk about the direction he was going in. A talk perhaps only Rachael could have given him at that juncture. However Emma Milton wasn't really interested in discussing perceived flaws in the album as

Cajmere was. So he had to swallow his feelings of disappointment and collude, half-heartedly in her chit chat about various industry figures and their exploits. "Did you hear that Dave Ashworth is back in rehab," she confided, wide-eyed. "He's been hanging out with that coke fiend A and R guy from Turbo records. Couldn't stop himself," Cajmere found himself zoning out as her trite observations and chatter about the dance scene continued.

Finally she registered his lack of interest in her conversational gambits. "Oh for crying out loud, what's wrong with you!? I could tell you were going to be boring tonight. You are doing my head in. Do you know what, I think you're a depressive and you just want to drag everybody down with you, that's what. I've had enough of this self-indulgent mood, I'm going out." And so she went off, into the night, into the world of bars and repetitive beats and bright lights. And Cajmere was left alone, even more disconsolate, cradling a warm glass of wine in his hand.

Alone, he began to brood on his misfortunes. Losing Rachael, the disastrous gig in Rotterdam, the creeping feeling of inadequacy he experienced with Emma Milton. He was on a downward trajectory. He felt worthless. He started wondering if he should carry on. He put his coat on and decided to go to a nearby off licence and get a bottle of whisky. Only a drink would ease the pain, he thought. It was drizzling outside, British weather in autumn, thought Cajmere, and guaranteed to depress you further. As he walked he found himself beset by a heaviness of gait, as though he were trudging thought thick mud. Even walking had become difficult. The mechanics of everyday living were breaking down. He pictured himself walking down this same street just about to sign his record deal some years ago. It was a cliché but life was so much easier then. There was so much to look forward to. And now, now it had all gone, drained away, every last drop. In the shop he handed over the cash for the whisky, it was a Middle Eastern shopkeeper. *This man has no idea that I might be using this bottle to end my life*, thought Cajmere. *And even if he did know – would he care?*

He was sinking now, sinking into a gloom that seemed to be unbearable. The lurch of his stomach reading those reviews earlier in the day had transmogrified into a deep trough of angst. The feeling was seemingly intractable. Only alcohol can alleviate this pain, he reasoned. And perhaps he was right. Back in the hotel, he began to painstakingly review his life thus far. This was like a reckoning, he thought. His casual bachelor days. Perhaps he hadn't treated people as well as he should have. In fact he knew he hadn't. His voracious sexual appetite. Those women he'd used and tossed aside like pieces of litter. The girl in the hotel room who'd passed out. Perhaps he should have gone to hospital with her and made sure she was okay. The crack whore. How low he had sunk. How arrogant he had been in dismissing the feelings of others. All the people he'd been rude to. Fans who'd innocently told him they liked his music, his bullying of Etta, a sweet nervous girl with a wonderful talent. It was like they were coming back now to visit him, in this lonely hotel room, to tell him how rubbish he'd made them feel. And then there was Rachael of course. Beautiful, pure, intelligent Rachael. She was just an innocent record shop girl. She had been kind and she had been trusting. She was sincere. She tried her best. He'd made her change, inveigled her into the Daniel Cajmere world, with lipgloss, high heels, glamorous clothes and international travel. And for what. Because he'd cheated on her with Emma Milton that night in Glasgow. He'd left her alone. If she hadn't been alone she'd have never taken the drugs. And if she'd never taken the drugs she'd still be alive. *I killed her.* That was one rumination that had been persistent since the dreadful event. I did it. Not with his bare hands of course, or a gun or a knife. But insidiously, subtly, inadvertently. *I killed her with my arrogance and hubris and selfishness.* The thought would not go away.

The bland greige of the hotel room didn't serve to alleviate the pain. Instead, the anonymity of it, the empty, clinical, inoffensive corporate-friendly character of it, served to exacerbate his angst. At this desperate juncture, he realised there was no one he could call, no one he could share this with. He was alone, totally alone. He had to face up to his life without any help. It wasn't an easy thing to face.

He began to run a bath, lining up the bottle of whisky, a tumbler and a couple of packs of his medication – SSRIs, anti-anxiety and sleeping pills. As he sank into the bath, his first thought was to take them to quell these awful feelings of guilt and sadness. Then that thought again – should he? Could he? Did he really want to end his own life? He had contemplated death before – but Rachael's death not his own. He had had points where he'd thought about joining her. Seriously. But only now did death seem like a serious consideration. He couldn't see an end to the pain, apart from that.

But really? Did he really want to do that. The usual thought – what lay beyond death or was it true finality. He could not bear, could not comprehend, the thought of nothingness. Yet did he believe in God? He didn't know. Did he eschew God entirely? He didn't know. There was no proof, after all, apart from the testimonies of people who'd lived two thousand odd years ago. And he liked science and scientific proof. He was invested in science – or at least it was an attractive trope for his music. But then, why build all those churches if there was no God. Could two thousand or more years of belief be for nothing? He wanted to believe so much. He wanted there to be an afterlife so that Rachael would live forever. And then there was the question, did he have the strength to kill himself? or was this purgatory, was he caught between the wretchedness of being alive and not quite being able to go through with it and kill himself. Yes, that was it. No mans land.

He lay there in the bath, 20 minutes passed, an hour passed and he'd drained half the bottle of whisky. He hadn't touched the pills. Yet. He looked at his hands - his skin was wrinkling, prune-like and now the water was barely warm. He let some of the water run down the plughole and ran piping hot water from the tap to replenish the supply. He soaped himself, feeling woozy and relieved. Then, just as it seemed all was lost, a voice came to him, or at least, he thought it did. It sounded like Rachael. She said '*Daniel, Daniel, don't lose heart, carry on, there is wonderful amazing music to be made and you must make it.*' He jolted upright. Was it a dream, this voice that had come to him at his lowest ebb?

But whatever it was, it lifted him out of his morbid dudgeon. Someone was watching over him. Someone wanted him to go on. He knew that he had been given a gift with music and it would be a waste of potential to turn the light off and die. What more lay ahead – who knew – but there were singles and albums to be made and remixes to be done and DJ sets to be constructed. He had to continue, if only for the sake of the music. It was his driving passion and it was what would save him.

Suddenly, albeit through a misty haze of Whisky-addled consciousness, it slowly dawned upon him what he must do. He needed to go back to Detroit, for good this time. He needed to sever his contacts with the major label – which should be easy enough as the two album contract had now been fulfilled. And he needed to go back to making music just for himself again and ignoring the commercial constraints and demands of the marketplace. Finally and perhaps most importantly he must split up with Emma Milton and be resolute about it. Not perhaps as easy as it seemed. For it was she whose insidious bullying had precipitated this evening's trauma. He hadn't realised it properly until now, but she was a negative force, damaging his sense of self worth. Lose her and life would hopefully improve.

Cajmere thought very carefully that night about how he would terminate the relationship with Emma Milton. He didn't want a scene and he hoped that vitriol and repercussions could be avoided. Although he couldn't predict how volatile she would be. Would she cry? He thought not. It was not her style. It occurred to him that she was one of those women who probably never cried. The best option would be to explain that he was going to go back to Detroit for good (apart from DJ bookings) and that he wouldn't be coming to the UK any more. It would then become clear he wasn't going to ask her to come with him. This would be a gentle way of letting her go. No more treating women badly, he resolved, whatever the woman in question happened to be like.

So, the following day he phoned her and asked her to come to the hotel after work that evening. Best to do it there, rather than anywhere else, he reckoned. No point in taking her out for an expensive meal for it to end in mutual antipathy.

"Hey Emma, wanna come over," he tried to be casual and not betray the serious intent beneath the invite.

"Yeah sure, as long as you're not going to depress me, has your mood lifted?" he felt relieved, it would be easier if she was in this intolerant frame of mind.

"I'm fine thanks Emma, I'm fine. It'll just be nice to hang out with you."

She sounded suspicious. "Yeah I mean you can hang out with me anytime, you know that."

She arrived about 7pm. Cajmere had bought a bottle of wine, he wanted to make this as civilised as possible.

She looked particularly gorgeous this evening, blonde hair tied back in a loose ponytail, subtle make up, maraschino lipgloss. For a minute Cajmere was taken in by her pulchritude. If only it had worked out. So much promise, If only. But he knew he had to unhook himself. Her appearance wasn't all. She was trouble and she could only cause him pain. He had come to that realisation – perhaps all too late he thought.

He poured the wine and they discussed her day, the frustrations of the office, the DJs that hadn't returned her calls. She had this way of making you feel she was hard done by at times, you wanted to be on her team. He almost felt sorry for her. Almost.

"So, I asked you here today because I want to tell you something,"

"Oh yeah, " she sounded bored already.

"As you know I've fulfilled my record contract – two albums – both of which have now been released. Well,' he took a deep draught of breath, "I'm going to be going back to Detroit. For good this time. No more coming back and staying in London. Apart from DJ dates of course."

"I suppose you're asking me to come back with you?" she sounded a bit more animated now, although it was hard to discern whether this was because she wanted to go to Detroit or whether she was gearing up for conflict.

He paused, he was about to try to explain that he would be going back alone when she cut in decisively.

"Well you know what, I won't be coming with you," she sounded sour now and resolute.

"Sure" said Cajmere, relieved that it was she who had said this not he.

"You can't ask me to live there. There's nothing there for me. It's a dump and it's boring. Even with you there. I've got my career here, my friends, I know everyone in London."

He didn't tell her he wasn't going to ask her, no point in being cruel. The days of cruelty were over now. He was a man that was going to be treating people with sensitivity, even if it did not always come naturally.

"Actually, if I'm going to be brutally honest, you bore me too. When I first met you I thought, here's this incredibly eligible bachelor. He's rich, he's handsome, he's famous. I wanted you. Big time. But now I feel nothing. You are boring and your music is pretentious. No one I hang out with would ever listen to it." She paused, as thought waiting for a second to deliver the zenith of her attack. "And you know what – you're rubbish in bed. You can't even please a woman any more. In my opinion you're career is over and yes, for me you are over Daniel Cajmere, or is it more? I'm over you."

He felt the sting of her whiplash tongue and was struck dumb. His breath had been taken away and he was enervated by her cruelty. The level of contempt in her voice was lacerating. He almost believed it now, perhaps he was boring and his music pretentious. Her worldview had infiltrated his consciousness so completely. Why did she have to end it like this? With nastiness? Why did it have to be so malicious? Why couldn't they be two adults just parting, going their separate ways, without spite. He guessed that just wasn't her style.

"That's enough," said Cajmere finally summoning the strength to put a stop to it. He held up his hand with finality. "I think you should go" ventured Cajmere calmly. "This conversation isn't going anywhere. I'm not going to sit here and let you insult me."

"Fine, that's fine. I am outta here. That's all I've got to say to you." She marched out of the door.

Cajmere heaved a sigh of relief and lay down on the bed prostrate with his arms cradling his head. She was gone now. There would be no more verbal assaults. He didn't have to endure that any more. Silence descended.

The next day he was going to swing by the record label, say goodbye to Wanstall and then catch his flight. He had to have some contact with someone civilised soon. Someone that did not have tantrums and abuse him. Someone decent.

"Hey there Dan, good to see you," he said patting Cajmere on the back fraternally. At last someone civilised, thought Cajmere. Someone who is not going to try and break me down. He felt a pang of emotion at seeing someone so nice, so friendly, after all the unbridled vitriol directed at him last night.

"You know what, it's *really* good to see you too," how much did he mean that.

"So I guess this is goodbye. You going back to Detroit today?"

"Yeah I am"

"And I take it that's it for us, you won't be coming back, apart from to DJ,"

"That's right,"

"Well it's been brilliant working with you, a real education, I mean that. Two brilliant albums. You've been a real asset to my roster."

"Thanks. Thanks a lot," he really needed that bolstering after Emma Milton's negation of all that he was.

They talked for some time about the current state of the music scene "It's all about Big Beat and trance now and of course the French stuff," observed Wanstall sounding vaguely depressed about it. "The dance scene has commercialised and fragmented to a point where you feel nostalgic for the days when there was that innocence and integrity and cohesion for all the genres." He continued. "Those days when you first signed me," smiled Cajmere, thinking back on his early trips to London and meeting Rachael in the record shop. "I think the commercialisation has become very cynical, big hooks, big cheesy samples and big drum breakdowns. It's like a formula now. " said Wanstall. "It's crazy when I'm saying that, I mean I'm the devil a major label. I've got to sign this stuff," he sighed.

"You still got a girl friend in London?" asked Wanstall changing the subject in cased he became indiscrete. "Oh we split up last night. She was a record promotions girl,"

"Oh some of those can be a bit vacuous Dan, it's probably for the best," Cajmere needed to hear that. Confirmation that she hadn't been right.

"That girl from the record store. Now she was incredible. It's such a shame you lost her."

"I know, sometimes I think I'll never really get over it."

"You will Dan, you just need to meet the right one, someone who's not fixated on shoes and the latest trance banger!" How did he know? It was like he was psychic, thought Cajmere, perhaps these girls proliferated in the industry.

"Look take care and do look me up when you're next DJing in London. I hope we're friends now as well as business associates."

"Sure thing," said Cajmere, he'd be sad to lose contact with Wanstall, despite being a major label A and R he was a good guy he reckoned. "And , you know, if you're ever in Detroit."

Cajmere headed for Heathrow. It was an inclement autumn day – windy and rainy and as the taxi sped through west London he was thankful to be leaving. Emma Milton's assault on him, hadn't just been limited to her few recent outbursts and her 'grinding' with another man in front of him in Ibiza. It had been almost continual; an insidious, creeping feeling that he was worthless inveigling his consciousness. By the end, he'd felt useless as a DJ and a producer and the dullest, heaviest, most depressive personality imaginable. But he was beginning to realise it was merely how she'd made him feel and these were not qualities intrinsic to him. Wanstall found him interesting, Carter King found him interesting, he still got booked for gigs. Hers was the view of one very wilful and dominating promotions girl. And that's all she was – a promotions girl. He needed to remember that. As Carter had ascertained, she was no Rachael. He would recover from this. He would leave it all behind.

Less than twelve hours later he was back in Detroit. The weather was just as bad as in London – oppressive leaden skies - but he felt relieved to be home. Back in his little Mies Van Der Rohe house he put on some music, some modern classical works by Messaien that Rachael had liked and he started reading a book. He was glad to be alone for the first time since Rachael had died. Tomorrow he would go to the studio and start to make a new single for his Rings of Saturn label. He would phone up his stable of young producers and he would start getting them to produce tracks for him. He felt galvanised. A world of music lay ahead.

Back in the studio Cajmere felt enthused for the first time in months. There was no longer the pressure of a major label bearing down on him. He didn't have to manufacture albums on a production line. He could do what he wanted – start experimenting with modern classical again, play around with some freeform jazz, or go back to classic Detroit techno. He was free and the opportunities were infinite. He decided to phone some of his fledgling producers and see what they were making. The label needed more input and tracks lined up for release.

He decided to tidy up his studio and alphabetically index some of his thousands of records. In going through them he would rediscover some treasures to sample and play in his sets. Cajmere was meticulously tidy if nothing else and within a couple of weeks the studio would be clean and orderly and the records catalogued – just as he liked it. He phoned Carter King and invited him over whilst he was doing this.

"Hey dude, how are you? It feels like an age," King ambled in wearing a baseball cap and a leather jacket. "What's been going on? I hear the album was released in the UK. Good reaction?"

Cajmere related the mixed reviews. "Yeah I knew it was a risk," interjected King. "Not everyone's gonna get that."

Cajmere told him he'd found it tough, taking something of a critical hammering for the first time.

"I've never had that experience," said King, 'but then I've stayed underground. Easier in some ways. Sure you don't get the big money deal, but then you never have to take a beating for entering the mainstream either. It's a difficult one. You made the leap, brave in some ways, but then you also paid the price for it." He paused "By the way what happened to the girl?"

"Oh yeah, Emma Milton, she's gone,"

"You get rid of her? That's good." King was pleased with his protégée. Cajmere told him about Ibiza, how she had openly flaunted herself on the dancefloor in front of him with another man.

"Man she was a ho! She was playing you for a fool." commented King – he had some unreconstructed views towards women.

"She was a challenge!" harrumphed Cajmere.

"Did she apologise for that?"

"No, we argued," explained Cajmere, and she claimed she was a free spirit and said I mustn't try to restrict her."

"And you took that?" At the time, like you said, I was hooked. But I've since thought better of it. We split up just before I left London. "She really ground me down King. She said I was boring, she criticised a lot of things I cared about." It was unusual for Cajmere to admit all of this, but he was trying to be more open as well as more sensitive. To express himself emotionally.

"Well we DJs can be boring! I don't mind admitting that," said King with a laugh. "All we really want to talk about is music and I for one, don't' care for clubbing any more. I've had enough of clubs. Clubs are work. I like restaurants and bars and cinema. My days of partying are long gone. These days I love a bottle of red wine and an early night. If you're gonna be a truly great DJ you can't behave like a drugged up clubber. Those DJs ain't serious man – they're jokers."

King had exposed the paradoxical at the very heart of dance music. A lot of the main players, in Detroit especially, had never taken drugs, even though they made music that was often the soundtrack of hedonistic abandon. The techno heads in the studio were enthused by keyboards and samplers and computers and not fired up by the chemical excesses of ecstasy and cocaine. And as many DJs got older they didn't want to lose it on the dancefloor with the kids, they settled down, had families of their own or immersed in reading books and watching films, like Cajmere. It wasn't boring, thought Cajmere, as Emma Milton had ascertained, it was just the process of ageing, the advancing of years, the increasing knowledge that you wanted to get things done in daylight, like making music for posterity's sake, rather than wasting night time and sleeping through the day.

"Do you think she might talk about me?" asked Cajmere, struck by a pang of paranoia.

"Only to her stupid commercial house friends. I wouldn't worry about it. Just idle gossip. They'll be onto someone in rehab next month," said King, dismissive. "Those kinda girls are predictable, they want some flash dude with money to splash around. Then when they've spent the money and partied some they're onto the next one. Let her tell the next sucker you were no good in bed, or whatever she's gonna say. Until they wake up and smell the coffee too."

Cajmere felt better with his friend's approbation. His ego had taken a battering being with Emma Milton, that and Rachael's death had made him re-evaluate his approach. Had he once been like Emma Milton – in a way – with her arrogance and hubris – thinking he was the centre of the world. That had to change. Rachael was the key to what he must become. Someone who didn't stamp on other people any more.

It was his passion for music that had pulled him through. Time spent in the studio was a pleasure to him and now he had his protégées on the label to mentor, that would prove rewarding.

"You working on some new tracks?" ventured King,

"Yeah I'm going to make a start," said Cajmere of his intentions. "Just going through my records to get some inspiration."

"I'm working on an album," revealed King.

"Really," said Cajmere "about time. You've been DJing so much and not concentrating on your recording work."

"I know and I've been thinking, with getting older, you know I wanna leave a body of work behind, not just some DJ mix tapes."

And that was it. They were getting older. The adrenalin of the scene no longer flowed through their days and nights. They wanted to settle down, get married, have children, not spend every night, up till dawn with a different woman. They were thinking about serious projects, things to leave their stamp on the world.
That week in between indexing his record collection and starting to work on a new track Cajmere decided to pay a visit to Reeves records and see Marvin. He wanted to talk about Rachael.

Marvin was skulking behind the counter, in his usual irascible frame of mind.

"Why you come here?" he questioned Cajmere "Now she's gone,"

"Because I wanted to remember," said Cajmere quietly. *Because I miss her and she was special* he thought to himself.

Marvin softened, like most men of a certain age he knew about loss – he'd lost his own parents. He started telling Cajmere about times when Rachael had been there and they'd been discussing music. "She opened me up to a whole lot of modern classical stuff I'd never considered before," admitted Marvin. "Me too, me too," agreed Cajmere. "And in return I taught her about jazz." He told him how Rachael and he had made jokes behind the counter about some of the regular customers "the head nodders, the aficionados. That girl wasn't frightened of no one, however knowledgeable and uppity they were and she was funny too." Marvin knew that Cajmere was a producer and he asked him about his releases and his record company contract. "I'm thinking Rachael had a lot of input into your music," he ventured. "She did," confirmed Cajmere, "she was a constant source of inspiration. She was my muse." They talked for a while about music. Jazz was Marvin's specialist area. He told him about some live jazz venues in Detroit that were worth going to. Cajmere made a mental note to see more live music – it could be useful for his production work. "Did you ever replace her?" he asked Marvin. "No I didn't bother. Can't think of anyone else I'd get on with so well. I may as well manage this place on my own now. It's not so busy these days."

Cajmere was thinking a lot about Rachael now that the toxic influence of Emma Milton was gone. But he was not pained any more; the acuteness of the grief had dissipated with time passing and the events with Emma Milton. It was a nostalgic wistful yearning now, vague echoes, traces of memories he was trying to excavate.

A brief fleeting thought ran through his mind one day. Rachael had wanted to do youth work. Perhaps he would look into doing that. There were community projects around Detroit he could get involved in. Doing some part time work with kids would mean he didn't get too solipsistic and involved in his studio and DJing work. It would ground him. He would be giving back something after the prodigious good fortune he had experienced. And it was a way of remembering her.

He went to the state department offices and enquired. He then spent a day making phone calls to various organisations in deprived areas. Eventually he found somewhere that needed volunteers. "Hello Sojourner Truth community centre," a woman's voice answered the phone. "Hi yeah, my name is Daniel Cajmere and I'd like to volunteer to do some youth work and mentoring."

"Do you have any experience with our age group, 11-18?" "Uh, not really," admitted Cajmere. "But I'm keen to learn. Also I'm a DJ, I thought I could pass on my skills and help the kids get into music." "That sounds great," replied the woman, why don't you come in and see me about it, we can look into getting you started, my name's Laetitia. Come along next Tuesday, 2pm and we'll see what we can sort out."

Sojourner Truth was in a deprived area south of where he lives in Lafayette. He took the bus there rather than drive his car, he was wary of his car being broken into. The community centre turned out to be a low-rise one-storey building with pillar-box red tubing running around it built in a nondescript style probably in the 1980s. There was a childrens playground outside and a small park adjacent.

Laetitia turned out to be a big middle aged black woman with wide eyes and a glossy mahogany-hued weave trailing down her back wearing a large fuschia jumper, jeans and trainers. Cajmere was relieved to meet a normal woman, rather than a fashion obsessed record label girl, or a zoned out club kid, for once. "These kids are vulnerable," she went on, " for a lot of them there's no hope. They're from deprived homes, single parent families, the projects. If we don't offer them something constructive leisure they're going to get into gangs and end up shooting each other. You know what a dead end Detroit can be. You live here."

She explained that what was needed was volunteers who would mentor the kids and take an interest in them. Play sports with them, work on their reading and writing skills, inspire them to continue with their education and introduce them to the arts – music, films and books – and even graffiti if it was done in a controlled environment and not on public property.

Cajmere thought he had a lot to give. His reading and writing skills were good. Although he'd left school at 18 he could have easily gone to University. He was a prodigious reader and proficient at writing. He hadn't played sports since he was at school but he'd been good at basketball and sprinting, he figured he could coach some informal basketball games quite easily.

"I think one of the best things I could do for the kids would be to bring my decks along and show them how to DJ, I reckon even the real hooligans could get into that. We might even find some genuine new DJ talent here. I've got some hip hop and R and B records in my collection that I think they would like."

Life in Detroit was getting back into a rhythm. He was taking pleasure in everyday life once more – cataloguing his record collection, going to the supermarket, playing music in his studio and at home. He was helping Carter start work on his album and planning future releases for Rings of Saturn, his own record label. It was winter now. Detroit winters bit hard. But Cajmere felt optimistic about the future for once. He had been set free from a toxic relationship and now he was able to determine his own destiny. The DJ bookings had subsided for the time being, although he'd got an intermittent residency at a bar in Detroit, a favour to a friend. He figured the DJing would pick up in the spring. And he was enjoying being in one place, rather than jetting around the globe itinerant, for once.

He was still enthused by photographing the ruins. He went through all his existing pictures and made an album, he also made a large cork pinboard to hang in his living room with blown up black and white and colour shots. One day, when Carter came round to his house, he showed them all to him. "Man I didn't know you were doing all of this," Carter exclaimed, as though Cajmere had a secret life unbeknownst to him. "It's the tragedy of Detroit and the melancholy beauty of the ruins. The ashes of the capitalist dream." Mused Cajmere, almost to himself. "Yeah, well, whatever." Said Carter, he never quite knew how to respond to Cajmere's more philosophical utterances.

That week Cajmere decided to photograph more ruins. On a cold winter's day he wrapped up in his puffa jacket, loaded his camera and drove to an old theatre he knew was disused and falling down. Inside it was a narrative of destruction. A ghostly light was pouring in through the fallen in ceiling. Rubble was strewn over the once plush red velvet seats. Ionic columns at the sides of the proscenium arch were cracked and crumbling. Latticework moulding on the walls was smashed and crumpling in on itself. This is the grandest ruin yet, thought Cajmere, thinking he could almost hear the roar of the crowd, echoes of laughter, the ripples of applause, resonating around the interior. And now, nothing. He trudged along the stage, aiming to get interesting angles. Click, click click, the sound of his camera seemed to be amplified in the emptiness and the brightness of the flash lit up the gloom – a robotic luminescence. Finally, when the cold became unbearable on his ungloved fingers he decided to go home.

He started doing two evenings a week – Tuesdays and Thursdays - at Sojourner Truth. Some of the teenagers were initially thrilled to meet a real live DJ, although others were sceptical. One girl asked him if he knew TLC, breathlessly. "Do you know Lil Kim and Puff Daddy?" "Oh boy I gotta tell you I don't smiled Cajmere beneficently. But I do DJ all over the world – Berlin, Ibiza, Holland, London." "You are cool," deemed one tracksuit clad black kid of about twelve. "I don't believe you're a DJ" said one obstreperous teen. "I think you're just fronting it." "Well wait and see when I bring my decks, then you'll know" In general they made him laugh. Gradually he would get to know them all. Laetitia and a mid forties guy called Ralph oversaw the community centre in the evenings. Then Cajmere and various other mentors came in and took smaller groups of kids, played games with them, tried to do educational exercises, art classes, allsorts of activities that would keep them off the streets. "I'm gonna bring my decks down next time, " he told his little group, "But you've got to be careful with them. I don't want you breaking them." The kids were excited. "Are we going to have a party?" said the 12 year old who was called Wayne. "Yeah, if Laetitia allows it, you can show me your breakdancing and body popping. " What's body popping?" asked Wayne. "Ah it was a kind of dancing from the eighties when I was growing up," explained Cajmere.

Cajmere felt the first evening was very rewarding. The tough ones would soften, he hoped, once he could get his decks down there. Yeah they were young and a bit rough but they had a lot of energy and passion that just needed to be channelled into the right activities. He felt, in a very small way, that after documenting the ruins, he was helping to rebuild Detroit. Give its underprivileged children some opportunities. Spread his good fortune to those who had little hope.

The next time he took his decks down there and set them up with a sound system. He took a carefully picked selection of hip hop and R and B chart hits he'd been sent, that he thought the kids would know and he began to play them and mix them to demonstrate to the kids. Some of the girls started dancing in front of the speakers as he dropped the tracks. "Can I try can I try next" a trio of adolescents crowded round behind the decks jostling to have a go at Djing. He instructed the kids to be very careful putting the needle on the record and showed them how to play a record and demonstrated phasing in one track and phasing out the other. Best to teach them some very rudimentary techniques first, he thought, before getting them to beat mix. The kids were mixed in their adeptness at doing this. One tall boy was a natural, deftly operating the controls with confidence 'he's better than me' thought Cajmere.

After the evening's activities were finished and the teenagers had gone home and Cajmere was clearing away his records, Laetitia and Ralph came over. "Hey Daniel, the kids loved you!" exclaimed Laetitia. "You were a hit! Did you enjoy doing that?" "Yeah it was great," nodded Cajmere enthusiastically. "It was really good fun, I got so much out of it." "We've decided we definitely want you on our team now. Twice a week yeah," she continued, "can you do that." "Sure I can, it would be my pleasure," replied Cajmere. "Do you want to come for a coffee with Ralph and I just now?" asked Laetitia. "We can get a drink from the vending machine over there," she said pointing to a vending machine. They talked about their lives. Laetitia was a social worker with grown up kids who wanted to help improve the lives of other children in the community. Ralph was a teacher who also had grown up children and was trying to reduce violence in the neighbourhood. Laetitia asked Daniel what had made him want to do voluntary work. "I mean you must be really successful at what you do. How did you end up here. How come you care about us, some poor kid community centre in the projects?" Cajmere explained that once, someone he cared about very much had wanted to start doing this, but he'd lost them and that had inspired him to do it himself. He found himself very open with Laetitia and Ralph, they were good people who didn't judge, even the most feral of teenagers, he'd noticed. He also intimated that he'd had a lot of good fortune in his life and that he'd had time to assess what he'd done with his life and that he wanted to make a contribution. "Detroit's in ruins right," he ascertained quite rightly. "I guessed it was time we started rebuilding it and giving kids some hope." Laetitia and Ralph explained that it was difficult for them to get funding – the state department and the mayor just didn't want to know. Money had been mismanaged and the city was broke. "For me, I don't care if there's higher taxes," said Laetitia, I just want the vulnerable people taken care of. And there are a lot of desperate people in this city. Some of these are their kids. Hell knows I've even heard about people living in the ruins recently, just to get shelter and a roof over their heads." Daniel was shocked. Even though he had not come from a wealthy background, in his privileged multimillionaire realm he hadn't realised how tough things were. He had an idea, photographing all those ruins, that the city was in chaos. But about people's lives, other people who were not successful DJs and producers, he had no notion.

That night he went home feeling he was embarking on something important. Perhaps more important essentially than all the DJing and producing – although of course it was the proceeds of this lifestyle that had enabled him to volunteer. If he was going to be cynical, he would say that it was negligible whether one person could make much of a difference. But it was a start and maybe if he could do it, he could persuade others to do it and it would spread like a virus. However he had to be honest, he didn't know how many twentysomething DJs would really want to involve themselves in something like this.

The next time he went there the kids were ready to learn beat mixing. Cajmere put on Faith Evan's Love Like This at full volume and started to show a couple of girls how to segue one beat into another. *I never knew there was a love like this before....*

Suddenly a loud female voice could be heard shouting over the music, "Excuse me, can you just turn that down, you're distracting my graffiti art class."

Cajmere looked up from the decks to see a twentysomething white girl with long dark hair scraped back in a ponytail, approaching him. Close up, he could see she was striking looking, although completely unembellished by make up. She had clear arcs of black eyebrows, creamy skin, full lips and long thick eyelashes framing almond shaped green eyes. She was undeniably beautiful – although completely unglamorous. He couldn't make out her figure because she was wearing a paint splattered grey hoodie.

"Sure," he said taken aback by her loudness and quickly shifted the volume control.

"Thanks," she said briskly and turned her back to go back to her art class.

After the evening's activities had finished and he was unplugging the decks ready to take them away, she came over again. "I'm sorry if I was a bit brusque earlier,"

"No it's fine, really," said Cajmere, curiosity awakened. "It's just that the kids need relative calm to concentrate on their artworks. I mean a little music is fine, but too loud just deafens everyone."

"Yeah I know," said Cajmere," and its not really good for my kids learning to beat mix either. I think I just got carried away."

"What's your name?" the girl asked with an air of openness and approachability.

"Daniel" said Cajmere.

"I'm Karen," she held out her hand to shake his.

They talked for a while. She wanted to know what brought him to Sojourner and what he did for a living. "A DJ wow, not something I know anything about!" She, in turn revealed that she was living at home with her parents and studying for a Masters degree in philosophy. He figured she must be about 25. "I haven't seen you here before," she said. "Why did you decide to do this?" For some reason, he decided against mentioning Rachael, it didn't seem appropriate. So he told her about the ruins photography and how he'd become interested in Detroit's decline and how that had prompted him to wonder how he could help rebuild it. "You're good with the kids," she'd observed. "I think they just hero worship DJs!" he admitted. "Anyone with two decks is a source of novelty for them."

He wondered what sort of music she liked. "Classical and jazz," she responded. "I know very little about contemporary music I've got to be honest. I'm more likely to be listening to Stravinsky and reading up on Malebranch or the Frankfurt school." "I respect that," he said, it was refreshing to meet someone so outside the fashionable world of clubbing, a young woman who was engaging with the city's problems and academia rather than relentlessly purchasing the latest clothes, trainers or records. It suddenly occurred to Cajmere that he might like to study too, in the future, to put his prodigious reading habit to some use. "I don't have a degree," he admitted, "but I do read a lot, I know my Nietsche from my Heidegger." "Good for you" she urged, "well its never to late to get into academia. I did my first degree then waited a couple of years to do my Masters. You can go into these things as a mature student you know." It was as though she had read his mind. The kernel of an idea was there, he could take time out of producing and go back to college.

Cajmere went home with the thought of Karen imprinted on his mind. He had hoped he might meet new people doing this voluntary work, but he hadn't planned on meeting a beautiful smart woman. That had been the last thing on his mind. He could sense she was very grounded, the opposite of flighty Emma Milton. He wanted to see her again. He decided to ask her to come to the downtown bar where he played a jazz set. He would see her next week so he would ask her then.

The next Tuesday evening he helped at Sojourner Truth she wasn't there, she must only help on Thursdays he thought.

But he was getting to know the teenagers anyway. This time, he organised a basketball match, although it nearly ended up in a fight, with one boy wrestling another to the ground to get control of the ball. Cajmere almost had to intervene physically but Laetitia came to his rescue. She took him aside "erm we don't touch the kids or discipline them physically, even during sports," she told him. It's one of the rules. It can lead to escalating violence and repercussions apart from anything else." He took it very seriously, but he realised he was going to have to shout at some of these teenagers at times. Some of them needed a firm hand that they obviously weren't getting from their parents. Others, however were charming. "Do you get to go on an airplane?" Wayne asked him "and stay in hotels?" "Yeah I do," laughed Cajmere, joking "up there, way in the sky, half way across the world." Really" asked Wayne wide eyed, :"what countries have you been to?" Oh lots of places Wayne, Germany, Spain, Holland, the UK" "Wow that's amazing," said Wayne breathlessly. "I think you're the most exciting person I've ever met!"

The next time he went to Sojourner, Karen was there. He went to speak to her after they'd finished with the kids. "D'you wanna vending machine coffee?" he asked her hopefully. "Yeah sure, I'd love one," she replied, friendly. They talked for some time about the various kids in the groups. "How do you cope with the feral ones?" he was interested to know how a woman of relatively small stature could control some of the more challenging adolescents. "I don't have too much of a problem because a lot of them really like graffiti. I'm just encouraging them to do it on these boards rather than on public property, trains and disused buildings. Sure, some of them were difficult at first, but once I got to know them I found out what motivated them individually, and then it became a whole lot easier." "I organised a basketball match last time, and I nearly had a fight on my hands," he related, "that was tough," "Yeah I'll bet, that's the last thing you want, although I bet you can handle yourself," she said with a glint of flirtation in her eye.

"But seriously though, I'm a pacifist, I would never wish to see anyone fighting."

Finally as they were packing up to leave, Cajmere decided to ask her to come to his jazz night. "Do you know Reeves records?" he ventured, "I get my jazz tracks from there." "I know it well," she said with a broad smile. "And I'd love to come. Next Friday yeah?"

Cajmere was elated. He didn't know, right now, whether they were going to be friends or something more, but he was full of hope, the future panned right out in front of him with clear blue skies. His life was evolving in directions he never could have predicted. And now this new person in his life. Who knew where it would go?

Friday came around, they convened at the downtown bar with red neon in the window. Cajmere played his jazz records and Karen sat near to him, nodding her head intermittently and sipping a beer. She hadn't really dressed up, Cajmere noticed, just wearing a skirt, a hoodie and trainers, but she was strikingly attractive and he thought to himself, that this time, if something were to transpire between them, he would demand no change of image. She was a natural beauty and it was also all about what was inside her head. When Cajmere's set ended they had a long conversation about design and architecture, in which she had a passing interest. The night ended and Cajmere offered to drop her home in his car. She lived with her parents in the 'burbs. As she readied herself to exit the car she suddenly caught his eye. He very gently touched her arm and drew her closer. Ever so softly, on the front seats of the car, their lips locked, epidermis pressed against epidermis, tongues intertwined. Something was beginning.